BEACON
of LOVE

Ann Roberts

Bella
BOOKS
2010

Bella Books, Inc.
P.O. Box 10543
Tallahassee, FL 32302

Printed in the United States of America on acid-free paper
First Edition

Editor: Katherine V. Forrest
Cover Designer: Linda Callaghan

ISBN 13:978-1-59493-180-2

Acknowledgments

This story is as much about friendship as it is about love, particularly the friendships of our youth. I was fortunate to have many wonderful friends during high school, including my buddy Suemeree, a writer who just happened to wander back into my life as I was finishing this book. Thanks to her for her support and comments. I was also fortunate to have Katherine V. Forrest again as my editor. I always learn from her suggestions and guidance. It's a true privilege. Finally, I'm grateful to Bella and Linda Hill for the opportunity to reach so many readers. And as always, to Alex and Amy, the most important people in my life: they've trudged through marshes, walked many miles down dusty roads and climbed thousands of steps just to reach the top of all the lighthouses I wanted to visit.

About the Author

Ann Roberts is the author of the romances *Beach Town*, *Brilliant*, and *Root of Passion*. She's also written *Paid in Full* and *White Offerings* featuring real estate sleuth Ari Adams, as well as *Furthest from the Gate* for Spinster's Ink. She lives in Phoenix with her family and can't wait to move to Eugene, Oregon, in the future. She can be reached at www.annroberts.net.

Author's Note

The settings for this novel are the magnificent Heceta Head Lighthouse and the great city of Eugene, Oregon. For those of you who have been fortunate to visit Heceta or stay at the bed-and-breakfast, you'll recognize that I've taken some liberties with my descriptions. And as for Rue, the Grey Lady Ghost, she is indeed rumored to walk the halls of the bed-and-breakfast.

CHAPTER ONE

June, 1992

"I wish you could understand, Steph," Paula sobbed.

Some of her tears fell on the paper that rested on her knees—Steph's acceptance letter from UC Berkeley. Steph resisted the urge to yank the key to her future out of Paula's hands. She knew Paula needed time to accept what was happening—that after ten years as inseparable best friends, she would be leaving their hometown of Eugene, Oregon, and moving to California for college.

They'd situated themselves behind the large rock that according to Steph's father, divided her parents' property from the adjoining woods. She was rather certain they owned all of the land that stretched to the road and cut through the base of Spencer Butte, but her father had declared the rock as her personal boundary when she was five. She'd always yearned to explore the thicket of trees that grew southward, but that youthful curiosity disappeared when she was old enough to see over the rock and recognize its beauty and its potential as a privacy barrier between her and her parents.

She and Paula had no desire to venture beyond the backside of the rock, which proved to be a perfect place for private talks, smoking their first cigarettes and drinking Scotch—both of which sent them flying into the woods to vomit. Recently they'd spent much of their free time hiding behind the impenetrable granite curtain touching each other in delightful ways.

Most importantly it was a fabulous hiding place from Steph's mother, who refused to journey past the redwood deck. Steph always knew she was safe up the little hill since her mother would never venture that far from the liquor cabinet.

Paula sniffled and Steph sneaked a glimpse at her watch. It was after five. She peered down the hill toward the back door. It was still closed. *That's good. Mom's still watching TV, probably Donahue.*

She gazed at Paula's dejected face. She'd been put on the Berkeley waiting list last winter and had nearly given up hope of acceptance—until a letter arrived two days after graduation. She'd dreamed of becoming a Golden Bear since her freshman year of high school, convinced it was the perfect place for a pre-med student. She was euphoric but it had taken her a week to summon the courage to tell Paula, and after an hour of crying, Paula still couldn't accept what was happening.

She checked the back door again. Still closed.

"Paula, I don't understand why you're all worked up. I know I'm leaving but San Francisco isn't that far. We'll call and write."

She squeezed Paula's hand and her sobs faded away. They'd held hands for years but Steph knew that any touch now had lost its innocence, replaced by a desire that crept up on both of them like a virus infecting their bodies.

Much of Paula's profile was obscured by her long chestnut-brown hair, but it was impossible to miss the incredible eyelashes

2

she constantly fluttered and the full mouth that readily met Steph's whenever they were alone.

"I know we'll keep in touch but I just can't believe you're leaving."

"Yeah, but you'll still have Emilio to hang out with," she added, referring to their other best friend.

Paula scowled and she blushed. It was an insensitive comment. "Sorry," she said quietly.

Paula's face softened and she stroked Steph's hand with her thumb. Steph closed her eyes, enjoying the connection. She'd secretly admitted that she savored Paula's caresses and her touch could make her shiver as if she were standing naked in an Oregon downpour. Although they'd known each other for a decade, it was only in the last three months that they'd tiptoed across the line of friendship into a place that scared Steph to death.

But she wouldn't think about it—couldn't think about it, even as Paula's lips found the curve of her jaw and traced it with butterfly kisses. Steph melted under the delicate gesture. Paula giggled as her lips continued their journey to Steph's mouth. Paula pressed her against the rock, unbuttoning her shirt and fondling her breasts. Steph knew what came next. Paula pulled off her T-shirt and unhooked her bra. She was consumed by Paula's determined tongue buried deep in her mouth, and it wasn't until Paula's nipples pressed against her own that she realized they were half naked.

Paula kissed her completely, as if she were leaving for California in just a few moments. When Paula unbuttoned her shorts, she didn't pull away as she had in the past. Paula's tongue was too persuasive and she pulled Steph's yearning to the surface. Her hand crept between Steph's legs and rested on her mound.

"More," Paula whispered, breaking the kiss and shattering Steph's lust.

Steph gently pushed her away. "We can't today. My dad's home and he'll come looking for me if I forgot one of my chores."

Paula frowned and her eyes gleamed with tears. Steph didn't know if she was upset at losing the moment, or the letter from

Berkeley or both. They'd never talked about Steph's fear. Paula's soft lips confused her terribly. She wanted to run away—right into Paula's arms. She'd created an emotional circle that she couldn't escape but her sexual terror trumped the guilt over leaving her.

"It's just…" Paula stammered.

She sucked in air but failed to complete her thought.

"It's just what?" Steph asked impatiently, peering around the rock, willing the back door to stay closed.

She stared at Steph for a long time before she said, "I'll miss you a lot."

She immediately looked down and Steph exhaled, not realizing she'd been holding her breath.

The screen door squeaked. After a flurry of redressing, they peered over the rock. Steph's mother, Debbie, tottered out, highball glass in hand.

"Steph! Stephanie! Yoo-hoo! C'mon, Stephie, where are you? John, are you home?"

She was wearing a silk negligee, having changed out of the leggings and oxford cloth shirt she'd worn when she'd greeted Paula an hour before at the front door. The thick blond tresses Steph had inherited were stacked on the top of her head with a black clip and her customary deep-red lipstick proved a stark contrast to her ghostly white skin.

She glided back and forth across the deck, scissoring her legs in one of her old dance moves. Her lithe body shifted effortlessly and the alcohol did little to thwart her natural grace. She'd told Steph a hundred times she'd given up a theatrical career in New York to be with her father.

Periodically she'd stop and take a serious drink and then sweep across the deck in the opposite direction. They watched her performance and Steph thought that without her glasses she couldn't see them. Steph hated that Paula was there but she loathed the prospect of babysitting her mother so she stayed behind the rock. Her father was obviously ignoring her mother—at least for now—and Steph couldn't blame him. He was a saint, constantly caring for her mother, suffering her abuses and enduring the

4

public embarrassments she caused the family. There wasn't an adult resident of Eugene who didn't know Debbie South, the drunkard, and her unfortunate husband, John.

He kept his sanity by frequently traveling his sales route through the Midwest where he sold medical supplies to hospitals. Steph missed him but she understood his work. They'd had long talks about her departure for college and she felt horrible about abandoning him, but he assured her everything would be fine and she had nothing to feel guilty about.

"I wish I could dance like your mother," Paula said, interrupting her thoughts. Steph knew Paula admired Debbie, despite her weird quirks and antics, but Paula couldn't see what she did. Steph thought Paula's mother, Francine, was the epitome of a great parent and she'd sought refuge at the Kemper house hundreds of times over the years.

Debbie pirouetted and stopped short of falling over the balcony railing. Hopefully she would give up soon and go back to her La-Z-Boy recliner and the bottle of Jack Daniel's she'd bought yesterday.

She serenaded them with music from the *Rocky Horror Picture Show*, a movie she'd seen dozens of times. As long as she kept her clothes on—which wasn't a guarantee—Steph didn't care. They lived at the top of a cul-de-sac at the base of Spencer Butte. It afforded them a privacy they frequently needed—like today. Steph took comfort that their closest neighbor, old Mr. Crick, wouldn't be able to check out Debbie South's latest performance.

Paula wrapped one of Steph's blond locks around her finger in a playful gesture of understanding. It was her trademark. She never offered pitiful looks or spoke in a sad tone because she knew it made Steph feel more pathetic. Paula always distracted Steph from her misery by filling her heart with Paula's own optimism and logical view of the world.

"I know you won't miss this when you're gone. Debbie is just...Debbie."

Steph turned away, hoping Paula couldn't see how the simple gesture affected her.

5

Debbie hit a high note and raised her hands to the sky in a big finish. The glass slipped through her fingers and crashed to the deck but she didn't seem to notice. She held the pose, obviously hearing thunderous applause in her head. With her arms outstretched the silk clung to her curves.

"She's beautiful," Paula sighed. "I hope I look that good when I'm in my forties."

Paula and their friend Emilio had seen Debbie drunk often and they'd all laughed together about some of her antics, like the afternoon she staged a pickle rolling contest, offering twenty bucks to the winner, who turned out to be Paula. Her friends always understood Debbie and it was why they were the only people who ever visited during high school.

John South emerged from the house, the breaking crystal more than he could stand. Debbie took her bow and her ample breasts slipped out of the negligee. She drew herself up before she saw him standing next to her.

"Want a little action, Johnnie?" she asked loudly, jiggling her chest in his face.

Steph thought she might be sick.

"God, Debbie, you're trashed," he scolded sharply, turning away from her and gathering the large shards from the deck.

She looked ashamed and she readjusted herself without looking at him again. As she opened the screen door, she glanced up toward the rock and Steph wondered if she'd known they were there all along.

Once John went back inside they scrunched down again behind the rock. Paula closed her eyes as if she were meditating. Steph didn't know what to say. Her mother had interrupted an important emotional moment they couldn't get back, and now Paula seemed to have slipped away into her own private world. She fidgeted uncomfortably while Paula remained still. It was an unusual twist since usually she was the quiet one, lost in her own thoughts while Paula chatted endlessly.

The silence became too much. "Paula, are you okay?"

When Paula's eyes fluttered open, a few tears escaped before

6

she said with a laugh, "Nope." She reread the letter, quietly folded it into thirds and handed it to her. She wore a look of sad resignation. "I really am happy for you, Steph. We've always wanted the best for each other and I don't want that to change."

"Thanks," Steph said, relieved.

She leaned closer and Steph could smell the Chanel No. 5 she'd given her for Christmas. "But if you're going away then I think we need something special to remember each other by. I want more, Steph, right now. Your mother's in the house and your dad is preoccupied. No one's coming. I want to be your first. Please," she begged.

Paula nuzzled her neck until Steph was blinded by sheer ecstasy. Their clothes were shed again in a matter of seconds and Paula hovered over her, wearing only her underwear. She was beautiful but Steph sat limp against the rock, like a discarded rag doll. She didn't know what to do.

Paula crawled to her and kissed her softly, her body flowing against Steph's. She lay her down on the soft grass and traced circles on her belly. When her hand swept under Steph's waistband, it was as though an alarm sounded. Steph sat up and Paula fell backward.

"Paula, I can't." When her eyes remained unconvinced, she added, "I love you as a friend but I don't want you like that. I thought you understood."

Paula's jaw dropped and it seemed to Steph that her mind floated away from the moment, from anything that had existed between them. She remained motionless for a long time as if absorbed fully in herself, long enough for Steph to hear the cars racing home on the road beyond the little forest. Suddenly Paula reached for her clothes and hurriedly dressed as if she were late for curfew.

She started down the hill quickly, Steph trailing after her. They walked around to the front of the house and into the sunlight. Paula put on her sunglasses and looked up, as if a spotlight had been turned on her. Her hair shimmered and her creamy skin relished the attention of the sun. Gone were the tears of an hour ago, replaced by a mask of self-assuredness.

"Well, goodbye, Steph."

She was puzzled. Paula was spending the summer in Seattle with her grandparents but she didn't leave for a week.

"What's with goodbye? We'll see each other before you go, right?"

She looked away. "Actually I'm leaving tomorrow. My grandfather asked me to come early and help with the chores."

Steph knew Paula's grandparents were third generation fishermen who owned their own business on the Washington coast. Paula loved visiting them and had invited Steph along one summer. It was the best summer she could remember.

"Oh," was all Steph could say, unable to right herself from the emotional whiplash she felt. In only a few seconds it was as if the last ten years vanished.

Suddenly it was all overwhelming and the clear path of her future was covered in fog. She opened her mouth to say— something. But Paula turned away, her face impassive, and headed down the sidewalk. Steph watched the sunlight sparkle against her hair for as long as she could, until Paula rounded the corner to her street and disappeared.

CHAPTER TWO

April, 2009

The gray-haired, tiny bathroom attendant at the Troon North Clubhouse watched Stephanie Rollins fling open the door and burst into tears, and she quickly led her to a corner of the sitting room with a box of tissue. No doubt she'd seen her share of crying wives after their catty friends had revealed over Blood Mary's that their husbands were having affairs.

Steph dabbed her eyes, determined not to ruin her makeup. She took a deep breath and stared at the expensive paintings that adorned the little sitting room filled with deep cherry wood settees and stuffed chairs. Classical music muffled the unrefined toilet flushes and the gossipy whispers of the trophy wives huddled over the granite sinks reapplying their lipsticks. It was amazing they could outline their lips and simultaneously stab a non-present club member in the back.

She leaned against the wall, listening to pieces of their conversations—the sudden chuckles and droll remarks, all at the expense of someone else. No one mentioned her, so at least her news from the dining room hadn't traveled that fast. After nearly eighteen years of living as a doctor's wife, she'd heard and said it all. She'd learned quickly that there wasn't a high road to take and survival in the upper social stratosphere was reminiscent of Roman gladiators—only these warriors sported three hundred dollar haircuts and hundred dollar manicures.

She needed to focus on the facts. Lawrence was having another affair, according to her tennis buddies. It had taken three rum and Cokes to pry the information from Leslie, her doubles partner, but she finally admitted that she'd seen him and Steph's Bosnian twenty-something domestic, Marta, naked and humping like rabbits in the Rollins' Olympic-size pool. Apparently Leslie had wandered into the house looking for Steph the day before and got an eyeful from the living room window. When she started to describe their antics under the beautiful waterfall that Steph had designed, Steph excused herself to the restroom, which she now decided was the nicest public restroom she'd ever entered.

She thought about leaving but the chaise lounge seemed to wrap its arms around her, coaxing her to stay. More than likely the real culprit was the three whiskey sours she'd consumed with lunch. She was pleasantly toasted and had no desire to rise; however, she knew that her window of opportunity was closing. She checked her Rolex and verified that it was two thirty, still an hour before Eric arrived home from school.

The thought of her son embroiled in the family drama was enough to drag her to her feet. She sought out the full-length mirror on the opposite wall. She'd never had one in her bedroom when she was a kid, Debbie decrying vanity as the root of all evil. But after years of living with a plastic surgeon in an environment where attention to physical beauty was essential to proper breeding, she automatically assessed her appearance, like a complex mathematical equation, the answer to which verified her worth.

She saw a thirty-five-year-old woman who still got carded when she went on a "girls' night out." *Plus.* She had a great haircut and her hair was free of gray. *Plus.* She remained a size six and her long legs were still her best feature. *Plus.* The boob lift she'd given Lawrence for *his* thirtieth birthday present was losing to gravity. He'd hounded her to go back under the knife but she refused. *Minus.* Tiny varicose veins peeked out from under her tennis dress, threading their way down to her ankles. *Minus.* And speaking of her ankles, they'd soon be cankles. *Minus.*

Not bothering to do the vanity math, she rushed out of the bathroom, ignoring her friends who were probably ordering their fifth or sixth cocktail. The hunky valet waved at her approach and went to retrieve her Beemer.

"How are you today, Mrs. Rollins?" he offered as he pulled up.

She noticed his eyes probing her body as she slid into the driver's seat. "I'm fine, Curtis, and you?"

"Never better," he said with a model-like smile. "Anything else I can do for you?"

She shook her head. "No thank you."

She sped away and recognized the irony of the situation. Curtis had indeed done many other things for several of the bored club wives—but not for her. After Lawrence's second affair, she'd thought turnabout was fair play, but sleeping with the head waiter didn't make her feel better about his cheating and it made her feel worse about herself. And in the end, when she'd announced her affair to Lawrence, he'd had the poor guy fired. She decided then that affairs weren't her style—at least with men.

A year later the club hired a new tennis pro, an incredibly attractive redhead whose personality was as powerful as her serve. They flirted for weeks but Steph was too chicken to do anything until she happened to attend a luncheon in downtown Scottsdale one afternoon and Lawrence walked past the restaurant's front window, his arm wrapped around the waist of a very young woman. Steph knew she was a temp in the billing department but it was clear from their groping that the relationship wasn't professional.

The next afternoon the tennis pro offered her a rubdown after their workout and Steph accepted. She'd never been with a woman, although there had been several ladies who'd caught her eye over the years. None was as bold as the pro, who came into the massage room wearing only a robe.

"Climb up on the table," she'd instructed.

Steph held her towel against her chest and lay on her stomach while the pro kneaded her muscles from head to toe for over half an hour, soft jazz music preventing any awkward conversation between them. The afternoon was clearly about their bodies.

Steph was so relaxed that she quickly turned over on her back when instructed to do so. The powerful fingers that had released all the tension from her back muscles caressed her face and breasts lovingly. It was an hour Steph would never forget and their weekly liaisons continued for several months until the pro got a better job offer and left Arizona. The entire affair made Steph think of Paula—often.

They'd never seen each other after that summer day when Paula walked away in the sun. During the many intervening years the image of her hair glistening in the light took on an ethereal quality and Steph elevated her status to angel. The story of their past had gilded corners on each page. All of it was romantic and beautiful—even the moment when they said goodbye.

Her dreams of med school and an amazing experience at Berkeley had lasted a mere year. She'd been lost without Paula and embraced the first clique of co-eds that was kind to her, a group that included the sister of Lawrence Rollins, her future husband. According to the therapist who would treat her for depression years later, she hooked up with Lawrence to forget Paula and the feelings she secretly harbored for her.

He was a third-year med student, destined to join his father's lucrative plastic surgery practice in Scottsdale, Arizona. He introduced her to the wealthy crowd—frat boys, sorority girls and the elite athletes. It was intoxicating, as was the alcohol that she enjoyed whenever it was offered. By the time she returned to Eugene for spring break, she was pregnant. Lawrence had realized

Steph could be persuaded to do most anything when she was under the influence, such as give up her virginity. Unfortunately, when he got drunk he also experienced lapses in judgment—like forgetting to wear a condom. Their son Eric was living proof that pregnancy can happen the first time.

She wound the Beemer around the golf course path, grateful for the easy drive when she was drunk. She parked a few houses away and walked the distance. She was on a stealth mission and wouldn't give herself away.

She dropped her keys at the door, swearing softly as they clinked onto the terracotta entryway. She fumbled for the right one and the door opened. Eric stood there, his arms crossed, frowning. He was still too thin but he'd put on a little weight in the last few months and bulked up from lifting weights. She was grateful he no longer dressed entirely in black as he had during his grunge phase, although Lawrence hated his new wardrobe just as much since most of it was second-hand. She never complained when he spent Saturday morning combing the thrift stores with his friend Jameson because it meant he wasn't out doing drugs.

Today he sported an old mechanic's shirt and ripped jeans. His dark curly brown hair was long again and she couldn't see his eyes, which she imagined were filled with disapproval. For a seventeen-year-old, he often acted middle-aged.

"You're drunk," he said.

She worked to control herself but she was rather certain that her body was swaying, as if she were dancing to a song on her iPod.

"What are you doing home?" she asked, ignoring his statement and sweeping past him. "It's only two thirty."

He followed her into the kitchen, took her purse and set it on the sideboard. "It's the third Wednesday of the month. I have early dismissal, remember?" No, she didn't remember but she nodded anyway.

"What are *you* doing home?" he asked, annoyed. "It's your day for tennis and a massage."

"I decided to skip the massage," she said, already heading for the stairs. "Why don't you run down to Sal's and pick up a pizza or something for dinner?"

"Dinner's not for four hours," he said, going to the refrigerator. "Why don't you sit with me and I'll make us some Arnold Palmers? And we can eat some of your amazing muffins."

He pulled out the lemonade and iced tea pitchers and grinned at her. She loved that grin and Arnold Palmers, their favorite non-alcoholic drink. "Um, just give me a sec to change, okay?" She figured she could confront Lawrence and because Eric was home, he wouldn't make a scene, but he would be *caught*.

She'd climbed to the first landing when Eric overtook her, his hand clasping her arm. "Mom, don't go up there right now."

They stared at each other and his eyes were filled with knowing. He was an old soul and the calmness of his nature was contagious. She let him lead her down the stairs and out to the patio. She imagined his plan was to have a pleasant conversation with his mother while his father finished pleasuring himself and the maid and sneaked back to work, thinking his stupid wife and former-druggie son were none the wiser.

They planted themselves in the lounge chairs, enjoying the tepid weather, which wouldn't last much longer. Within three weeks the persecuting heat would kill all of her flowers and drive the humans inside. Even the pool wouldn't be enjoyable, the Arizona sun practically boiling the water.

"It's not too hot yet," Eric said, reading her mind.

"No, but it will be," she said sharply. "God, I hate it here."

"Then why don't you move?"

She looked at him, astonished by the question. "What are you talking about?"

He pulled his long legs off the lounger and faced her, his arms resting on his knees. He looked more like a father than a son, someone who was about to begin an important lecture. He'd certainly heard enough of them from the drug counselors who'd helped him kick the cocaine habit he'd developed while attending an elite private school. Steph had tried to tell Lawrence that private didn't equate to better, but there was no way his son would go to public school. It was beneath him. Eric's three-month stint at Charter Hospital changed his mind. Afterward, Eric received straight-A grades after only a semester at Desert Mountain High School. If he took summer classes, he could still go to college at San Diego State in the fall, although he couldn't participate in his high school graduation ceremony, a fact that broke Steph's heart. Seeing her son in his cap and gown was one of the images she'd clung to throughout his youth when raising him seemed incredibly difficult and she wondered if she was a good mother.

"Mom, you need to leave Dad." His voice was firm, the tone even.

She couldn't look at him. Yes, he was right. She needed to leave Lawrence. She hated him. She'd never loved him but now she *hated* him. Such a thought, though, wasn't supposed to be voiced by her teenage son.

"Listen," he continued, "when I was in rehab we talked a lot about our parents and I think I understand you now."

She raised an eyebrow. "You do? What do you think you know?"

"That you gave up everything for me. That you never had any help. And since I was a *surprise*, as you call it, I don't think you ever loved Dad. I think you tried," he added quickly, "but you can't force yourself to love someone just like you can't stop yourself from falling in love."

For a fleeting second she thought of Paula and the fire that burned in her belly every time they'd met behind the rock.

She was impressed by her son's understanding of the world. How far that extended she was unsure. Of course gay topics only warranted fleeting mentions in their rare family dinner discussions and Lawrence usually had the final homophobic word.

She looked at her son, a young man she admired and pitied at the same time. He'd grown up into a fine person in spite of his parents. Steph blamed herself for his stint in rehab but he'd denied she'd played any role in his addiction to drugs. But Lawrence hadn't fared so well. While Eric never blamed him, he never excused him either. Lawrence was a doctor. He should have seen and known the signs.

"Son, I appreciate your exceptional and rather uncanny understanding of my situation but I'm not leaving you. I've sucked enough as a mother and I'm not going to add abandonment to my list of faults."

He laughed heartily. "Mom, you're not abandoning me. In a few months I'm out of high school. I'll be abandoning you. I've already told you I'm going to San Diego. I figure Dad's good for that much cash since he's gotta feel a little guilty about missing out on every single thing I ever did in school and countless birthdays. Or, I could join the military," he added, knowing that topic made her blood boil. She simply pointed a finger at him and he backed down. "I'm just saying it's time for you to live your life and to hell with Dad. Go back to Oregon. You've always talked about how much you miss the rain and the trees."

So true. She gazed out at the sprawling deep emerald green golf course that lay before them. She'd agreed to build their mini-mansion here because of the view. The lush trees and grass reminded her of home. But she was assaulted by the dreariness of the desert each time she drove out of her garage.

"You could live with Grandma," Eric suggested.

She offered a pained smile. She knew he was trying to be helpful. "You know Grandma lives in an assisted living setting, sweetie. It's not really an option."

He laughed again, knowing all of her issues with Debbie. While her parents had always been good to him, particularly when John was alive, she'd always felt closer to Francine, Paula's mother. Francine had been instrumental in Steph's decision to keep Eric and they still remained close through phone calls. She'd never say it out loud but Francine had been more of a mother to her than Debbie.

He spent another half-hour lobbying for her departure, and she finally asked him if he was trying to get rid of her. He dismissed the idea with a wave and she knew he had no ulterior motives such as returning to his life of hard partying. She pondered his offer seriously until the back door opened and Marta appeared. In the distance Lawrence's car left the garage. She almost laughed. How stupid did he think she was?

Marta had told them she'd been a model back in Europe and since her body was nothing but curves, Steph believed her and Lawrence instantly hired her. Her hair was wet from the shower she'd taken after they crawled out of *Steph's* bed, and the smile that spread across her face could only belong on the face of an adulterer.

"How you doin' Marta?" Eric asked, lifting his drink.

She flashed a wide smile and Steph bristled. Marta had been eyeing him ever since she arrived and Steph worried that she'd make her way into his bed too. Steph knew that he'd lost his virginity to a woman ten years his senior during a church summer camp on abstinence and addiction.

"I'm great, Eric," she said, refusing to acknowledge Steph. "In fact, I'm perfect."

"Is that what Lawrence says, or is that your own over-estimation of your ability in bed?"

She'd said the words before she could stop herself.

Marta stared at her, her eyes the size of golf balls.

Steph looked at Eric and his broad grin.

"Damn it."

CHAPTER THREE

Steph's exodus from Lawrence and her socialite life in Scottsdale began the moment she confronted Marta. The maid had gasped and run back into the mansion, no doubt phoning Lawrence immediately. Steph could easily predict how Lawrence would spend the rest of the afternoon. He'd leave work early to buy her an expensive gift and two dozen roses—and practice his begging on the way home. It was a poker game they'd played several times.

When he arrived home carrying *three* dozen roses and presenting her with a Cartier watch, she knew he'd realized the stakes were higher and he'd upped the ante. But she was ready to fold—forever. Eric magically disappeared with fifty bucks in his pocket and Lawrence ordered Chinese over the phone, not bothering to ask Steph what she wanted. He assumed he knew her tastes as he assumed many things, including her forgiveness.

He went upstairs to shower and change, and when he returned wearing jeans and a sweater, she sat regally in the Queen Anne chair, her legs crossed at the ankles. She wore a silk blouse with deep cleavage and wide-legged black dress pants. Her makeup was flawless and she'd adorned herself with some of her finest jewelry to create a look of power and confidence. They'd performed this play many times and Steph had always dressed the part, hoping that her beautiful exterior would give her the inner strength, but it had never worked before and she'd always forgiven Lawrence after he'd worn down her resistance and tickled her fear of being alone.

He knelt before her like a royal subject in front of his queen. He took her left hand and kissed her wedding ring.

"You know how much you mean to me."

She remained calm and still. She didn't answer and she didn't pull her hand away, not even when he brought it to his lips and kissed each finger.

"I'm sorry about Marta, Steph." He kissed her wrist and forearm, murmuring, "It's just you've been so distant and I've felt so lonely. It feels as though you'd rather spend time with Eric or your club friends than with me." He stared into her eyes and her frozen expression. "You understand, don't you? I work so hard to provide for you and Eric and I just needed a *release*. But you're my wife, my love."

He burrowed his face into her cleavage and squeezed her breasts. Just as he started to unbutton her shirt, the doorbell sounded.

"Shit," he said, rising and grabbing his wallet from the sideboard while Steph brought two plates and a small basket to the dining room table.

"What's that?" Lawrence asked, pulling the boxes of takeout from the brown bag.

Steph smiled. "Homemade Chinese fortune cookies."

Lawrence grinned and plucked one from the basket. "You

19

know I love these." He cracked the cookie and pulled out a slip of paper. "Five million. What the hell is this?"

Steph shrugged. "I'm not sure. Maybe you got a bad fortune. Why don't you open a different one?"

Lawrence frowned and cracked another cookie. "You're a dickhead." He took a deep breath and met her icy stare. "Okay, I probably deserved that."

"Open another one," she said flatly, her arms crossed.

There were two left in the basket and he crushed both of them at the same time and pulled out the slips of paper. Her smile grew wide as she watched him digest the words on the papers. *I'm leaving you. I want a divorce.*

He leaned over the table, shaking his head, laughing. "Oh, Steph, you're such a card. Like you'd ever really leave me."

She grabbed her purse and keys from the sideboard and glanced at him over her shoulder. "I'll be staying at the Troon Bungalows for now."

His shoulders sagged slightly but he wore a smug smile. "You'll be back."

She shook her head. "I don't think so. You know that first fortune you opened, the one that said five million? That's what I want—half of your practice."

Only when she was certain that Eric was fine and his summer classes were underway did she point her Beemer north and begin the trek back to Oregon. She'd loaded the car for the long drive across the southwest, taking only the essentials, since she didn't have a real plan. After eighteen years of filling Daytimers and social calendars with Lawrence's and Eric's activities, driving out of Phoenix's city limits was liberating. But six hours later, as she turned north onto I-5 outside of L.A., anxiety sat in the pit of her stomach. She'd been a marionette for her entire adult life, dancing each time her doctor-husband moved the controller. At one point during her drive—somewhere outside of Sacramento—she'd actually gazed down at her legs to make sure they were really her own.

As she crossed the Oregon border, she should've been celebrating the sight of the green trees and the cool weather. But she felt sick and was ready to barf by the time she drove through Eugene. She wasn't prepared to see her mother the way she was feeling so she turned left and kept driving—all the way to the ocean. She eventually wound up in Yachats, a popular coastal town.

After three days of sitting in a motel room staring at the tacky blue wallpaper and sobbing periodically at the mess she'd made of her life, she ventured to the store for groceries.

A woman stared at her as she roamed up and down the aisles, and she assumed it was because her eyes belonged on a raccoon and her hair was horribly disheveled.

"Stephanie?"

She turned around slowly to greet the smiling face of a woman wearing jeans and a Windbreaker.

"I thought it was you." The woman stepped forward, a hand over her heart. "Caroline Bickford? We went to Eugene High together. Do you remember me?"

She nodded. She remembered her and that she hadn't been very nice to her either. Over the years she'd found herself reflecting on her behavior during school and she wasn't impressed. She'd been a snob. Caroline hadn't been beautiful then and she wasn't now, but she was nice looking with bobbed brown hair and a pleasant face. She'd always been a little heavy—and still was—and her physical features ensured Steph and her cheerleader friends wouldn't bother to know her.

"Are you here visiting Debbie?" she asked, as if she knew what the answer would be.

"Uh, yeah, partly," Steph hedged. She held a box of Wheaties tightly against her chest like a security blanket.

"I ran into her at the park a few weeks ago. She just raved about your wonderful marriage and your growing medical practice."

She nearly dropped the box but caught it before it hit the floor. Her chest heaved with sobs.

Caroline quickly escorted her outside.

"I'm sorry, Caroline. That was very inappropriate."

Caroline reached into her purse and handed her a tissue. "It's no big deal. I'm sorry I upset you."

"Don't be. It's just that Debbie isn't well and she tells stories."

Caroline nodded, understanding. "I see. Reminds me of high school," she said softly. When Steph composed herself, Caroline said, "So, what's the real story, if you don't mind my asking."

"I'm not a doctor. I've left my husband. I'm a terrible mother and I don't know what I'm going to do with my life."

She'd spewed the truth like an exploding geyser and she was prepared for Caroline to walk away, dismissing her as a nut.

Instead she stuck her hands into her jacket pockets and sighed. "Where are you staying?" she asked.

"The motel up the road."

"C'mon," she said. "You're coming home with me, but we should probably go back and pay for that cereal," she added, motioning to the box Steph had strangled between her arms.

After they checked out of the motel, Caroline took her home.

"You live here?" Steph asked incredulously as they drove up the trail to a lighthouse keeper's house, which had been transformed into a bed-and-breakfast.

"Yup. My husband and I bought the bed-and-breakfast about six years ago. We came up here for a romantic weekend and fell in love with the place. Then we found out the couple who'd owned it for years were ready to retire. It's our pride and joy."

She parked in the back of a large, white Queen Anne style house, complete with a gorgeous red roof. An enormous weather vane twirled slowly in the light breeze, emitting a soft creak that harmonized with the wind whistling through the trees.

The porch stretched across the front, providing a beautiful view of the churning ocean two hundred and fifty feet below. Steph turned to the west and gazed at the Heceta Head Lighthouse, its beacon flashing intermittently. She'd only visited it once on a class field trip and she remembered it was the most photographed lighthouse in America. It sat atop a bluff at Devil's Elbow State Park and at sunset no picture was its equal. Heceta Head was the image Americans associated with lighthouses.

She stared at the tall sentinel, tempted to drop her bags and run up the trail to greet it.

"She has that affect on people," Caroline commented, smiling at her. "You see whatever you need to see in her—love, comfort, even strength. This was the picture that drew us here."

Caroline touched her arm and Steph followed her into the bed-and-breakfast. She shook hands with Caroline's husband, Rick, who was nothing like Lawrence. He was sturdy and reminded her of a lumberjack. Then Caroline picked up Steph's luggage and led her into a small room off the kitchen that Steph imagined had once been used for storage.

"It's not much," Caroline apologized, setting her bags on the small twin bed.

"It's fine," Steph replied, and she really meant it. She didn't miss her six thousand square-foot house at all. Guilt consumed her and she said abruptly, "I'm sorry. I'm sorry about high school."

It was entirely impromptu and if they'd been much younger, denials and obsequious flatteries would've followed, but they weren't young.

Caroline looked at her with a smile borne of years of experience and said, "Apology accepted. I'll let you get settled and then we'll talk."

She left the room and Steph checked her cell phone—three messages. Eric wanted to know how she was doing, Lawrence screamed into voice mail that she was a fool, and Paula's mother Francine wanted her to call because Lawrence had called her.

She quickly unpacked and joined Caroline in the kitchen. Caroline gave her a tour of the house, showing off the amazing parlors, fireplace and dining room. They toured the bedrooms upstairs, each one bearing a different name because of its place in Heceta history. She stopped at the last bedroom, her hand on the doorknob.

"This is Victoria's Room and it's the most unique of all."

"Why is that?"

"It's haunted."

After a week Steph's life settled into a pleasant routine. She called Eric twice a day, helped Caroline with the chores, ignored Lawrence's messages that became more terse and shrill with each call and debated when she would announce her presence to her mother. She was desperate to see Francine, who finally agreed to a visit after several rounds of phone tag and one cancellation. Steph sensed that something was going on but Francine had sounded like her usual cheerful self.

Steph wasn't prepared for the woman who greeted her at the door. She was emaciated and her cheeks were hollow. Her skin had yellowed and the steel-gray hair Steph remembered from high school had been replaced by white cottony tufts. She realized Francine was in her eighties. She'd been so much older than the other parents, having given birth to Paula at forty-three.

Francine hugged her and Steph returned the embrace gently. It was like squeezing a humming bird and she worried she would break her.

"Come in," she said, and moved slowly back into the house.

Steph followed her to the sofa, replaying the last time she'd visited—the night she came to ask her advice about her pregnancy. Francine had listened carefully and told Steph to keep the baby and marry Lawrence, holding her hand and assuring her that she was making the right decision. She'd gone with Steph to tell her shocked parents, a gesture Steph would never forget.

The place was exactly as she remembered it, including the plastic that covered the sofa and loveseat. Francine was of a different generation than her parents, one that practiced frugality as a science. The faint smell of menthol hung in the air like a hospital. Steph gazed at the photos that covered every flat surface in the living room. Most of them were of Paula—Francine and Paul's only child—but a few eight-by-tens featured Paul in his dress blues, holding a young Paula in his arms and standing beside a small plane. He'd been a pilot, first in the navy and then for a commercial airline. He'd been killed by a drunk driver when Paula was ten.

Her eyes settled on Paula's senior picture and a kaleidoscope of images filled her mind—her laugh, her voice and their first kiss. She'd imagined her face nearly every day of her adult life but she rarely took the time to pull her box of memories off the top shelf of the closet in Scottsdale and retrieve any of the old photos. The price for her laziness was a hazy remembrance of Paula's true self—the richness of her blue eyes, her aquiline nose and the dimple in her chin. She'd forgotten about that entirely.

Francine slowly settled next to her, every movement conveying her frailty. Her demeanor was still that of a lady. She wore a simple skirt and blouse, for it would be inappropriate to receive guests in a housecoat or jeans. Steph instantly thought of her mother who would open her front door dressed in her underwear.

"Would you care for something to drink? I've made iced tea."

Francine started to rise slowly but Steph jumped up. "Let me get it."

She retrieved the serving tray from the kitchen, cringing at the effort Francine must have exerted to prepare the refreshments.

Steph joined her again on the sofa and they sipped the tea. Steph knew there were things Francine wanted to ask but she'd never broach sensitive topics without an appropriate segue, one that was polite and correct. Francine smiled again, waiting for Steph to start.

"I've left Lawrence, for good," she stated.

Francine frowned and her face conveyed further disapproval. "I'm sorry, Stephanie. I know Lawrence is a difficult man. Is there any hope it could work out?"

"No," she said firmly.

"I see."

Steph was uncomfortable with her tone. She knew Francine believed that people married for life. Her insistence that she keep Eric had been rooted in that traditionalistic attitude and she knew her effort to rally her in support of marriage was borne from the same belief.

25

"It's not that I haven't tried, Francine, but the man's had several affairs. Even Eric thinks I should leave him."

Francine raised her eyebrow at this news. "Well, I don't know how much stock I would put in the opinion of a seventeen-year-old, particularly one who hasn't always exercised good judgment."

Although she jabbed with the blunt side of her blade, it still hurt. They both knew she was referring to Eric's drug addiction.

Steph felt the need to defend him. "I know Eric's made mistakes but this time I think he's right."

Francine sighed heavily and Steph could tell she was wearing thin of the conversation and the visit. Her hands shook slightly and her eyes were tired. Although Steph had only been there a few minutes, she needed to leave and let Francine rest.

Francine patted her on the arm and said, "I know you'll do what's right. How long are you staying in Eugene?"

She shrugged. "I don't know, indefinitely I guess."

The wheels in her mind were turning. Sitting in the room, Steph could feel the difference in their ages.

She took a sip of tea and asked, "Stephanie, you haven't spoken to Paula recently, have you?"

The question was asked innocently but Steph sensed it was rhetorical.

She searched for words to explain why her childhood friend of ten years had been absent for her entire adult life. Then she simply said, "No."

"I never knew what happened between the two of you. Would you care to tell me now?"

She spoke to the coffee table in front of them, an extraordinarily odd gesture for her. As children she'd always remind them to look at adults when they were engaged in conversation. To do otherwise was rude.

Steph's mouth started moving but words wouldn't come. After three false starts she cleared her throat and issued a planned response. "Francine, what happened between me and Paula was unfortunate. I blame myself for losing touch with her. She was a dear friend and we had a ridiculous argument but it's all water under the bridge."

Steph cringed at her use of a hackneyed cliché but she couldn't tell her the truth. Francine met her gaze with a hard stare. When Francine finally looked away Steph noticed her hands shook and her shoulders sagged.

"You look tired and I should probably be going. Next time I'll visit in the morning," she said, thinking that perhaps Francine would be better rested after a night's sleep.

Francine offered no protest and followed her to the door. They hugged again and Steph could hear her heavy breathing. She wondered if she was sick and if so, how bad was it?

When they parted, Francine dabbed at her eyes with a handkerchief. "You're like my other daughter. You know that, don't you?"

The comment implied a connection between her and Paula, one that hadn't existed for seventeen years and Steph was touched.

Francine took a breath and set her jaw before she spoke. "Steph, I want you to do something for me."

"Of course."

Francine put her hands on Steph's shoulders and looked her squarely in the eye. "I know you haven't seen Paula for a long time. Someday I want you to make up with her. I want you to promise me that by the time you're as old as I am, the two of you will be friends again. You can do that, can't you?"

In her eyes Steph could see how much she'd hurt Paula. *Does she know we kissed? Does she know we almost went to bed together?*

When Steph said nothing, Francine asked again. "Can you promise me, Stephanie? Will you do this for me? Someday?"

"Yes, of course. Someday."

"Do you really believe it's over with Lawrence?"

She asked it as a question but Steph sensed a different tone—hope. And she was bewildered.

"Yes," she said emphatically. "It's over."

Francine nodded, as if she approved, and closed the door.

CHAPTER FOUR

"There's no easy way to say this, Paula, so I'm just gonna put it on a paper plate and set it on the table. I'm not dressing it up with garnish and sliding it onto Grandma's fine china."

Paula smiled congenially at her boss who sat at his ornate desk, constantly smoothing his silk tie. One of the downsides of working at a PR firm was the overuse of metaphor and spin. And no one could decorate a Christmas tree the way Christian Marcum could. Christian was constant motion and while Paula worked tirelessly, he still arrived before her in the morning and was rumored to have fathered the baby of one of the night custodians because she was the only woman he ever saw consistently. He was a bona fide workaholic, one who couldn't stop moving. He tugged at his cuffs and shifted in his seat.

She'd worked at CM Connections for nearly three years, putting in an average of seventy hours a week—more than any other employee—to endear herself to the man who was regarded as Seattle's premier PR guru. And it had worked. She'd slowly ascended the food chain to account executive, overseeing two of his most important clients, FitnessPro and Cyberlink. She loved the folks at Cyberlink, but the FitnessPro exec, Lenore Kerry sat at the heart of Christian's bad news. Lenny was a power lesbian who often clashed with her. Their relationship ran hot and cold—until Lenny had made it very clear how hot she wanted it to get. But Paula found her totally unappealing, the complete antithesis of a beautiful woman.

Paula was totally turned off by Lenny's clownish makeup and manly suits. She preferred femmes and their sweet perfumes and delicious curves. So after Lenny made a play and Paula rebuffed her, their meetings had become uncomfortable.

"Paulie, I need to let you go."

"What?"

It was only eight thirty in the morning and she'd barely finished a cup of coffee so she was certain she'd misheard him.

He held up his hands, wrists together. "I'm a prisoner here, shackled by the almighty dollar. I've got to think of the company."

"What the hell is going on?"

He gasped at her reaction. She'd always used a sing-song tone and when she had to discuss problems or challenges with him, she spoke in euphemisms. He swallowed the jagged little pills easier that way.

"Paulie?" he cried.

"Christian, I need answers."

"Paulie, I don't have a choice. Lenny is threatening to pull the account."

"Is that what she said?"

"I'm not sure we need to go there."

"Of course we need to go there. I've worked my ass off for you for the last three years. You've seen me more than my lover, a fact she throws in my face on a regular basis. I've been abandoned by a ton of women over this job. If you're firing me, I think I deserve a full explanation."

He leaned back in his chair and tented his fingers. "Lenny claims that you engaged in inappropriate verbal banter with her during one of your meetings."

She sighed. "In English, please."

"Lenny says you sexually harassed her by making lewd suggestions about hooking up."

Her eyes widened. Lenny had turned the entire situation around, making her the aggressor.

"You don't believe this, do you?"

He scowled. "Of course not, but that's not the point. FitnessPro is a huge account for us, you know that. You also know that Lenny *is* the face of FitnessPro. They go hand in hand." For emphasis he clasped his fingers together.

"Why can't you just take me off the account instead of firing me? I wouldn't like the idea of losing it but it'd solve the problem."

He grabbed his reading glasses from the table and picked up a letter from his desk. "Not according to Lenny. She states that seeing you during a visit to CM would be terribly distressing and she doesn't think she could bear it."

"You've got to be kidding." She reached for one of the stress balls that he kept in a bucket on his desk and squeezed it, pretending it was Lenny's head. "She's just a manipulative bitch. She actually came on to *me*. And it wasn't just with words."

He showed no surprise or reaction. He released the letter dramatically and it floated to the desk. "Put yourself in my shoes, kiddo. What would you do if you were me, and before you say anything rash," he quickly added, "remember I know you want to be *me*. You want to sit in this chair. So what do I do?"

He tapped his finger on the desk, waiting for her to answer the rhetorical question. She flashed to Lenny's visit the month before. She'd staged an elaborate scenario, requiring Paula to deliver some important documents to her hotel suite late at night. The moment Paula crossed the threshold she knew it was a setup. Lenny greeted her in a satin robe, the lights were dimmed and a room service tray sat on a table with predictable foods for a sexual encounter—strawberries, chocolate sauce, whipped cream, cherries and a bottle of champagne.

She'd tried to hand Lenny the documents and go but Lenny insisted she stay for a glass of champagne. Before she popped the cork she discarded her robe, revealing a lacy bra and panties that exposed most of her body—and the muscles Paula were rather certain derived from steroids. She apologized profusely for potentially sending the wrong signals and left immediately. Apparently the apology hadn't satisfied Lenny or her libido.

"So is there anything I can do to reverse this decision?"

He shook his head slowly. "No, unfortunately not. Of course I'll give you a fabulous recommendation. This won't come up again. I know it's bogus, Paulie, but that's part of the game. We're in PR," he said dramatically. "It's all about pleasing the clients, kissing their asses. Hell, we build them a new ass if necessary." He stood and held out his hand. "I'll give you two weeks to hand over your accounts, and I'll write a great recommendation and offer a terrific severance package. I'm truly sorry."

She wandered back to her office threading her way among the cubicles of people on computers and phones, and loudly slammed the door. She'd never been fired before and she wanted to scream. This wasn't even her fault and it was totally unfair. She sighed. She might hate her predicament but she knew Christian was right. Corporate PR was all about pleasing the clients. If she wanted the big bucks and the corner office, she had to keep the clients happy.

"Damn that bitch," she muttered.

Her phone rang. *Shelby.* She took a deep breath before she answered. "Hey babe, how's the opening coming?"

"It's crazy but I'm so psyched! We've got all my paintings hung and Gemma even cleared out an extra space for my mural. Isn't that fabulous?"

Paula gritted her teeth at Gemma's extra attention to Shelby's art. She suspected Shelby was stepping out on her but she didn't have proof, only the experience and knowledge of one who'd made excuses during most of her own relationships.

"Look, I've gotta run and I won't be home till really late tonight. Gemma invited some bigwig investors to the gallery, kinda like a private preview. Everything okay with you?"

She knew it was a rhetorical question and Shelby expected a simple answer. "Fine," Paula said, dismissing the past twenty minutes with her boss.

After Shelby hung up Paula gazed out the tenth story window and the view she was about to lose. She doubted there was a special preview scheduled and she imagined Shelby would spend the evening between the sheets with Gemma. But she couldn't fault Shelby for sleeping with her benefactor. Monogamy wasn't a skill Paula herself had mastered and she'd begged more than a few girlfriends for a second chance after she slipped. She believed relationships should be able to get past affairs. Yet she was learning that most women didn't share her liberal view.

She put her head on her desk, thoughts of Shelby vanishing. She'd lost her job in a shaky economy. She knew Christian would give her a glowing recommendation and she'd leave quietly in return. He'd make up some story about creative differences. She'd survive but this would definitely derail Shelby's hope of cohabitation.

Shelby wanted Paula to support her while she created art. Paula had said she'd consider it but that was out of the question now and she was relieved. She dreaded everything else—retuning her résumé, job hunting, filling out applications, finding a head hunter and interviewing. It also dawned on her that she might need to leave Seattle, a fact that depressed her immensely.

She reviewed her messages—eight from the same unknown number in the Eugene area code. Just as she was about to hit voice mail, the phone rang again.

"Hello, Ms. Kemper? This is Lettie Gunn, your mother's next-door neighbor. Your mother gave me your cell number in case there was ever an emergency and I've been trying to call you for the last hour."

"Is my mother all right?"

There was a long pause on the other end of the line and Paula could hear Mrs. Gunn wheezing. "I'm so sorry, sweetie, there's been a terrible tragedy. Your mother had a heart attack this morning in the front yard. I hate to tell you this but she's passed away."

CHAPTER FIVE

When Steph saw the door to the church social hall, a nineteen-year-old memory clicked into place. Debbie had insisted Steph's sweet sixteen birthday be a huge production and most of the junior class had been invited, people that Steph, Paula and Emilio secretly called the outer circle. As they'd scurried to finish the preparations, Paula picked up the enormous custom sheet cake Debbie had designed and created—one arm supporting each end—and it folded in half, as if she were closing a book. The picture of Paula and Steph that had been drawn in the middle was ruined, an enormous frosting crease splitting them apart.

"I'm so sorry, Steph," she cried.

Steph assured her it was no big deal. She wasn't superstitious and seeing the picture divided by a pile of confectioner's sugar meant nothing. She never thought that moment could be slightly prophetic, but much like the cake everything had fallen apart after she went to Berkeley two years later. She'd never called Paula before she left for her grandparents' place and the words certainly didn't come easier as more time passed. Steph learned that Paula had never returned to Eugene, deciding to settle in Seattle permanently and enroll at the University of Washington. Her life had ascended into the stratosphere of corporate success while Steph's plummeted into the toilet.

Over the years the tenderness of Paula's lips had faded from her memory as she reinvented herself as a doctor's wife and socialite. The greedy monster that was time ate up their friendship and left Steph with bittersweet memories that only surfaced by accident, surprising her at unexpected moments. She'd see a woman who resembled Paula or she'd stumble upon a lesbian couple kissing as she channel-surfed late at night and she was drawn back to the afternoons behind the granite rock.

Now she sat in the Beemer while water pellets plopped onto the windshield. Francine's mourners slowly made their way into the church, most of them native Oregonians oblivious to the light rain that dusted their dark clothing. The visitors were obvious, with their sheltering umbrellas as they hustled toward the doors.

She debated whether to join them and face the awkward reunions she was sure to find inside the vestibule, particularly with Paula. Would she be angry? Would she throw her out? Unlikely. Their friendship was the anchor to the past and gave her permission to intrude on this intimate occasion. She was here for Francine—her friend, her second mother. She couldn't believe it'd been only a week since she'd visited her. Francine had obviously been very ill, but she'd still wanted to see Steph. And Steph had promised to make amends with Paula.

She sighed and reached for her compact. She glanced through the windshield at a balding, handsome man with a buff physique standing in front of the car. It took a second to recognize her old friend Emilio Santos. He'd been one of only two boys brave enough to join the cheer squad, and she and Paula had instantly befriended him. On many Friday nights he'd literally held her life in his hands as she vaulted to the top of the pyramid at the end of a routine. He was always the base and she was always the cherry on top, according to Paula.

He held out his arms until she got out of the car and hugged him tightly for a long time.

"I expected a phone call from you about fifteen years ago," he said. "I've missed your homemade muffins," he added, referring to the blueberry muffins she traditionally brought to practice.

She gazed into his chocolate brown eyes. He'd always had the face of a model and time had been kind. Traces of gray marked his temples and laugh lines outlined his mouth. She suspected he spent life with a perpetual smile on his face, like the one he offered her now.

"Would you believe me if I said I'd been kidnapped by wolves and living in the Amazon?"

He laughed. "You know that wolves are not indigenous to the Amazon?"

"Caught."

She blinked away tears and he chuckled. He made an approving sound while his eyes wandered up and down her body.

"Girlfriend, you look hot. Is this Armani?" he asked, gesturing to the simple black silk dress she wore.

"No, it's Chanel."

"Ah, well, it's perfect on you."

He kissed her on the cheek and it wasn't until that moment that she realized how much she'd missed him. They'd dated for a short time during junior year but it never felt right and she couldn't explain it. Like everything else, Emilio just accepted it and they went on as friends until she abandoned him along with Paula. Years later she learned he'd come out of the closet and their dating frustrations finally made sense.

He took her hand and they climbed the steps leading into the vestibule. "You know that I called and wrote?"

She nodded. "This is all on me." She stopped and stared at

him. "You don't know how many times I've thought of you."

"Yeah, I do." He wrapped his arm around her shoulder and said, "So I expect us to catch up, but for now will you be my date to this gig?"

"Is it appropriate to bring a date to a memorial service?"

He peered inside the church at the multitude of people, only some of whom she vaguely recognized. "I'm figuring that you want an escort."

She took a deep breath. "You got that right."

"Have you spoken to Paula?"

She nearly tripped and he steadied her. "Not since high school."

He offered a wise, sad smile and led her down the center aisle. In a group clustered near the front she recognized Paula's gorgeous chestnut hair from the back. A throng of acquaintances separated them. Etiquette demanded she acknowledge the others, greeting each one with warm courtesy. She was certain that they'd stayed in Paula's life, for she'd always been fabulous about maintaining relationships. Steph imagined Paula had a few hundred friends on Facebook and Twittered regularly while taking pictures with her cell phone was a struggle for her.

The outer circle of friends had grown and multiplied. Many had married and their children wriggled between Mom and Dad. Steph knew none of their names, and in many cases she was totally unaware that they existed. She felt old in an instant, despite the fact that she was the parent of a teenager too.

As she engaged in pleasantries with these virtual strangers, her gaze flitted to Paula constantly. While she herself was a tiny blonde, Paula was her opposite, a tall, olive-skinned, dark-haired beauty. Her black pantsuit was clearly tailor-made and clung to her curves perfectly. She looked fit, as though she could lead everyone through a cheer at any moment. Her Blackberry rang and she drifted away from the group to take the call.

A younger woman dressed in a button-down shirt and dark pants moved next to her and wrapped her arms around Paula's waist. She immediately removed the woman's arms and stepped out of the embrace but a pang of jealousy pinched Steph.

Before Steph could approach her, the organist's sad melody began, signaling everyone to their seats. She'd intentionally arrived with only a few minutes to spare, to avoid lengthy, painful introductions and non-sequiturs that could never bridge the many years of distance that separated her from the high school crowd. But now she found herself longing for a moment alone with Paula before the emotional goodbye to Francine.

There wasn't a casket at the front and Steph remembered that Francine had mentioned often that she wanted to be cremated and scattered somewhere near the ocean. Her love of all things nautical, particularly lighthouses, had brought her to Oregon years before and probably accounted for her attraction to her husband Paul, a Navy man.

The program reflected Paula's attention to detail and her intelligent nature. Many of the outer circle read poetry and sadness tugged at Steph's heart. She was no part of this, although many years before, she and Paula had been practically sisters, as close as any two people could be. When one of their fellow cheerleaders read *Thanatopsis*, Francine's favorite poem, Steph knew that if she were still a part of Paula's life, she would have been awarded that honor.

Movement caught her eye and she noticed a well-dressed man had slipped into the pew across from her. She watched him carefully, trying to place him. He wiped a hand across his face and she realized he'd spent a lot of time at Paula's house. He was Francine's attorney—Ted something—and a good friend apparently.

As the poetry reading ended he removed a handkerchief from his suit jacket and dabbed at his eyes. It was such a touching show of sentiment and she couldn't pull her gaze away. His shoulders hunched and he hung his head. *He's sobbing.* Apparently overcome with grief, he hurried out again.

When it was Paula's turn to speak, her voice cracked as she shared some memories of her mother, and Steph felt they were once again united in their mutual loss of a parent. She learned things about Francine she'd never known. She'd been questioned by Joe McCarthy in the fifties and met her husband while she worked for the CIA overseas. Steph knew Francine was nearly forty when she'd finally married, and the first time Steph met her, she'd mistaken her for Paula's grandmother.

The age difference between their parents often made for some funny stories, because what Francine thought was hip or popular, such as furniture or clothing choices, was about fifteen years out of style. Steph knew the generation gap had caused Paula some embarrassment over the years, like the time when her mother gave her an Etta James record rather than Rick James's latest album.

As Paula recounted a humorous anecdote, a cell phone chimed and everyone glanced about, wondering who was callous enough to leave a phone on.

"Sorry," Paula said quietly, checking the Caller ID before turning it off and continuing her eulogy without losing a beat.

She spoke about her mother's love of lighthouses and reading but Steph sensed a detachment in her voice. She remembered Francine hadn't mentioned Paula when she'd visited, except to ask her to reconnect with Paula. She wondered how long it had been since Paula had visited her mother.

"I guess the most important quality my mother possessed was her helpful nature…" Her voice trailed off when her eyes locked on Steph. She fumbled with her notes until she found her place. "Sorry, again," she said absently before she continued.

After the benediction everyone filed out into the rain, which had become thicker during the service. A lunch was planned in the social hall and the procession of mourners filed out, passing a picture display depicting Francine's life, a great span of time Steph knew nothing about back then and never cared to know. They were young and their parents were old. It was painful enough to endure their own family anecdotes but to subject their friends to each other's boring histories would've been unthinkable and uncool.

Another acquaintance cornered Emilio while Steph flipped

through the old photo albums, finding many pictures of Paula and herself and the years leading to their graduation. Steph's sudden absence in the later photos was probably noticeable to no one but herself, and she wished a pictorial existed that could explain what had happened and at what exact moment they abandoned their friendship for good. When had too many years passed to send an *I'm Thinking of You* card? And why had she never sent her an e-mail?

"I wouldn't be angry if you ducked out."

Paula's voice surprised her and she jumped slightly before she turned around. Paula greeted her with a strained smile, so unlike the innocent grin she'd always worn as a cheer captain. Her eyes were tired and her expression was tainted by the emotional upheaval of losing a parent.

They embraced and Steph whispered, "I'm so sorry."

Paula held her at arm's length while her eyes probed her body. Steph couldn't breathe. She was accustomed to men leering at her but a wave of energy surged through her as Paula jumpstarted her libido and reminded her that she was still sexy.

"You look...great. It's good to see you but like I said, if you want to go, I'd understand."

"Do you want me to leave? Would that be easier?"

Paula was clearly shocked by her bluntness. It was a quality Steph had only developed in the last ten years after learning to stand up to Lawrence about his affairs.

"Is the luncheon that bad?" Steph added.

Paula laughed slightly and the tension broke. "I could always count on you, Steph. You made me feel better whenever I was upset."

"Well, not always."

Paula's gaze swept about the room, assessing the other mourners. She touched her collar absently, a nervous habit she'd picked up senior year when she quit smoking.

"I want to catch up but I don't think I have time for the entire seventeen years. So I'll just ask if you're okay."

"I'm fine. You need to make the rounds. Go."

"Are you staying for lunch?"

"Um, well…"

Steph hadn't intended to stay this long but she'd been caught in the line of people headed to the display. The thought of old friends peppering her with questions she had no desire to answer was not appealing.

Paula drew her into a corner, away from the crowd. "I imagine it's difficult to be back here but it means a lot to me that you came."

"I had to be here," she said honestly.

Paula looked away again and Steph followed her gaze, toward the woman in the button-down shirt and chinos. She was talking to Melissa, a fellow cheerleader from high school. The stranger whispered something and Melissa burst into laughter.

"Who's that?" she asked.

"My girlfriend, Shelby." Paula's expression remained neutral, free of jealousy despite the open flirting that was occurring between the two women. "She insisted on coming even though my mother had no idea she existed and half the people here had no idea I was gay until now." She added with a sharp tone, "It would help if she'd stop announcing to everyone that she's my lover."

"It's not a big deal," Steph said casually. "I didn't even know, at least not officially," she added.

Paula flashed a wry smile. "That's because you and I haven't spoken for nearly twenty years. A lot of these people send me Christmas cards, stop by and visit when they're in Seattle or e-mail me regularly. They didn't need to find out I was a lesbian at my mother's memorial service. This is supposed to be about *her*, not me." She held up her hands and shook her head. "Why am I telling you all of this?"

"Because you can tell me anything."

Steph thought Paula might cry. The years of separation crumbled around them and they stood surrounded by the past.

"God, Steph, I've missed you so much."

"I've missed you, too."

Paula glanced back at the mourners before she said, "Come with me."

She led Steph through the back door to the meditation garden. Fall flowers burst around them, enjoying the slight drizzle the rain had become.

"It's nearly stopped raining," Steph observed as they sat on a bench away from the windows.

Paula shook her head. "Please don't talk about the weather. I know we haven't spoken in forever but let's not sink that low. There are a hundred different things I want to ask you and another hundred memories I'd like to share with you again. But I don't want to pretend or be casual."

"Okay," Steph whispered, not knowing where to begin.

After seventeen years she was inches away from Paula. Suddenly everything she remembered about her flawless skin, full red lips and deep blue eyes seemed a ridiculous caricature compared to the natural beauty who sat beside her. She'd envied Paula's effortless good looks through high school and time had sculpted wisdom and laugh lines that added to her loveliness.

Paula leaned against her and sighed. "I've missed you," she said again in a dreamy voice.

She brought Steph's hand to her lips and Steph thought she might fall over after the first kiss. She suddenly felt dizzy and grabbed the edge of the bench.

Paula's fingers traced the rings she wore—a diamond and a ruby in each respectively. While Steph had removed her wedding ring, she wouldn't surrender the ruby Lawrence had bought for her thirtieth birthday or the simple diamond chip that Eric purchased for her thirty-fifth.

"You've obviously done well for yourself," she said.

"Rich husband."

Paula raised an eyebrow. "Really?"

Steph glanced back at the social hall, wondering what Shelby would think of this moment. Or Francine.

"You don't think your mom ever suspected you were gay?" she thought to ask.

"No, I was very careful. I treated myself like one of my own PR clients, someone who had to be sold to an audience, namely my mother. She had to believe I fit a certain persona."

"So what did you do to sell yourself?"

Paula laughed. "All kinds of things. I had fake boyfriends and we took fictitious vacations and there was even a pretend proposal that just didn't work out. And of course I never brought anyone home for her to meet except my fake boyfriends."

"Didn't you feel like you were living a lie?"

"Absolutely, but I certainly couldn't tell her. Steph, you have to remember that my mother was born an entire generation before everyone else's parents. She never fit in." She leaned back, craning her neck upward, exposing the fine curve of her chin. "My mother was so backward that she still called black people 'colored.' Can you believe it?"

"Well, I know she was a little old-fashioned—"

"A little? When I got my period, Mom was so out of touch she didn't know about tampons. For two months I wore those thick pads. Until you finally got your period. *Your* mother was the one who showed us how to use tampons, remember?"

Steph nodded, thinking about that Saturday afternoon when she'd gotten her period while Paula was over at the house. She was mortified but Debbie never blinked. Fortunately it was early enough in the afternoon that she was still sober. She huddled in the bathroom with them and pulled out her box of Tampax. They were mesmerized by the process and asked several embarrassing questions that Debbie answered with true sincerity. It was her mother at one of her best moments.

"Francine could barely say the word menstruation," Paula said. "She would have fainted if she'd walked in on us with your mom holding the tampon over her vagina." They both laughed, imagining the usual pained expression Francine wore when confronted by a nouveau idea that shocked her.

"Look, I know that it was politically incorrect for me to keep this from her, but I just couldn't tell her and I don't regret it. Maybe it would've been different if my dad hadn't died…"

43

"Did she ever give you a hard time about grandchildren?"

She made a face. "Sometimes. She blamed my career and told me that I worked too hard and that's why I couldn't keep a man."

"So is Shelby your wife?" she asked reluctantly.

"Oh, no, she just came down to help me with the house. We're in the midst of deciding about our relationship."

"Deciding what?"

"Whether we're ready to take that next step—living together. It's a long story."

It's a long story. That's what you say to someone you hardly know and don't want to bore with the details. Steph realized they were strangers. Seventeen years had flown by and they'd evolved into different people with new biographies, new views on the world and probably different tastes in music and art. If she had to step into a store and buy her a gift, she wouldn't have the slightest idea what to purchase.

"I should really go," Steph said and pulled her hand away. "I loved your mom. She was a great lady and always so kind to me."

Paula started to cry. "Thanks." She took a breath and centered her emotions again. "How long are you in town? Maybe we could get together?"

Her cheeks warmed. "Actually, I moved back a few months ago."

Paula made no attempt to hide her shock. "You live here? I'd have thought a world-famous doctor with a degree from Berkeley would be practicing in New York or Chicago."

"Not quite," she whispered. "I'm not a doctor. I only went to Berkeley for a year."

"What?"

"It's like you said. It's a really long story. I need to go."

Steph started to leave but Paula grabbed her arm. "Oh, no, wait a sec. You don't get to leave after that, no matter how long the story is. You're not a doctor?"

"No."

She obviously sensed her embarrassment. "Doctor's assistant?"

Steph chuckled slightly and shook her head. "Nope. Doctor's wife."

"Ah," she said. "Happily married?"

"Getting divorced—finally," she added, but she didn't know why. That one word caught Paula's attention and she raised an eyebrow. "I do need to go," Steph said again, glancing at Paula's fingers gripping her forearm.

She let go but stepped closer until their lips were only inches apart. "Steph, can I ask you one more question?"

"Sure."

"You knew I was gay, right? After everything that happened between us?"

She nodded. "Yeah, I thought it was obvious. And that's why after all these years I find it hard to believe that your mom didn't suspect. Her beautiful daughter never marries—"

Paula ran a finger down her cheek and her touch burned a path to Steph's chin. "You think I'm beautiful? I've always thought you were. I loved wrapping my finger around your hair and just…being near you. Do you remember the afternoons behind the rock?"

Steph knew she was blushing and the memory of their last afternoon together flooded her mind. The two of them half-naked. Paula's hand between her legs. When she finally looked up into Paula's intense blue eyes, she couldn't answer. Her mouth felt as if it were filled with glue.

Paula lifted her chin and the heat between them intensified. *Just walk away, Steph. That's all you need to do.* But she couldn't move and she couldn't speak. When Paula brought their lips together, the nerves in her toes reacted. It was an easy, comfortable kiss, reminiscent of the ones they shared years ago.

She looked into her eyes. "Well, you didn't run away screaming and you're not swearing at me. Those are positive signs. Maybe I'm crazy but I've thought about kissing you every day for the last seventeen years."

Steph stepped back. "You shouldn't read too much into…
that. You caught me totally off guard. And what about Shelby?
Should you really be kissing me? We're at your mother's *memorial
service.*"

She shrugged. "I'm not sure it matters to Shelby. She's having
an affair with the woman sponsoring her art show. Maybe it's just
business but I'm not sure."

Steph couldn't understand how sex equated to business. It
was clear that Paula lived in a different world, one where the two
intertwined. Steph's experience with Lawrence had taught her
that sex was recreational, his escape from work and his life with
her.

Paula took her hand again. "I don't want to talk about Shelby.
And you didn't answer my question. Do you remember our last
afternoon behind the rock?"

Steph looked down at their intertwined fingers and laughed.
"Seriously, Paula, you know I'm not gay. I was married for almost
twenty years. I have a son."

How many times during their youth had they grabbed each
other's hands and run across the playground? During high school
Paula routinely took her arm as they walked through the halls,
always laughing and giggling. They were inseparable.

"I know you think I'm crazy and maybe I am. I just got
through telling you that I was pissed at Shelby for outing me to
our friends, and yet here I am holding you in my arms wanting
to kiss you again *at my mother's memorial service.*" She looked up
with a sardonic expression. "Sorry, Mom."

But Steph could sense she wasn't sorry at all and she heard
that detachment again. She willed herself to move away or run to
the parking lot but she couldn't. Given the choice between the
comfort of distance and the emotions crackling between them
each time they moved closer, she chose nearness.

Paula parted her luscious lips and licked them. *Please kiss me
again. I want to feel something inside.* Instead she whispered, "Steph,
honey, you may have been married and you *may* be straight, but
you kissed me back."

CHAPTER SIX

Paula's kiss had changed everything, bringing forth memories Steph had packed away years before. Standing in the garden and staring into her gorgeous blue eyes had been like opening the door and locating something she'd lost—passion.

She blushed when she thought of what might've happened had Paula invited her into the church, tool shed or the backseat of her car. She gripped the steering wheel tighter as she zoomed down the highway, realizing that she probably would've done anything with her, ignoring the sacred place or the solemnity of the occasion.

But Paula had restrained herself and walked Steph out to the Beemer. She asked to see a picture of Eric, who, she declared, was as perfect as his mother. She'd invited Steph to help with her mother's house the next day and quizzed her for another twenty minutes about her life. Before Steph had pulled away, she promised to tell Paula more details of her real life, essentially undoing all of Debbie's stories, and Paula promised to kiss her again.

Steph's fingers absently touched her lips. It was ridiculous but she still felt the heat of her kiss. Her lips were the epicenter and the rest of her body swirled in desire. She took a deep breath and shifted in the bucket seat.

She enjoyed driving highway 126 the artery that connected Eugene with the coast. The road stretched through a long valley dotted with wineries and towns like Veneta and Walton. Along the hillsides endless rows of grapevines ensured that the Willamette Valley would remain a supplier of fine Pinot Noir. It was always a battle to stay focused since the drive was easy, the entire ribbon of highway visible for miles. Few patrolmen monitored the Valley since accidents were infrequent and speeders would easily recognize their cruisers half a mile away.

The Siuslaw Mountains loomed in the distance and the straightaway eventually became an obstacle course of winding uphill curves. She navigated the turns, passing the tiny hamlets that dotted the highway until she ran out of land. She turned onto the 101, the Pacific Ocean straddling her left shoulder. The road meandered along the coast and up a hill toward Heceta.

She found Caroline in the kitchen preparing apple strudel for tomorrow's breakfast. Every room was booked primarily by straight or gay couples looking for the same romantic experience that had initially enchanted Caroline and Rick.

"How can I help?" Steph asked, shedding her purse and keys onto a sideboard.

Caroline's gaze swept about the room, assessing progress. "At this point I've got it all under control. The rolls you made earlier are baking for dinner and you got a great compliment this morning from the Steiners. They absolutely adored your banana bread and want some to take with them when they leave tomorrow morning."

"So noted. I'll make two loaves tonight."

"But that's it for now. In another hour I could use you. I'll be ready to set the table. How was the funeral?"

Steph grabbed an apple from a bowl and studied it, avoiding her gaze. "It was nice. Paula did a great job celebrating Francine's life."

"And how's Paula?"

She took a bite and stalled. How could she answer that? *She's more beautiful than ever and we dishonored her mother by kissing in the garden.* Although Caroline knew nothing about the details of their destroyed friendship, she'd asked enough general questions to surmise they were no longer in touch.

"Under the circumstances, I'd say she's holding up pretty well. They were always so close."

Caroline nodded. "I know. I'd see Francine in Eugene periodically and she talked incessantly about Paula. 'Paula just got a promotion,' or 'Paula's managing some big accounts now,' or 'Paula just bought a great condo.' But she never said it in a stuck-up way," she quickly added.

Steph knew what she meant. Francine didn't have a pompous bone in her body.

"Damn it, where's the salt!" Caroline looked about, her hands on her hips. "I used it right before you came in."

"Maybe Rue took it."

Rue was the famed Grey Lady ghost that haunted Heceta Head and preferred Victoria's Room. Everyone had seen her except Steph, and although she believed Caroline and Rick were perfectly sane people, until she saw the old bat herself she wasn't buying it.

Caroline whipped open cupboard doors, cursing under her breath. Steph almost laughed when she checked the oven but the laugh died in her throat when she opened the freezer—and found the salt shaker inside. She waved it at her, knowing Steph was a nonbeliever.

"Still think we're all nuts?"

Steph decided to take a run before dinner preparations began. It was always a wonderful sprint down the mountain to the shore and then back up, past the B and B to the lighthouse. It wasn't much of a workout but she felt refreshed by the time she reached the edge of the cliff. If it was a slow tour day, she'd climb the tower steps to the light and stare through the glass, imagining what it would've been like to live here as a real keeper. But today it was crowded so she avoided the obvious picture spots and found a quiet patch of grass to be alone with her thoughts of Francine—the only person other than her parents who ever knew the truth about her abrupt departure from college.

The day she'd returned to Eugene that fateful spring, she couldn't fathom what she would say to her parents, so she'd driven to Francine's house. During high school she routinely shared her problems with Francine before she took them home. Francine was great at finding just the right words that wouldn't send Dramatic Debbie over the edge.

Four hours later Francine had convinced Steph to keep the baby and accept Lawrence's proposal. When she went with her to tell Debbie and John, Steph wondered if they'd be upset that she confided in Francine first, but she suspected that her mother would be finishing her fourth or fifth drink and her father would be too stunned to care. She was right. Her father, although furious, agreed with her decision and her mother fake-cried for about fifteen minutes before she fell asleep.

A gust of wind sailed across the cliff instantly chilling her. Oregon wasn't known for its warmth. She glanced up at Heceta, its beacon flashing every thirty seconds, as it had for over a hundred years, protecting sailors from crashing into the shore. It was constant and dependable, ameliorating the fear of death.

She was envious of the strong conical structure. When she'd learned she was pregnant, she'd turned to the person she thought was the strongest, who would protect *her* and eliminate her fear. At the time she was too young and too distraught to recognize Francine's tactics were rooted in her own fear. She'd planted seeds of doubt, convincing her that the newborn could wind up

50

in a poor home if she put it up for adoption, or worse, her soul would be damned if she got an abortion.

Years later she realized what she was most afraid of—herself. If she'd pursued either an abortion or an adoption, the reins would have been returned to her and her life would've been her responsibility again. She rationalized that she'd told Francine first because Debbie couldn't handle it, when in fact she herself couldn't.

Francine had given her the traditional, predictable and desired answer, whereas Debbie would've viewed the situation for the complexity it had, forcing Steph to stand in the sea of gray and leave the shore of black and white. After the yelling had stopped and Debbie had sobered up, Steph would've had a choice.

Standing at the base of Heceta, she realized it had been nearly a decade since she'd thought of that afternoon with Francine and it had taken her death for the memory to surface. She'd made the right choice, perhaps for all of the wrong reasons, but she wouldn't undo parts of the past if she could.

As she watched the twilight loom over Heceta and the dark of night pressed the day to end, she thought of the gray in her life, the possibilities with Paula, her divorce and Eric. She looked up at Heceta, yearning for its strength.

CHAPTER SEVEN

The weight of the past three days crashed onto Paula as she and the silent Shelby drove back to the motel. She leaned against the headrest and closed her eyes, hoping Shelby could navigate in the dark. When a wave of sadness overtook her again, she turned toward the window and whimpered softly. Her mother was gone but oddly it was her father she missed. He'd always seemed almost superhuman and she wasn't certain if it was because of his true greatness or the romanticism of childhood. Didn't all little girls think their daddies were perfect?

She comforted herself by thinking of the people around her. After Mrs. Gunn's phone call, she'd immediately Tweeted all of her friends, who rallied to their support and promised to attend the service.

Emilio was his usual upbeat self when he responded. *She's happier than she's ever been, Paula, remember that.* And then he'd used the rest of his one hundred and forty characters to write, *Did you contact Stephanie? She needs to know.*

Paula had called the care facility where Debbie was staying, and after much cajoling she was able to get Steph's cell number. She wasn't brave enough to call so she'd sent a text with the funeral arrangements. Steph had replied with a brief, consoling message, but Paula was disappointed that she hadn't said more, like a few hints of what she'd been doing for the last seventeen years.

Her own behavior at the service was a mystery. She couldn't fathom what had come over her when she'd seen Steph. Shelby, less than fifty yards away, and Paula had kissed another woman. And not just any woman—the one. And she wanted to do it again. She didn't understand how the intervening years could disappear in a single conversation but they had. It was like they had never been apart.

She reminded herself that Shelby was probably sleeping with Gemma and she'd also caught her making out with a bridesmaid at a wedding they'd attended a month before. Shelby had blamed the strong tequila but Paula thought her libido had as much to do with the *transgression*, as Shelby liked to call it.

She opened an eye and glanced at Shelby, who was yawning as she drove. The woman was ten years younger than she, and their different perspectives on life reflected the years of experience that separated them. Now that both her parents were dead she was painfully reminded of her own mortality and isolation. Shelby, on the other hand, had barely turned twenty-five and had two very young and healthy parents. While she was sympathetic to Paula's situation, she couldn't empathize or grasp the depth of the loss.

"I'm an orphan," Paula had said as they waited in the airport for their flight to Portland.

"No, you're not," Shelby replied. "Orphans are little kids like in that *Oliver Twist* book. You've had your mother for your whole life. I mean it's sad," she quickly added, "but come on, babe, she was old, really old. It's part of life."

Face it. Shelby doesn't get it. You can't talk to her about it. Thank God you have Steph.

The vision of Steph standing in the lovely little garden made her smile. She'd seen Steph enter the church with Emilio but she was so stunned that she quickly turned away, knowing a vacuous conversation was the last thing she desired after so many years of separation. She needed time to collect her thoughts, to ensure that she made a good *second* impression on the woman who still held a place in her heart.

Throughout the service she glanced at Steph, whose beauty over time had matured into elegance. She'd always been a knockout, but now she was glamorous, savvy about her looks and the clothes and makeup that accentuated her features. She was a true femme—Paula's exact type.

She might not have found the courage to speak to her if Emilio hadn't literally pushed her toward Steph as she admired Francine's picture display. And the more they talked the more selfish she became. She forgot about the other guests. She wanted Steph all to herself. It had been thoughtless to lead her into the garden, brazen to kiss her—a married woman—and shameful to want more.

"You okay?" Shelby asked, massaging her neck.

"Yeah," Paula lied. Guilt erased the vision of Steph as she tried to focus on Shelby and her recent good deeds.

She'd grudgingly agreed to come since it meant she had to postpone the gallery opening. But since they'd left Seattle she'd been quite helpful, performing every task that Mrs. Gunn assigned to her without much complaining.

Mrs. Gunn had saved them. She was Francine's best friend and when they arrived, she presented them with a thin white envelope. Inside was a message:

Paula, I wish to be cremated and placed at the Tillamook lighthouse. You may have a service if you desire, but please don't allow people to eulogize me with their own memories. It's rude to the audience. You'll need to see my attorney about my will. I love you. Mom.

She was stunned by her mother's entire lack of sentimentality, not that she'd ever shown a tremendous amount of overt compassion. Francine Kemper was regarded as polite, helpful and practical. The only person she'd ever been particularly gentle and kind toward was Steph. Paula had long ago rationalized that Francine felt sorry for Steph, a victim of her mother's antics.

When they arrived at the motel, Shelby headed for the shower and Paula crashed onto the bed, not bothering to remove the dingy comforter. She was too tired to care. The Elmwood Motel was beneath her usual standards, but there'd been nothing else available on such short notice.

"Why can't we stay somewhere nicer?" Shelby whined.

"This isn't a huge city," she explained. "Eugene is a town and there's not a lot to choose from during football season."

Of all the weekends to need a motel, Francine had managed to die during the week before the Oregon Ducks played at home against UC Berkeley, an arch rival.

Thoughts of Berkeley reminded her of Steph's acceptance letter and their last meeting. She'd been so angry and hurt. How could Steph not understand the depth of Paula's feelings—or even her *own* feelings?

She glanced up at the motel ceiling, listening to the hum of the shower. She'd been certain Steph loved her in high school but hadn't been ready to accept it. Over the years her friends had shared tidbits of information obtained from Debbie—apparently all false—about Steph's rise in the medical profession. Based on these nuggets, Paula had written her own story of Steph's life, one where she'd become a respected pediatrician, met an amazing psychotherapist who helped her accept her lesbianism, found an upstanding girlfriend and adopted a couple of kids from a foreign country.

The truth floored her. She couldn't believe Steph had walked away from academics. Steph was the smartest of students, explaining calculus to her while they lay on the bed, although she never quite understood it. *Maybe that's because you spent most of the time looking at her tanned legs and smelling her shampoo.*

Her cell phone chimed and she knew another text message awaited her from Christian. She'd been gone less than thirty-six hours and he'd already called or texted twelve times, including once during her eulogy for her mother. She glanced at the message, a question about the FitnessPro account. *He'll have a lot of fun trying to manage Lenny all by himself.* She punched in the answer and tossed the phone back on the nightstand.

Shelby emerged from the bathroom, naked and drying her hair. "Are you taking one?"

"I'm too tired and I can't move. Every part of my body hurts."

"Why? It's not like we hiked or anything today. All we did was stand around."

She lifted her head and narrowed her eyes. "You don't understand what it's like to have your body start rebelling against you. You've never met back pain or arthritis." Then she chuckled and pointed a finger. "Ah, but you will, young'un, you will."

Shelby crawled onto the bed, hovering over her. She shook her breasts and kissed her on the mouth. "How about a little nookie?"

She couldn't believe it. "Shelby, I appreciate the interest but my mother just died. I'm in a bit of emotional turmoil. I think I'd be a little too distracted to enjoy it."

"But I wouldn't. You could give me something." She took Paula's hand and placed it against her center. "See, I'm already wet. You need to just finish me off."

"Not tonight."

She pulled her hand away but Shelby grabbed it again and thrust it against her clit. "Baby, please," she cooed. "I need it."

"God, Shelby! Your lack of sensitivity is appalling."

Shelby looked like a child who'd been smacked in the face. She rolled off Paula and went to her suitcase. "Fine, if you don't want it, I'll do myself."

She retrieved the vibrator, which Paula hadn't known she'd packed, and headed for the other double bed. Apparently not only would Shelby please herself, she'd be sleeping alone, too.

And that was fine with Paula.

She still hadn't told Shelby she'd been fired. Shelby would be very upset and pressure her to find a job immediately so they could resume The Plan. Then she could devote her time to her art and Paula would support her. She believed Shelby had talent, and while Shelby seemed incredibly grateful that Paula would show her love in this way, Paula questioned her motives, almost certain that once she found her footing in the Seattle art world, Paula would be history, a stepping stone left in the pond once Shelby sold something significant.

But you're not really in love with her either. You've only been in love twice.

She turned away, determined to block out Shelby's soft moans of ecstasy. The last time she'd been in a motel room was her previous visit to Eugene the year before to see her mother. It was supposed to have been a healing visit. She'd left angry and they'd never fixed it. The tears came again and she wept into her pillow. As a teenager she never would've believed her relationship with Francine would be as strained as Debbie and Steph's.

"Can your mother adopt me?" Steph had asked once.

The request came after a particularly embarrassing episode at the market when Debbie had brought a can opener with her and insisted on personally checking all of the canned olives for botulism. The manager found her on the floor after another shopper alerted him that there was a wacky woman sitting in the condiment aisle surrounded by fifty open cans.

"I don't think my mom's allowed to adopt you," Paula said. "But you can just keep coming over a lot."

Steph threw her arms around Paula and kissed her on the cheek, sending a pleasant shiver down her back.

At the time she was flattered that Steph thought so highly of Francine because she thought her mother was practically perfect. Every time she hauled Debbie up the stairs with Steph and John, or when she saw Steph's face turn crimson after a public embarrassment, she was grateful for Francine's quiet, reserved nature even if she was old-fashioned.

It had taken several years before she realized she'd gladly trade places with Steph. Debbie wouldn't have cared if Steph had come out. Paula thought about how it could've been between them if she hadn't walked away when they were teenagers. Instead she spent her entire adult life hiding from her mother, living in a fiction, lying and ruining relationships, avoiding some promising ones altogether, all because she couldn't tell the truth. She pinched her eyes shut, determined to succumb to her exhaustion and sleep.

CHAPTER EIGHT

Steph began her morning as she always did—gazing at Heceta. Fog hugged the ocean and cliffs but Heceta's beacon pierced the shroud, announcing its presence. The steady burst of light was hypnotic and brought her comfort. It was a survivor, despite the storms and rockslides that had pelted the tower for decades. She was envious. If only she could have a core of such strength.

It was Monday and that meant it was time to visit her mother at her care facility in Eugene. Since she'd returned she'd kept her promise that she would stop by at least once a week, regardless of how depressing and awkward it seemed. So far she hadn't missed a Monday and Debbie had recognized her most of the time—except for once when she thought Steph was Vic, the guy who owned Debbie's favorite liquor store. It'd been embarrassing listening to her plead for a free bottle of Jack. She assured Steph she was good for it, which only brought chuckles from the staff.

Quality time with her mother was usually preceded by an admonishment from the facility manager, who would inform her of Debbie's latest antics. The first week Steph learned Debbie had stood on a chair in the dining room and held up a placard that read UNION, ala Norma Rae style, when she thought the residents should unite against the facility's unwillingness to serve soy milk.

"Mom, you don't even drink soy milk," she argued with her later.

"No, but Mrs. Grunewalt does. She's lactose intolerant and she complains every morning that she can't have her Special K like she used to. That's not right. When you've got one foot in the grave, you should be able to enjoy the little things."

Steph couldn't argue with that but she apologized to the manager and Debbie promised she'd stay off the chairs. Interestingly, soy milk appeared on the menu after the incident.

While Steph dreaded another visit with Debbie, she couldn't wait to see Paula again. She imagined they'd be surrounded by other helpful Samaritans, including Paula's girlfriend, and there wouldn't be any further kissing. She knew yesterday didn't count. Paula had been distraught over Francine's death and kissing Steph was a side effect of her distress.

She dressed quickly and joined Caroline in the kitchen. "How'd you sleep?" Caroline asked as she cracked eggs into a bowl.

"Fine."

"You didn't hear the screams?"

"Huh?"

She frowned. "The Carters claim they heard Rue screaming last night in the attic. Rick and I didn't hear anything but we're down here. They're asking us to forgive a night on the bill."

Steph shook her head. People would do anything to get a deal, even invent a ghost.

"I wouldn't do it," she said. "They knew the place is supposedly haunted when they checked in. If they wanted a spirit-free lighthouse, they should've visited Yaquina Head."

"Now, you're just being sarcastic," Caroline said, pointing a wooden spoon at her face. "You'd better be careful. Rue might not like that you're making fun of her."

Steph touched her heart dramatically. "If you're listening, Rue, I have the utmost respect for you as a spirit and a woman."

Caroline chuckled and shook her head. "You'd better hope she's developed a sense of humor over the last hundred years."

They prepared breakfast for the guests, falling into a customary routine. Steph was in charge of all the breads and baking while Caroline handled eggs and beverages. Unlike many B and B's, Heceta Head served a full seven-course meal for its guests with choices like eggs Benedict and quiche. Steph had never eaten so well in her whole life. Caroline had learned quickly that she knew little about cooking—only baking—which in her mind was an entirely different experience.

After five years of living with a wife who could barely use the microwave, Lawrence had acquiesced and hired Mavis, his first live-in affair. He quickly realized that Steph's lack of domesticity could equate to a nearby mistress. It was the perfect answer for a busy doctor with a full calendar. Mavis eventually gave way to Alana, Rachel, Coral and finally Marta appeared.

Steph had known about Mavis but hadn't a clue that while she and Eric served food at the homeless shelter every Thursday night, Alana was serving Lawrence herself. Eric was the one who discovered their affair when he stumbled upon them humping over the washing machine one afternoon. Steph knew there had been dozens of women and she had given up looking for evidence of his periodic indiscretions; however, when Lawrence chose to have his affairs in her home, it was impossible to avoid and untenable.

"I'll be gone most of the day," she said to Caroline. "I hope that's okay."

"It's more than okay," she said. "You've hardly left this place in three months except to visit your mom. What are you doing today? Are you going to see Paula?"

At the mention of her name, Steph felt her cheeks flush. "Yeah, I thought I'd stop by Francine's house and see if she needs any help packing. And Emilio and I are going out to lunch and then to see my mom."

Caroline glanced up from the eggs she was beating. Steph waited for the wisecrack that she thought would follow, but Caroline said, "Has he seen your mom since high school?"

"No," she said.

"Should be interesting. What do you want me to tell Lawrence when he calls here after you don't answer your cell phone?"

Steph smirked and popped a warm muffin in her mouth. Maybe she couldn't do much but she could make a mean muffin. "You can tell him to go to hell," she said, and she meant it.

"I think I'll just tell him you're out."

Caroline went downstairs to the basement and Steph wrote herself a note to call her attorney. Lawrence's abusive phone calls were occurring daily and she wanted a restraining order. According to Eric he'd now dumped Marta and spent each night drinking by the pool and crying. She laughed when she thought of how many nights he'd made her cry. He'd need sixteen more years to catch up.

Once breakfast was concluded, she excused herself and practiced the little speech she'd prepared for Emilio when they arrived at Waverly Place. Basically, the poor man needed to be ready for anything, including a full frontal display of her mother's boobs or vagina.

The drive into Eugene only clogged in a few places, as the highway turned into Eleventh Avenue. She meandered through the heart of the city, past the University of Oregon area and south toward the suburban neighborhood that nestled against Spencer Butte. Before she climbed the hill to Francine's street, she wound her way through the familiar route that led to her parents' house. It had been three years since she'd last visited, when she'd spent a week moving Debbie to the facility and clearing out the house. The Goodwill people had been ecstatic when they saw the U-Haul pull up to the drop-off center. She'd given everything away, except for what Debbie needed and a few boxes of pictures. Her last act before she'd dropped off the keys to the Realtor was to sit behind the rock, their rock, facing the forest that kept all of their secrets. Memories of Paula rolled over her, giving her the fix she needed.

She parked the car and stared at the blue and white house of her youth. From the outside it looked inviting and friendly. The new owners had kept it the same color and she felt oddly relieved. Not much was different, as if in deference to her father and the endless weekends he toiled in the yard to plant trees and shrubs. Even the rose bushes, the ones he'd slaved over because her mother insisted on having them, still lined the front walkway.

"If walls could talk," she muttered, pulling away.

Paula's house was two blocks to the west. As the car ascended the hill, she thought of how developed their calf muscles became from trekking up to Paula's house each day to escape Debbie. They'd return whenever Steph's father would call. Usually each night by eight o'clock Debbie fell asleep in her chair after the Jack was gone, and it would take all three of them—John, Paula and Steph—to lug her up the steep flight of stairs. During the many nights when he was out of town, Debbie slept in the chair while Steph crept past her late at night after spending the evening with Paula.

There were no secrets from Paula. She knew who and what Debbie was.

Four cars with rental stickers were parked in front of Francine's house so Steph knew Paula was inside, sorting through an entire life as Steph had three years before.

She'd brought a basket of muffins and she was halfway across the street before she got cold feet. She hesitated, wondering if she was intruding. She stopped and swiveled back toward the car, unable to decide what to do.

A screen door shut and Paula emerged from the house lugging a large cardboard box to a rented Chevy Malibu. She looked like a typical Pacific Northwest girl—blue jeans, a denim shirt with a white T-shirt underneath and hiking boots. She'd pulled her hair back into a ponytail and could easily pass for eighteen again. Steph automatically smiled.

Paula set the box on the hood and looked at her quizzically. "Hey," she said. "What are you doing?"

Steph realized she was standing in the middle of the street between the car and the house. She looked ridiculous.

"I don't know," she answered. "Do you really want me here? I'll understand if you say no," she quickly added. "I'm sure you're already miserable and I don't want to add a heavy dose of weird on top of it."

Paula smiled sardonically. "I can take a little weird, but only a little. Muffins?" she asked, hopefully.

"Yeah, I thought everyone might be hungry."

Paula searched under the warming cloth until she found a banana nut. "So did you remember how much I loved these or is this an accident?"

"Of course I remembered."

Paula kissed her on the cheek and she felt her face flush. "Not quite the same as yesterday," Paula said softly and Steph almost dropped the basket. "Did you think about our kiss last night before you went to sleep?"

Steph stared at the ground, trying to steady her breathing. If she passed out, she wondered if Paula would catch her. "I never gave it another thought," she said coolly.

Paula chuckled quietly and nibbled on her muffin. "Right. How was I? Did I do okay?"

Her voice dripped with sarcasm and Steph cracked a grin, grateful she was playing along. To face the truth would be impossible while they stood in the street.

"Well," she sighed, "the kiss you gave me was passable."

She pulled Steph against her. "Then I'll need to try again. I won't have my reputation smeared by a rumor of mediocre lip locking."

Steph pressed her hand against Paula's lips as she moved in to strike. "Your girlfriend is inside and if she were to peer between those hideous curtains and see us, she'd probably run out here

64

and flatten me. I'm too old for a brawl."

"You're probably right," she agreed grudgingly.

Steph nodded and moved her hand away. Paula immediately planted a quick but passionate peck on her lips. "Sorry. I couldn't resist."

After she packed the box in the car, they lingered outside until Paula finished her muffin. "We've spent so much time talking about my mom but she doesn't need help anymore. She's in a much better place. How's *your* mom? I heard she went to live in a facility."

"Yeah, about three years ago. She told me she wanted to go and she didn't think she could deal with everything alone and she wouldn't accept my offer to move to Arizona."

Paula touched her arm. "That must've been hard."

"Very. But I think she's happy there most of the time. She's certainly the life of the party."

Paula chuckled. "I still remember the time she sang "Lady Marmalade" in front of the entire PTA."

Inside the house Paula introduced her to Shelby and she nodded at Hazel, Roman and Jeff, some people from the outer circle, who hovered over a box in front of Francine's curio cabinet wrapping knickknacks. Steph smiled when Emilio emerged from the hallway, carrying a large teddy bear named Mr. Piddle.

"Well, hello," Emilio said.

"Hey."

He turned to Paula and waved Mr. Piddle's arms. "What about this guy? Does he get to motor to the Emerald City?"

Paula touched his fur and frowned. Her dad had given him to her when she was very young. After he died she'd put him in her closet and never taken him out again.

"I don't think so," she said.

Emilio pushed the bear toward her, offering a kiss, but she swatted it away.

"E, don't," Steph said harshly.

Both of them looked at her and Paula offered a half-hearted smile. "Still defending me, huh?"

Her cell phone rang and she excused herself to a corner. Steph imagined she spent a lot of time with it glued to her ear. She took the bear from his hands and set it by the front door.

"You're a little touchy," he said, coming up behind her and squeezing her shoulders.

"Sorry. I don't know what I'm doing here. I don't belong."

He kissed her on the head. "Steph, you belong here more than any of us. Even Paula knows that. I can see how relieved she is that you're here. She needs you."

"Do you think so? You're not just saying that?"

He looked at her tenderly. "No, sweetie. This is all about the past and no one was more important to her than you." He leaned closer and whispered, "And I'm really hoping it's a bridge to a future for the two of you."

She kissed him on the cheek. "I should've married you."

He batted his eyelashes. "That's what all the fag hags say. Millie's the best."

They laughed and she followed him down a hallway toward Paula's room, which was lined on both sides with glass jars of various sizes and shapes filled with coins.

"What's this?"

"We're guessing this is Francine's lifelong change collection. We found them all over the house, in all of the rooms, the closets. Paula even found one in the toilet tank."

"You're kidding."

"Nope." He picked up a smaller one made of aqua blue glass. The cap was rusty and she imagined it was very old. "Jeff figures this Mason jar is worth fifteen or twenty bucks without the change."

"Wow," was all she could say.

"And one other thing," he said, leading her to the end of the hallway outside of Paula's old bedroom. "As you pack stuff you need to check it."

"Check it?"

"Yup. We're finding all kinds of paper money hidden in Francine's things—inside knickknacks, old purses, even the pockets of her coats and sweaters. There's money everywhere, so if you find some, just put it up here." He motioned to a small cardboard box sitting on a table. It was filled with crinkled bills of different denominations, including fifties and hundreds.

"I guess this is what Francine used instead of a bank," she said sifting through some of the cash. She picked up a twenty that was dated 1942.

"My grandmother used to do the same thing. She hoarded cash and kept it under mattresses and in kitchen cupboards. It was typical of people who lived through the Depression."

They went into Paula's room and she froze, staring into the past. Francine had left Paula's room exactly as it was the day she graduated from high school. Her corkboard hung over the oak desk where she diligently finished her homework and a purple beanbag chair sat in the corner. She resisted the urge to plop down, as it had been her customary spot whenever she visited. Paula would sit at her desk or lounge on the four-poster canopy bed that overwhelmed the small room and Steph would gaze up at her in awe.

Emilio handed her an empty box and gestured toward the bookshelf filled with all of the titles they read on demand during high school.

"Are we still going to see your mom later?"

"You can come if you want. I'm warning you, though, she's not the same."

"Does that mean she's stopped doing crazy stuff?"

"Hardly. Last week she hijacked the electric golf cart and took it for a spin. She said three orderlies chased her across the entire property and some woman in a walker had to jump out of the way."

He laughed heartily. "God, I love your mom. I still remember the time she put on your cheerleading outfit and came to practice."

Paula waltzed into the room. "Are we talking about Debbie?"

"I'm going with Steph to visit her this afternoon after we go to lunch," Emilio said.

Paula's face brightened. "I'd like to go."

"Why?" Steph scowled. When she saw Paula's shocked expression, she added, "I mean, won't it be a little upsetting for you?"

She shrugged. "Maybe it'll help to take my mind off everything. Would it be okay?"

Steph couldn't think of a reason to say no, but the thought of her mother and Paula meeting again after so many years made her somewhat uncomfortable.

"Of course you can come," she said, hoping she sounded enthusiastic.

They sat down in front of the bookshelf with a box and got to work.

"Thanks for helping," Paula said quietly. She glanced at Emilio, who'd busied himself with the stuff Francine stuffed in her closet after she'd moved out.

"It's not a big deal. I remember how hard it was to clear out my parents' house after we put my mom at Waverly Place."

Paula rolled her eyes. "I'm supposed to be back at work in a week. I'm not sure I'll even finish the kitchen by then. I can't believe how much cash my mother hid in this house." As if on cue, she held a book upside down and a twenty-dollar bill drifted to the floor. "She even hid money in *my* stuff."

Steph murmured agreement. She wanted to say something but she couldn't think of a way to start a real conversation.

"Steph, I need to ask a huge favor."

"Sure," she said automatically.

Paula paused and took a breath. "At some point I need to take her ashes up north to Tillamook. I was wondering if you'd go with me."

Steph stopped packing and looked at her. She was close to crying and her eyes glimmered with tears as if she wouldn't know what to do if Steph said no.

"Of course I'll go, but wouldn't you rather have your girlfriend go, or did you want both of us," she quickly added.

"No, just you and me." There was gentleness, an intimacy in

her tone that Steph remembered from high school when Paula was her most serious.

Steph pulled another stack from the shelf and noticed the title on top—*Pride and Prejudice*. Her mouth went dry and she glanced at Paula, who wore a little smile on her face.

"Do you remember reading that book?"

"Yeah," she said casually. "Do you?"

"Well, I remember that you made a great Elizabeth to my Mr. Darcy."

Steph chuckled and she laughed. And then they were both laughing hysterically.

"That does *not* sound like serious work," Emilio called from the closet.

Paula flipped through the book, which naturally spread open to chapter thirty-two, when Mr. Darcy proposed to Elizabeth.

"Well, that was a long time ago," she said, setting the book in the box. "So, where are you living?"

"I'm staying out at Heceta Head."

"You know, I've never been there."

"Really?" Steph was surprised. "I thought Francine would've taken you since she was a lighthouse lover."

"No, she always went by herself. She said that lighthouses were solitary creatures and it was a private experience for her. She just wanted to be alone and stare out at the sea."

She could barely finish the end of her sentence. She took a deep breath and avoided another crying spell. Steph touched her cheek and Paula pressed her palm against her face, holding it in place. She smiled warmly and kissed her palm before pulling away.

"How did you wind up at Heceta?" she asked after the moment had passed.

"Do you remember Caroline Bickford from high school?"

She searched her memory and nodded. "Vaguely. I've heard my mom mention her. Are you living with her?"

There was an odd tone in her voice and she seemed engrossed in packing the box.

"Actually, she and her husband Rick own the B and B. I ran into her at the mini-mart in Yachats a few days after I pulled into town. I guess it was just fate."

"Oh." She sounded relieved. "What's your plan?"

Steph shrugged. "I've got no idea."

Paula stared at her, clearly wanting to ask more questions but recognizing it was neither the time nor the place. Shelby called and she pulled onto her knees, her arms resting on the box.

"Um, we're not done talking about this."

"You mean my *plan* or lack thereof?"

Her lips curled into a seductive smile. "Yes, we definitely should talk about your plan, the last decade and a half—and maybe Mr. Darcy and Elizabeth."

Her cute little butt vanished and Steph searched the box for the old copy of *Pride and Prejudice*. She leaned against the wall and flipped through the pages, breathing in the old book's smell and gazing at the pink dust ruffle that decorated Paula's bed—the bed they'd lain on while they read and the place they first kissed when Elizabeth locked lips with Mr. Darcy.

CHAPTER NINE

After three hours of packing Paula's room they were famished. The others declined to join them for lunch, and when Hazel returned from the mini-mart with a twenty-four pack of Budweiser, Steph doubted that much more packing would occur.

They decided to revisit the Glenwood, a diner just west of the university that had been one of their haunts during high school. It was a converted house that served great coffee and decent meals. Emilio pleaded and flirted with the gay host to give them their old booth in the back. Once they were situated, Paula and Emilio caught up on life. They'd stayed in touch, referencing people and incidences Steph had never heard of, such as a lucrative job offer for Paula in Portland.

"Would Shelby go with you?" Emilio asked.

She shrugged. "I doubt it. Her art is really taking off in Seattle. It's hard to move and reestablish yourself. Frankly, I don't think I'm worth it."

He scowled. "Now, I totally disagree with that, honey. Right, Steph? Paula is totally worth it."

"Absolutely," she said. She realized if Paula had begged her to go to Seattle with her when they were kids, she would've had a hard time saying no.

She was equally envious of Emilio's scandalous life. He'd returned home from visiting a friend to find all of the furniture missing from his house. While he was gone his boyfriend had learned he was cheating and sought revenge.

"Did you call the police?" Paula asked.

He nodded. "I did, but they said there's not much they can do. It's not like Juan and I were legally married. And California is a community property state anyway. We owned all of that stuff jointly. It's just a fucked-up mess," he concluded with a dismissive wave.

Steph felt bad for him but she had a sore spot for cheaters because it made the other person look like a loser.

Her phone rang as their lunches arrived. It was Eric and while she didn't want to have a public conversation with her son, she hated missing his calls since he was incredibly busy.

"Hi, honey," she answered cheerily.

"Hi, Mom. How's it going?"

"Good. Everything okay at school?" She glanced over at Paula, who speared her Caesar salad, seemingly uninterested.

"Hectic. I got a job at Pizza Joey's to save some more money for college."

"Congratulations, son, that's terrific. Did you get the goodies I sent you?"

He made a disgruntled sound. "What I managed to pry out of Dad's hands. He recognizes your care packages and he'll open them before I get home. Last time I found him out by the pool sobbing over your blueberry muffins."

She shook her head at Lawrence's pathetic behavior. "Well, I promise I'll send you some more treats but I'll disguise the box. Your father won't think there's anything interesting to discover."

"Good. Go ahead and put a toxic waste symbol on it, too," he said, laughing. "And speaking of Dad, he wanted me to tell you that he's sorry for fucking Marta and he wants you to come home."

She laughed and when Emilio laughed too, she realized he and Paula could hear Eric.

"I doubt your father used those words."

"Might as well have, jackass," he added.

She cracked a grin. Lawrence typically threw Eric in the middle, thinking that the son he'd hardly acknowledged during his youth would side with him simply because they both possessed testosterone. Eric, though, was incredibly bright and she'd invested a lot of dinner conversation explaining her position.

"Don't let him get to you," she advised.

"He doesn't. I'm hardly home now and I'll be gone in a few months. So how's life at the lighthouse? Have you seen the ghost?"

"Nope."

"You know, I read once that spirits with a positive aura only show themselves when they feel comfortable with you or they think you need their help. You said Rue is a positive spirit, right?"

"Well, I think she's a tragic spirit. She committed suicide over the death of her daughter."

"Well, she's not giving off a negative or destructive vibe so you'll probably see her when she thinks you're ready."

"Thank you, Mr. Paranormal Expert. I'll let you know when it happens."

"It will," he said. "I gotta get to class, Mom. I love you. And don't feel guilty."

Her voice caught and she paused before she said, "I love you, son. I'll talk to you later this week. I can't wait for you to visit."

"I know, Mom. After exams, okay?"

"Yeah."

They hung up and she realized Emilio and Paula were waiting for her to fill them in.

"There's a ghost at the lighthouse and I'm the only one who's never seen her."

Emilio furrowed his brow. "I'm not sure that's a bad thing. Ghosts give me the shivers."

"I think it's kinda cool," Paula disagreed. "I'd like to have a ghost for a friend."

"She's not really a friend," Steph said. "She's more of a practical joker and she tends to run off the troublesome guests with her wailing."

Paula set down her fork. "Okay, Steph, it's time to fill in some blanks. Your soon-to-be ex-husband is a doctor—"

"Plastic surgeon."

She scrunched her nose. "That's a doctor, right?"

Steph shook her head. "Surgeons hate to be referred to as mere doctors. They're far more specialized and educated than a regular GP."

Paula rolled her eyes. "Sorry. Okay, so he's a plastic *surgeon* and your son is finishing summer school so he can go to college."

"Does he want to be a surgeon? Follow in daddy's footsteps?" Emilio asked.

"He's not really sure. Right now he's talking about genetics. He'd like to help cure diseases."

"He sounds a lot like you," Paula said, squeezing her arm.

She smiled. That was true. She'd always hoped to become a doctor who did a lot of pro bono work for the poor. Eric's affinity for helping those less fortunate was something he'd learned from her.

"So, what about you?" Paula asked, sipping her tea.

Steph looked from her to Emilio. Both of them were waiting for her big story, which didn't exist. She shrugged. "There's not much to tell. I used to take care of Lawrence and Eric."

"Did you work?" Paula asked.

She shifted in her seat. "I do charity work. I'm the president—

I *was* the president—of three different organizations and I volunteered in several capacities. I was rather busy with all of that," she said mildly but she willed herself to pass through the old oak top tabletop, just like Rue the ghost. Her life was nothing and it was completely embarrassing.

Paula took her hand under the table and whispered, "I'm sure you do a lot for everyone around you. That's how you are."

Paula kissed her cheek and she nearly sank to the floor. She glanced at Emilio who grinned.

"Excuse me," a voice said.

They all looked up at a waitress, a tray of dirty dishes resting on her shoulder. Her bobbed blond hair bounced when she moved her head and she had enormous lips. Steph knew they'd gone to high school together but she couldn't remember her name.

"What the hell are you guys doing here?"

Of course Paula immediately identified her while Emilio and Steph exchanged stupefied looks. "Gretchen Ellers, how are you?"

Steph was grateful Paula said her full name for their benefit. Paula's exuberance ratcheted up about five levels, reminding Steph that Paula was voted Most Popular in high school for a good reason. Everyone was a friend and everyone loved her. Steph had once read that the key to public relations was never burning a bridge and from what she could tell, Paula had bridges intact everywhere.

Gretchen smiled, obviously pleased that Paula remembered her. They exchanged pleasantries while she and Emilio smiled politely. She was keenly aware that Paula never let go of her hand.

"What about you, Steph, Emilio?" Gretchen asked. "How are you guys?"

"Fabulous," Emilio offered. "You?"

Gretchen sighed. "Hell, I'm still in Eugene working at the Glenwood. What does that tell you?" She flashed a smile at Steph. "Where do you practice medicine?"

It took a second for the question to register. At the moment it did, she felt Paula's grip tighten. She glanced at her friends, who looked at her compassionately.

"Not around here," she answered quickly, determined to keep the lie as simple as possible.

"Oh, are you one of those traveling doctors like the ones who work for Doctors Without Borders?"

She shook her head and Emilio saved her. "Hey, Gretchen, it's great seeing you but we know you're super busy. Could you find our waitress? We really need our check."

"No problem. It was great seeing you guys."

She headed off and Steph leaned over and kissed his cheek. "Thanks."

When they arrived at Waverly Place, Steph was greeted by Tammy, the head orderly.

"Honey, you're just in time to see Debbie in her element. And I see you brought friends to enjoy the show."

Before she could ask her to explain, Debbie's notable and extraordinary singing voice floated into the lobby with the opening line of "Tomorrow" from *Annie*.

"Oh, God," she murmured.

Emilio and Paula stifled their laughter as they entered the day room, where Steph had expected to find her mother engaged in a quiet game of bingo.

It was no accident that she came on Mondays during bingo to visit Debbie. It gave them something to talk about and limited other topics of conversation. It was hard for Debbie to tell stories from the past when she was listening for I-fourteen.

However, she was late and Debbie had seized the opportunity to make bingo about *her*. She stood at the front, holding the microphone and resting her other hand on the ball cage. The college volunteer who usually ran the game sat back in his chair, enjoying the show.

"Unbelievable," Paula said. "Some things never change. She looks and sounds great. How many guys does she have in her stable of love?"

Steph's eyes widened. "Are you serious? You really think she has a boyfriend?"

Emilio leaned closer. "Steph, your mother is totally hot for her age. It's not boyfriend, honey, it's *boyfriends*."

She sighed heavily, worried they might be right. Years of formal dance training during her youth had ensured Debbie kept her lithe physique. While other women in their mid-sixties donned polyester pants with elastic waistbands, Debbie's designer jeans and oxford cloth shirt hugged her fabulous curves. She'd earned a few more wrinkles and her blond hair, still fashionably coiffed, was streaked with gray.

Debbie shouted, "Everyone, with confidence!"

While several of the elderly and debilitated patients sat confused and disoriented, some sprang from their chairs slowly and joined Debbie, singing the final chorus terribly off-key. As the last note faded with their limited breathing, clapping and cheers erupted. Debbie took a bow before she grabbed the volunteer and kissed him on the cheek.

As the residents returned to their seats, Debbie saw Steph and Paula. She ran up the aisle and threw her arms around Paula, who squealed with glee.

"Let me look at you! You look exactly the same, darling."

"And so do you. I just told Steph how beautiful you are."

"We're also wondering how many boyfriends you have," Emilio said, giving her a hug.

She chuckled, clearly embarrassed, and Steph insisted they return to her room in case Paula's presence sparked any inappropriate stories that might possibly ruin Steph's reputation in Eugene or the entire Pacific Northwest.

In her room, Debbie offered everyone some cookies and Hawaiian Punch, her new drink of choice. "I'm sorry about Francine," she said immediately. "She was a great lady. I remember the time we took you girls to the shore and Steph got stung by the jellyfish."

Paula and Steph exchanged puzzled glances. No such trip had ever occurred but it had become common for Debbie to invent stories that intrigued or pleased her. They'd taken some car trips together during the summers but Steph had never been stung by a jellyfish.

"Yeah, that was a great trip," Paula agreed. "My mom always loved being around you," she said.

Debbie patted her knee. "I felt the same. Now you two tell me about your lives."

Emilio took a cookie and proclaimed, "I'm a queer man enjoying life in San Francisco. I have many friends, spend my days teaching the second-grade youth of America and partying responsibly at night. That's me."

"Hear, hear," Debbie said, raising her glass in a toast. "What about you, Paula?"

Steph was dying to know some details from the past two decades.

Paula took a sip from her glass and set it down. "Well, up until my mom died things were okay."

"Are you married?"

"No, Debbie, I'm gay. I came out in college."

"I knew it! All those afternoons you and Steph spent alone out in the forest…" Her voice trailed away and Steph spilled her punch on her pants.

"Shit," she said, rushing to the paper towel dispenser.

"Debbie, just for the record," Paula continued, "Steph and I were just close friends. Nothing really happened."

"It didn't?" Emilio asked.

Steph glared at him from the sink and he sank into his chair.

Debbie snorted. "It figures. Do you have a wife?"

Paula shifted in her seat. "Um, no. I've never come that close. I spend a lot of time at work."

"That's great," Mom said. "So what do you do when you're not working?"

Paula was clearly at a loss for words. "Work some more?"

She shook her finger at Paula. "That's not good, missy. Life isn't about work. That's what you do between fun stuff. She suddenly belted a line from a tune Steph couldn't recognize but it seemed applicable for Paula.

An orderly named Steve appeared in the door and applauded. Probably in his late forties, he was completely bald and muscles bulged underneath his white uniform shirt.

"Sounds great, Deb. What's cookin' good lookin'? You got time for me?"

"I've always got time for you, Stevie," she purred.

She turned toward Paula and mouthed, *Boyfriend*.

Steph rolled her eyes and stood. "We should probably get going so Steve can help you with...whatever it is he's here to do."

Her mother winked. "Sponge bath."

CHAPTER TEN

Steph and Emilio dropped Paula back at the house before zooming off toward the Sea Lion Caves, which Emilio desperately wanted to see before he returned to San Francisco the next day. When Paula noticed the other cars were gone except for her rented Malibu, she pulled the willing Steph into a lingering kiss and earned a cheer from Emilio. It'd been like that all day. She'd openly flirted with Steph while he watched. He never proclaimed himself a third wheel and he seemed happy for them.

She found a terse note from Shelby stating that they'd done what they could without her guidance but they didn't know what to do next and had headed to Neighbors, a gay-friendly bar. She was encouraged to join them—an opportunity that seemed entirely unappealing. She only felt a little guilty for leaving Shelby with Hazel, Roman and Jeff, since they loved art and drinking, Shelby's favorite pastimes.

She looked around at their minimal progress. There were several closed boxes by the door, an indication that something had been accomplished, but it was only a small punctuation mark in the prolonged sentence that was her mother's life and stretched throughout the house. The curio cabinet was emptied but the hutch and the shelves over the mantel still displayed Francine's extensive miniature lighthouse collection.

"This is gonna take forever," she muttered.

Unable to find a single beer in the fridge, she hunted through the kitchen cabinets to see if on the off-chance her teetotaling mother had kept any alcohol around for guests. She was more than a little surprised to find an unopened bottle of single malt scotch. It was covered in dust, suggesting Francine had bought it long ago and forgotten about it.

She found a tumbler and poured herself two fingers. "Thanks, Mom," she said, raising the glass in salute.

She went out to the deck. The rusty patio chairs obviously hadn't been used in years, but she found a rag and dusted the old vinyl straps, which had endured two decades of Oregon rains. She sat down carefully and closed her eyes, thinking of the general response her parents' house received whenever her friends had visited during school. It was the eighties, but the furniture, the housewares, even the beds, were circa 1964. They either quietly giggled behind her back or expressed jealousy that she got to live in a retro museum.

"Why throw usable things away?" her mother always argued. "Everything is cheap plastic now." Inevitably she would pick up something, such as the sturdy pink Sunbeam can opener, and hold it out for Paula's inspection. "Look at this! They don't make quality like this anymore. You'll inherit this when I die and you'll still be able to use it."

She took a stiff drink and thought of the can opener now in Jeff's possession. He'd asked to have it when she said she'd give it to Goodwill if he didn't take it.

"You've got a fortune here, Paula," he'd commented. "We should inventory everything and put it on Craigslist. You'll make a ton of money."

She wondered if she should consider the idea since she'd just lost her job. She wasn't too worried about money, but if she didn't find employment fairly quickly, she could be in trouble. She'd spent too much on her Mercedes and her loft in downtown Seattle, insisting when she purchased it that it had to be upgraded. She rationalized her expenditures with the knowledge that she really had no life—no hobbies, no vacation destinations, and until Shelby a few months ago, no real girlfriend. What she had told Debbie was the truth. She worked. All the time.

There would be a small inheritance from her mother, enough to keep the panic of unemployment from overwhelming her. She made a mental note to call back Ted Ruth, her mother's attorney, who'd been trying to reach her. He had the only copy of Francine's will and she was curious to see where she stood.

Francine had rarely mentioned her death to Paula, beginning and ending the subject with, "You're the only child and I have a lawyer. You get everything and you won't have any of the fuss."

Details were not discussed. As a member of the Greatest Generation, Francine subscribed to the notion that certain subjects such as financial affairs were confidential and private.

"I'm not sure why we abandoned that idea," Paula said out loud, thinking of how many times in her professional career she'd cleaned up a messy personal life after the paparazzi stalked one of her clients. She hated tabloid TV and all the gossip mongers who kept them in business, but she also knew she wouldn't have a job if no one cared which starlet was dating which actor.

Perhaps she'd work at a low-key company for her next gig and avoid the high-profile clients. It sounded appealing but it would guarantee a significant cut in pay to go from planning a multi-million dollar PR campaign to organizing local radio spots.

She had avoided the truth about her job and now she'd lied to Emilio, Steph and Debbie about a fictitious career in Portland. Maybe if she mentioned a promising job offer, they wouldn't quiz her as much about her current situation.

She felt slightly guilty that she hadn't told Shelby, but when she finally did, Shelby would be furious that she waited so long. As she sipped the scotch, staring out into the woods that were her childhood backyard, she realized she didn't care if Shelby got angry, or threw things or made a scene.

She just didn't care about Shelby anymore.

She wished Steph were here. The tiny kernels of truth about Steph's life were incredibly interesting. She'd quit school, been married and had a son. Those seemed to be the major plot points of her life but Paula wanted details and she wanted to laugh more. Today had been joyous and she couldn't wait to see her again.

She knew she could easily tell Steph about losing the job because she wouldn't judge her. She glanced at the other old patio chair and pictured Steph sitting next to her, her knees tucked under her chin, curled up in a ball. As teenagers whenever they'd venture outside into the chilly air Steph assumed that pose. She loved being outdoors even when it was cold. She appeared vulnerable and small and Paula had resisted the urge to throw her arms around her and hug her tightly.

Once, Paula had come home from a day of shopping with her mother and found Steph on the deck, asleep in the chair. She'd waited all day for Paula, avoiding Debbie who was on a tirade about money. She'd thrown all of John's fishing gear on the lawn after he'd criticized her spending habits, and Steph had snuck out and neither of her parents ever noticed she was gone.

Paula leaned back in the old chair, remembering how much she pitied poor Steph and her crazy mother. It wasn't that Steph complained about her life. Quite the opposite. Whenever she was embarrassed or hurt, she became quiet and distant. They often spent an entire evening just sitting on the chairs, hardly saying a word. There was nothing to discuss, nothing to change. Countless times Paula had counted her blessings about her mother while she watched Steph suffer the emotional turmoil from dealing with her own.

She finished the glass of scotch and went for another. Only

instead of returning to the deck she sat on the couch, listening to the plastic sheet crinkle under her weight. She hated that sound and whenever her mother had left for an overnight at a lighthouse, she'd removed the plastic and sat on the couch like a regular person.

"What the hell," she said. She stood and ripped off the plastic, mangling it into a twisted ball and throwing it into the corner. "Sorry, Mom."

It felt good to react and she wanted more. Everything in the house revolved around preservation and conservation and rarely had Francine splurged on anything. "Maybe if you'd spent some of that money rather than hiding it," she said loudly, her voice a mixture of fury and sadness.

She wandered through the rooms, looking for anything offensive that still remained unpacked. In the guest room she saw the curtains that were older than she was. Her mother wouldn't spend the money for vertical blinds and insisted on washing the drab and outdated drapes each year as part of spring cleaning.

She grabbed the cloth in both fists and yanked, nearly falling on her back as the fabric easily tore away from the rod. She took the pile out the back door toward the fire pit her father had built when she was a child. He was never home long enough to take a real camping trip so they often pitched a tent in the backyard and roasted marshmallows over the coals. She went room by room, pulling down all the curtains and adding them to the heap.

"What else?" she said, wiping the dust from her hands. Clearly her mother's yearly cleaning crusade had ended long before her death.

She immediately thought of her comforter, purchased when she was seven and covered in pictures of Tinkerbell. Despite her daughter's advancing age, Francine had refused to buy a new one and Paula always seemed to find other ways to spend her babysitting money. And once she knew that Steph didn't care that a fairy covered her bed, her embarrassment dissolved.

She yanked Tink from the old, lumpy mattress and dragged her out to the growing mountain of stuff. Next was her mother's comforter, an assortment of gaudy flowers in various purple patterns. Once Paula had made the mistake of saying it was ugly and Francine had yelled at her for an hour. She had a difficult time throwing it onto the mound because it was so large, and she almost retrieved it in deference to her mother's feelings. But a sense of freedom prevailed and she grinned at the huge flowers suffocating Tinkerbell and the hideous drapes.

For the next hour she collected every obsolete and revolting object her mother had ever owned and threw it on the pile. She added eight-tracks, old wooden bowls and a velvet painting of dogs playing poker. By the time she was done she'd created a disgusting retro mountain, full of possessions that no one at Goodwill would ever want, things that she'd already heard her friends remarking over as they packed. In the process she also acquired another three hundred dollars in cash, which she thrust in her pockets, deciding it would buy some great bottles of wine.

There was only one other place to look for things—her mother's closet. She opened the doors and was assaulted by the rack of polyester.

"Mom," Paula had said frequently, "fashion changes and you need to change with it."

Francine disagreed. "That's a myth perpetuated by the industry in its quest to make money. Nothing is out of style unless I say it is. If I enjoy wearing an article of clothing, others will understand and accept it because they accept me. I decide fashion, not the idiots on Madison Avenue."

It took three trips but Paula dumped every dress, pantsuit and clunky sandal on the mound. She went to the kitchen and rummaged through the odds-and-ends drawer and found a book of matches. She also retrieved the fire extinguisher from under the sink, which no one had yet packed.

A giddy excitement overtook her at the prospect of destroying everything from childhood she hated. It was almost cathartic, a way to rid herself of this set of memories, while still preserving everything she loved, all the things that were important from her life and her bond with Francine.

Without another thought she lit a match, touched it to the rest of the book and tossed the entire burning mass onto the pile of detritus. Always conscientious, she immediately grabbed the fire extinguisher and held it with care, prepared to use it should the fire threaten the house or the woods. She'd been careful not to include anything that wouldn't burn or was highly combustible. She wanted a little catharsis not a forest fire.

The heap, much of it withered with age, burned quickly. She imagined the fibers in the drapes, comforters and sheets were broken down long ago, threads that barely held together. She stepped back as the fire grew, the intense heat warming her face. Watching the burning pyre was exhilarating and dangerous but her sense of caution quickly overwhelmed her. She waved the extinguisher's nozzle back and forth until she thought her arms would fall off, laughing hysterically. Hopefully the neighbors hadn't called the police since she was rather certain she'd broken a few laws.

She left the powdered mountain only after she'd taken the hose and thoroughly drenched the remains. In the glow of oncoming darkness she saw remnants of many discards and she wondered what Steph and Shelby would think when they returned in the morning to continue the packing. Fortunately everyone else would be gone. *They'll probably think I've gone insane.*

"Well, I've saved us a little work," she muttered, climbing back into the Malibu.

She stared at the house, gripping the steering wheel between her hands. *Don't cry. Don't start again.* But it didn't matter. It was like the first five seconds after jumping into a cold lake. Her body shook with unexpected emotion, a rush she couldn't control. She sat there for a long time until her cries turned into soft hiccups. When her breathing returned to normal, she leaned back in the seat.

She drove back to the motel concerned that the crying fit was guilt over the bonfire. *You've never done anything like that in your life!* And it was true. She wasn't a violent or destructive person, and although she chastised her mother for her extreme frugality, she believed in thrift, recycling and simplicity, but she'd never sleep on the same sheets for twenty years.

She thought of the fire consuming all of Francine's detritus. She thought about the house now, free of the decrepit curtains and endless curios. During childhood she'd felt claustrophobic because Francine kept so many things. It seemed different to her now, more appealing, open. She wondered what it could be worth if she fixed it up. She pictured the walls with fresh coats of paint and the hardwood floors shining after a refinishing.

On a whim she turned onto a residential street near the university and followed it until it curved into another. She drove absently up and down the streets, familiarizing herself with the landmarks she'd forgotten long ago—the café where she'd had her first cup of coffee with Steph, the movie theater where they'd each kissed a boy, and Autzen Stadium, home of the University of Oregon Ducks, the place where she and Steph had spent endless Sunday mornings cleaning up after football games to earn community service credit.

She smiled as she drove by the players' entry. On a few occasions the Eugene High cheerleaders had been invited to join the U of O line. One cheerleader had pulled Paula into a bathroom stall and whispered, "There's this great party I want to take you to. Will you go with me?" She'd kissed Paula's earlobe and squeezed her ass. Paula mumbled an apologetic no and quickly excused herself. Later she recognized that beyond her initial shock lay an intense curiosity that later developed into remorse.

Could she ever live in Eugene again? Doubtful. It would probably be too painful and the place was too small. She imagined Steph was here for the short term and she would probably move wherever Eric landed or like so many women who claimed to be straight, she'd go back to her worthless husband simply because he was familiar.

"But maybe she's different," she whispered. Despite her impeccable fashion sense and designer jewelry, Steph had kissed her back. Dressed in Chanel and full makeup, she'd readily returned Paula's affection, pressing that expensive lipstick against Paula's cheap Carmex lip balm.

She wondered if a future with Steph was possible and immediately shook her head. She probably wasn't cut out for relationships or life in a smaller town. She herself had left so long ago and sworn she'd never come back, but her mother was dead now, taking Paula's anger with her to the grave, a fact that troubled her immensely. Francine had died thinking Paula hated her. She started to cry and headed back to the motel. She could only handle so many memories at once.

She found Shelby lounging on the bed eating takeout. She'd obviously showered and wore only a teddy and some briefs. When her eyes remained glued to some reality show, Paula knew she was incredibly pissed. A little anger usually translated into clipped dialogue but fury equated to silence. Happy to avoid confrontation, she slipped into her sweats and crawled onto the bed. Her eyes were red with tears and a wave of exhaustion crashed into her body. It wouldn't be long before she was asleep.

A takeout carton sat on the nightstand containing her favorite, orange chicken. "Thanks," she said. "It's been a long day. I'm not sure we'll ever get through that house."

Shelby swiveled to face her. "If it's been such a *long* day, then where the hell have you been? It's nearly ten."

"I went back to Mom's after we visited Debbie. I took care of some stuff. Did you have fun at the bar?"

Shelby snickered. "This place is nothing compared to Seattle. No wonder you left. Why didn't you come over? Were you still with Stephanie?" she asked suspiciously.

"No, she dropped me off."

Shelby snorted in disapproval. "If you ask me, there's something wrong with her," she slurred, and Paula could tell she was a little drunk.

The comment stung. While Paula hadn't revealed all of the details, she'd told Shelby that Steph was the first girl she kissed. "There's nothing wrong with Steph. She's going through some serious shit right now with her marriage. Her husband left her for another woman. Have a little compassion."

"I am compassionate. Don't get all defensive on me. I'm your girlfriend, not her. Not that she ever would be," she laughed. "Silly straight girl. Boy, you sure can pick 'em," Shelby said, poking at her takeout.

"I picked you."

"And what the hell is that supposed to mean?"

"Just what I said. If you think I'm such a bad judge of women you need to look in the mirror."

Shelby leaped off the bed and threw her dinner into the trash on the way to the bathroom. "You are a fucking bitch," she called before the door slammed.

Paula heard the toilet flush and Shelby reappeared, her finger pointed. "You remember what I gave up to come with you. My show was supposed to open and instead of getting my big break, I'm packing ten gazillion lighthouse models."

"And clearly resenting every minute of it," Paula said.

"That's not what I resent. What I resent is that you'd rather spend time with your old girlfriend than me. It's bad enough that I've spent our entire relationship hiding from your mother, but now that she's gone, I'm still playing second to her. You left me with all of your friends today to go visit *Stephanie's* mother. I don't even know these people!"

"You were okay to go drinking with them."

"What the hell else was I supposed to do while you go off flirting with your ex?"

"I wasn't flirting."

Shelby threw a dismissive wave. "That's crap. I've seen the way you've been looking at her. Everybody else has noticed it, too. There's nothing worse than coming on to someone else in front of your current girlfriend."

Paula automatically shook her head, feeling slightly guilty, but Shelby the hypocrite had no right to say anything about her connection with Steph.

"You obviously think it's wrong to flirt when you're with someone else but is it okay to fuck somebody else?" she asked acidly.

Shelby contorted her face into a look of indignation. "What does that mean?"

Paula sighed. "I'm too tired to argue with you or massage your hurt ego. I've known for over a month that you and Gemma have been fucking. Is that how you got her to show your stuff?"

Shelby's face turned bright red and Paula knew she'd hit below the belt—hard. She'd dismissed Shelby's indiscretion for the sake of art but now the conversation had wandered onto a dangerous precipice and Paula didn't care what happened. She'd kissed Steph twice and she wanted to keep kissing her. She'd just have to convince Steph that she wanted to *be* kissed—and touched.

"I think you need to get out," Shelby spat.

Paula poked at her chicken languidly. "You're forgetting that I've paid for this room, pretty much like everything else. But you should also know that the free ride is ending. I lost my job."

Shelby's eyes widened and she dropped onto the other bed, the fight clearly forgotten. "When did this happen?"

"About twenty minutes before I found out my mom had died."

"Aw, babe, I'm sorry," Shelby said.

Paula knew she was sincere. Shelby's self-centeredness was often balanced by her compassion. They sat quietly listening to the highway outside and the audio from the TV. After a particularly annoying wave of canned laughter, Shelby grabbed the remote and hit mute. She stretched out on the bed and faced Paula, her face full of concern.

"No more games. No more fights. Yeah, I slept with Gemma but that was *after* she'd promised me the show. We just had a connection. And it's time for you to fess up. If there was a knock on the door right now, who would you want to find on the other side?"

Paula swallowed hard, surprised by the question. "Well…"

"Who? Angelina Jolie? Maybe Megan Fox? Lady Gaga? Or would you pick Stephanie?"

Paula felt her face flush just hearing her name. She shrugged in embarrassment.

Shelby chuckled. "Wow. Your arm must really hurt."

"What do you mean?"

"Seventeen years is an awfully long time to carry a torch around."

CHAPTER ELEVEN

The darkness that settled around Sea Lion Point broke when the beacon showered the ocean with a reminder that land was close by. The stupendous effect occurred every thirty seconds when an enormous Fresnel lens magnified a tiny bulb housed in the tower.

Steph loved watching Heceta work, and when she couldn't sleep she walked to the cliff and stared out at the water which glittered under the power of the light. It was hypnotic and after a half hour of watching the show, her eyelids grew heavy and when she returned to her bed sleep came easy.

Tonight was an exception. She'd situated herself on the bench along the path to Heceta, a view that allowed her to alternate her gaze between the shore and the tower. But after an hour of following the revolving lens her body still wouldn't rest. Her mind turned like a clock at quarter hours—Paula's beautiful face, the joy of youth, her destroyed marriage and the blank sheet of paper that was her future. Each image carried its own emotional baggage and collectively it should have exhausted her.

She glanced back at the B and B and noticed Rick and Caroline's light was out, which wasn't surprising. It was after midnight and they usually turned in early, a natural consequence of preparing breakfast for twenty others on a daily basis. They hadn't made it past ten p.m. since moving to Heceta.

It had been a strange day. Emilio had regaled her with stories of his past trips to Sea Lion Caves. She'd told him about her marriage, Eric and her pending divorce on their way back to his motel.

"I know it was a different time, Steph. Believe me, I remember the Eighties but I don't think you ever should have married him. Francine should've stayed out of it."

"It was my decision."

He cocked his head. "Are you sure about that? From what I recall Francine was a staunch pro-lifer. I remember one time she and Paula really got into it."

"It doesn't matter. I got Eric out of the whole thing. Francine could've forced me to watch *The Silent Scream* and it would've been the right thing to do. My son is my life."

He patted her shoulder and changed the topic. "So have you slept with Paula?" She almost drove off the road. "Whoa, steady there, girl. Is that a yes?"

"No," she snapped.

"Hmm. Well, how many times have you kissed?"

"Enough," she said through clenched teeth.

He howled and stomped his feet in the car. "Goooooooo, Steph!" he cheered.

She laughed. It felt good to tell someone about Paula. They'd parted with a promise to e-mail regularly and keep in touch. As he jumped out of the car he said, "Steph, you're thirty-five years old. You still have more than half your life to live and with your great genes, probably even more. Make the most of it, sweetie."

She'd arrived home to a shrieking phone call from Lawrence, who'd received the divorce papers and wasn't happy with her request of fifty percent of their assets. She figured that since she'd stood by him through med school, residency and the establishment of his practice, she was entitled to her share. But she'd said little during the conversation and hung up on him when the swearing began.

The oddest event happened after dinner.

"I thought you were making another loaf of banana bread for the Steiners?" Caroline asked.

She looked at her quizzically. "I made it last night. I put it in the breadbox so that you'd be sure to find it when they left."

"Well, it wasn't there."

"What?" she asked, searching the breadbox. It was empty.

She turned to Rick, who was known for baked goods thievery. She pointed at him and he put his hands in the air.

"Don't look at me. This time I didn't take anything. I learned my lesson after you scolded me for eating your cupcakes."

"That's only because you ate half a dozen," Caroline said dryly. She turned to Steph and said, "When I couldn't find it, I told them that you'd been really busy with a funeral."

"Well, if it wasn't Rick, then I'd say that one of the other guests had a snack before dinner."

"There is one other possibility," Rick offered.

She turned and faced him, her hands on her hips. "I seriously doubt that Rue enjoys banana bread."

Caroline put a friendly hand on her shoulder. "Honey, I think you sell yourself short. There's something heavenly about your baking."

Steph smiled appreciatively and searched the kitchen, checking all of the other rational possible places she might have set it—refrigerator, cupboard and pantry. She knew she'd been distracted thinking of Paula so anything was possible.

But she never found the loaf and despite her friendly interrogation of several guests, none of them admitted taking it.

She was more frustrated that the Steiners had been disappointed but Caroline had promised them she'd mail another loaf soon.

A passing ship's horn jerked Steph awake and she realized she was falling asleep on the bench. She headed back up the trail to the B and B and her little room. It was always much darker moving away from the water toward the house through the woods. She gazed up and saw the glow of the bedside lamp from Victoria's Room, where the Steiners had stayed. It hadn't been on before—she thought. Perhaps they'd been forgetful but she didn't think so. She was almost certain the light had been off when she walked down the trail.

She stared at the window, unwilling to take her eyes away until something—anything—happened. A silhouette passed by the window and she nearly jumped out of her shoes. It was gone in a second and she blinked, unsure if it was real or just another shadow created by the moonlight. She concentrated on the window for another minute, staring at the warm yellow radiance above but nothing happened and she decided she'd been imagining things.

She trudged up the stairs to turn off the light before she tried to go to sleep. Her heart was racing and she guessed she'd be awake for the rest of the night, mulling over her life, the apparition she may or may not have seen and the missing banana bread. The door was slightly ajar and the soft light crept into the hallway.

She moved slowly forward, anxious at the thought of encountering a ghost. Just as her hand touched the doorknob, she felt a tap on her shoulder and screamed.

"Shit!" a voice said.

She whirled around and faced Paula, who was bent over to retrieve the bottle of water she'd dropped on the floor. "You scared the hell out of me," Steph gasped.

"Well, you scared me."

"What are you doing here?"

"I'm a guest!"

Feet raced up the stairs and Rick and Caroline joined them,

pulling robes over their nightclothes. A few other doors opened and startled faces appeared.

"What's going on?" Rick asked. "Steph, are you okay?"

She couldn't get her breath for several seconds. "I was checking on the light." She looked at Paula. "What happened to the motel by the university?"

She smiled wryly. "I needed a place to stay. Shelby and I broke up. It was just too awkward so I called Caroline and she said she had a vacancy."

Paula motioned to the room and everything clicked into place. It wasn't the ghost who turned on the light. It was Paula. It wasn't the ghost's silhouette she'd seen. It was Paula.

Paula pulled her into a loose embrace. "I'm sorry I scared you."

"It's okay," she said, stepping away. "I just wasn't expecting you."

"Okay, we're going back to bed," Caroline announced, leading Rick down the stairs and waving goodnight to the other guests who closed their doors and returned to bed.

"I suppose I should let you get settled. Do you need anything?"

"Just some rest," Paula sighed.

She looked exhausted and Steph imagined the stress of the last week was nearly unbearable and now she'd lost her girlfriend.

"I know it's none of my business but do you want to talk about it?"

"There's nothing to talk about. We just fizzled out."

Steph nodded and waited to see if she'd share anything else. She played with the collar on her shirt and wouldn't meet her gaze.

"I'll see you in the morning," Steph said, reaching out and smoothing her gorgeous dark hair.

Paula pulled her hand to her lips and kissed her palm.

Desire radiated throughout her and Steph moved against her, pressing her lips against Paula's neck. "You smell so good," she murmured.

Paula chuckled. "You think I smell good. It's nothing compared to you. All that expensive European perfume and French soaps."

Steph raised her head and looked at her. "How did you know I used French soap?"

Paula's eyes danced. "I used to have a French girlfriend."

"Really? How many girlfriends have you had?"

Paula ignored the question and cradled Steph's face between her hands. "It doesn't matter," she whispered. "Stay with me, Steph. I want your lips on my body."

I want your lips on my body. The words echoed in Steph's head and she floated into Paula's room.

Paula lowered her onto the bed, their mouths dancing against each other. They moved slowly, Paula taking the lead. Steph had told her about the tennis pro so Paula knew she was experienced, but this was different, delicate. This was the past joining with the future.

Paula touched her innocently at first, her hands asking permission before her lips set Steph on fire. She stroked her breasts through the thin cotton T-shirt until Steph's nipples stood erect and she murmured a tiny, "Please." Only then did Paula push up the T-shirt and suck lovingly on each mound, as Steph panted for more.

She wanted to be the aggressor but she couldn't. She needed to be claimed. She writhed on the bed, half-naked, her eyes partially closed, as Paula's warm fingers sculpted her belly. Her gasps turned to moans when Paula's lips followed the path of her hands, between her legs, helping her shed her jeans, leaving only her little pink panties. Paula grinned when she discovered what Steph already knew. They were completely soaked.

Paula sat up and gazed at Steph while she peeled away the panties. Steph stared at her, entranced by the lust in her eyes. And when Paula's lips and tongue touched the core of her being, it was as if a secret had been revealed, something she should've known all along.

And once she'd learned all she could in that moment, she rolled on top of Paula and said, "I want my lips all over *your* body."

Much later, after Paula was asleep, Steph dressed and headed to the kitchen. She made some tea and looked for the banana bread again, uncomfortable that she'd lost something, but she couldn't find it anywhere—not even in the freezer. If Rue had it she'd probably eaten it.

She knew she'd never sleep now, not after—that. Knowing Paula was only two floors away heightened her senses, her awareness of her and the past. She resisted the urge to race back up the stairs and take Paula again. She shook her head. *How old are you?*

The memories were flooding back now. Every time she looked at Paula something rose to the surface. When they'd sat on the floor of her room packing books, she'd turned her head and Steph saw the tiny scar at the bottom of her chin, the one she'd acquired when Steph's fishing hook caught her in the face on the campout the summer after eighth grade.

She went to her purse and removed the copy of *Pride and Prejudice* she'd taken from Paula's room. She stared at the cover and sipped her tea at the kitchen table, listening to the ocean nearby, restless, thinking of Paula. She could still feel her lips on her face, her breasts—everywhere. The memory of her body was no different. Their lovemaking had reminded Steph of their intimacy. Maybe that was the secret.

Paula had told Debbie they'd never gone all the way but they'd spent several afternoons touching and kissing, satiating their curiosity that had developed from years of friendly hugs, handholding and quick pecks on the cheeks.

It started one afternoon when Paula invited her onto her bed, and Steph had abandoned the safe distance of the beanbag chair forever after. Lying next to Paula every day was sexual even if she didn't recognize it. Their bodies frequently collided during tickling matches and innocent embraces. On some occasions the façade of lightheartedness would crumble and their true feelings were obvious, even if they remained unspoken. If Steph's shirt rode up from their horseplay, Paula's hand lingered against her exposed belly—a gesture of preoccupation that signaled an interest beyond simple friendship.

Paula would circle her bellybutton with her index finger and she'd watch her face, enamored by the act, her lips slightly quivering. Of course, Steph's whole body was trembling from her touch but she said nothing. She watched, exhilarated that she wielded such power over Paula's heart and emotions.

Eventually it was too much and Steph would roll off the bed comically or make a joke such as, "Have you found any lint in there?"

And Paula would reply, "I've found more than lint. Really, Steph, you need to wash your bellybutton a little more. There's a fungus forest in there."

And then one day their senior English class was assigned *Pride and Prejudice*.

"I think we should read it out loud to each other," Paula said, turning to chapter one. "You can be Elizabeth and I'll be Mr. Darcy. And we'll alternate all of the other characters."

It had sounded like a good idea, a fun way to make a dreary old book seem interesting. Yet as the plot progressed they fell in love with the romantic tension between the main characters. They were so involved in the story that they didn't notice their legs tangling together or their fingers lacing as they lay on the bed, sharing a single copy of the novel for nearly three weeks.

"When do they kiss in this novel?" Paula asked after they'd completed nearly thirty chapters. "When is it gonna get really good?"

"I don't think Jane Austen wrote it that way. It's proper British stuff."

"Oh, so they're not going to have any fun," she mocked, using a fake accent that sounded more Southern than British.

"I'm sure they'll have fun eventually," Steph said, thumbing through the last chapter. "Probably after the book ends."

"I'm not waiting that long. I think we should improve it," Paula announced.

She laughed. "You don't *improve* Jane Austen. This is a classic."

"A stuffy classic." Paula pushed her down and fell on top of her. "Elizabeth, I must have you."

Steph laughed hysterically at her ridiculous accent and the funny face she made, attempting to be serious.

"I'm going to kiss you, Elizabeth. But I promise I won't use my tongue."

Her laughter faded as Paula's face moved dangerously close to her own. She was paralyzed, trapped beneath her body, staring into her blue eyes. Paula carelessly smashed their faces together and quickly pulled away. Steph thought she might have a bruised upper lip.

"Ow."

"What do you think of my kissing?"

"It hurts."

"Then we need to do it again."

She closed her eyes, prepared for the worst, but when Paula's lips softly touched hers, her skin drained away from her bones. She kissed her several more times, each one tantalizing her senses in a different way—the feel of Paula's slick tongue in her mouth, the slight creaking of the bed as their bodies shifted and the look in her eyes when she pulled away. It was as if someone had laid them over a blank mask. Steph saw nothing else of her face, only the wildness in her dark blue irises.

Paula sat up and removed her Joan Jett T-shirt, exposing her lacy black bra. "Take yours off, too," she said, using a voice Steph had only heard in the movies—low, breathy and very sexy.

Steph hesitated for only a second, too nervous to think and too excited to disobey. Paula flung Steph's Polo shirt onto the floor and cupped her breasts.

"Do what I do," she said in that same infectious voice.

She circled her nipples with her thumbs and Steph mimicked the action, her mind fractured by the sensations of giving and receiving pleasure. She couldn't decide which she liked better until Paula's fingertips stroked her exposed cleavage. Her hands dropped to her sides and she closed her eyes.

"I can't keep going," she mumbled.

"That's okay. I can."

Paula pushed her down on the bed and unclasped her bra. "I've always wanted to do this," she said, before her mouth covered her chest with kisses. "You're beautiful, Steph."

Paula took off her own bra and they spent another hour kissing, their nipples pressed together until they heard her mother's car drive up.

They didn't speak of it again, but each afternoon their tickling sessions evolved into kissing that led to stripping off their tops. Eventually they discovered that making out behind the granite rock was equally fabulous and they alternated locations. One afternoon Steph arrived at Paula's house and found her in bed— completely naked. Steph stood in the doorway, torn between terror and delight.

"C'mon, Steph, get in here with me."

Gone was all of the subtext and the situation was as bare as she was. Mr. Darcy and Elizabeth had been abandoned back in the nineteenth century. It was too much. Steph ran out of the room, worried that she had destroyed their relationship.

But the next day Paula arrived at her house, smiling and acting as if nothing had happened. She took her back behind the rock and kissed her passionately, assuring her that they were okay. Then the Berkeley letter came.

Steph finished her tea and returned to her own room, still lost in the memory of Paula's perfect breasts. She flipped on the lights and quickly leaned against the doorjamb to steady herself. On a table next to her laptop was the missing loaf of banana bread.

CHAPTER TWELVE

Steph's alarm buzzed an hour after she'd fallen asleep, reminding her it was time to get up and prepare breakfast for the guests, which now included Paula. She glanced at the banana bread sitting on the desk. If she showed it to Caroline, she'd never hear the end of it. Rue had finally played a practical joke on her, and if Eric was right, then she was trying to tell her something.

Paula's laugh floated into her room and she lingered at the door listening to Paula and Caroline rehashing old high school memories. She glanced at the dresser mirror. She couldn't stop smiling and giggling. She tried to readjust her expression to something less incriminating but the memories from the past night flickered and the smile returned. Caroline would know. She hid her face in her hands, counted to five and made her entrance into the kitchen just as they finished a story about Old Lady Lumpen, the cafeteria lady who dropped her dentures into the soup.

When Paula saw her, she immediately stopped laughing—and stared. "Hey."

Steph was positive the goofy smile had returned and she didn't care. "Hi."

"Earth to Stephanie!" Caroline called. "Hello!"

"Huh?"

She whipped her gaze toward Caroline who was chuckling and shaking her head. "I've said good morning three times."

"Oh, sorry," Steph replied, totally embarrassed.

Caroline sighed. "No comment. But let's get to work."

Steph busied herself with preparing the breads, trying to ignore the sparks that continued to fly between her and Paula, who leaned against the counter in an incredibly sexy pose while she bantered with Caroline.

"Do you remember the day Mr. Kring's hairpiece nearly fell off during the music performance?" Caroline laughed.

"Oh, that was so funny," Paula agreed. "He was bobbing his head up and down while he directed the orchestra. I don't think he realized what happened until it fell into his eyes and he couldn't see the music."

"And then he ran off the stage," Caroline said. "I played the cello that year and I was sitting in the front row. I was trying so hard not to miss a note, but I was laughing—everyone was."

"He couldn't get it back on," Paula added. "He ran to a corner where there was a mirror and tried to center it but it looked like he was wearing a dead squirrel. I think he gave up then."

They laughed until Rick walked in, scanning the pegboard for the keys to the truck. "What's so funny?"

"You don't wear a hairpiece do you?" Paula asked, pointing at Rick's thick head of hair.

They laughed again and Rick looked at them like they were stupid. He quickly found the keys and headed for his morning ritual at the gym.

"How's the house coming?" Caroline asked pleasantly.

"Not well," she said, sipping her coffee. "It doesn't look like we made a dent."

"You did," Steph said, joining the conversation, "but there's a lot of stuff. Your mom saved everything for decades."

"Do you remember my Tinkerbell comforter?"

Caroline glanced up at Steph, a slight smile on her face that only she could see. "Yeah."

"Well, don't report me to the sheriff but last night I took a whole bunch of stuff and made a bonfire in my backyard."

"Whoa!" Caroline exclaimed. "That's pretty radical. You're not harboring some terrible angst from childhood are you?"

Steph knew it was meant as a joke but Paula's smile evaporated. "No, growing up was fine," she said slowly. "I just hated all of the outdated stuff my mom kept, like that set of funky wooden chip bowls or the ten cent salt and pepper shakers she won at the market when I was seven."

"You mean the ones shaped like fish?" Steph asked.

Paula nodded slowly. "I thought they deserved a proper death. Anyway, I'll just keep packing until it's done."

"How long do you have off work?" Caroline asked absently, emptying a bowl of beaten eggs into a muffin pan for frittatas.

The question hung in the air and Paula didn't answer at first. She finally said, "I have a week and then I need to go back. I'm thinking about changing jobs. There's a prospect in Portland."

"Portland's a fabulous city," Caroline replied. "Personally, I like it better than Seattle."

Paula shrugged. "I don't know. My life is there."

Steph busied herself with a batch of muffins, avoiding her gaze. She knew Paula's departure was inevitable. Her life was somewhere else and Steph's life was nowhere. She just needed to enjoy the moment.

Paula sidled up next to her and wrapped an arm around her waist. "Do you think you could help me today? I need to go to the lawyer's office and I imagine Shelby's heading home to move out. And after last night with you, I'm glad."

Steph smiled automatically but quickly caught herself. "I'm sorry about Shelby. I know what you're going through."

"And you've got it worse. My relationship was destined to crash and burn."

Steph was confused. "Then why get into it? If you know it isn't right, why subject the other person to misery?"

Paula pressed her lips together and Steph could tell she was debating her response. When she spoke it was slowly and carefully. "At the risk of having another woman scream at me, I'm wondering if you could ask yourself that same question."

Steph's mouth went dry and anger swirled inside of her.

Paula saw her expression and caressed her cheek. "Hey, this is me, Steph. No secrets."

She took a breath and nodded. "I'll be happy to help you today."

"Thanks. And maybe we can catch up some more." She pecked her on the lips before she headed up to her room to change.

Circling the pile of charred remains covered in white-gray soot, Steph was concerned that Paula was losing it. The pile was large but it was apparent that she'd doused the fire before it got too big, leaving much of the detritus totally intact. Most of the fringe items, though, were incinerated. She recognized the corner of a hideous end table that Francine had brought home from a garage sale, a swath of ugly green drape—and Mr. Piddle's eyes.

"You burned Mr. Piddle?"

Paula didn't answer. She looked down and kicked some of the powder with her shoe.

"Jesus, Paula, you could've burned down the whole place."

"Don't be dramatic, Steph," she said, hurrying into the house.

Steph assumed the tears were flowing again so she gave her a second before she followed behind. Perhaps she was regretting the bonfire or at least destroying one of the last memories of her dad. She waited in the kitchen and realized there was far less clutter than the day before. She imagined the reason was sitting in the white pile outside.

"Can you come here," Paula called. Steph found her in the office, squatting behind her mother's old desk. "Take a look at this." She looked calm, composed She'd opened a cabinet, revealing a small safe. "Do you know anything about safecracking?"

"Not really. You haven't found the combination anywhere?"

Paula shook her head. "I've gone through all of her personal papers and I haven't seen any random sets of numbers. I'm sure it's here somewhere but I'll probably be dead by the time I find her hiding place."

"Maybe the attorney has it."

"That's possible but he didn't mention it when I spoke with him this morning."

"Have you tried all of the obvious combinations—her birthday, your birthday, her social security number…"

She nodded. "I've tried everything I can think of but I don't know it."

"Maybe we should call a locksmith."

"I'll do that if we don't stumble upon the answer today but I'm not sure I want to know what's in it. Does that sound bizarre?" she asked as they stood up.

Steph thought of the jars of coins and all the random cash. "No, I understand what you're worried about. Your mother is totally exposed now. There aren't any secrets left and you're probably not going to like everything you learn about her."

She nodded and smiled. "You always get it, Steph. You've always understood me."

They held each other, listening to the radio Paula had switched on. Journey's old song, "Don't Stop Believin" wailed through the house.

"I know how hard this is. I want to help, Paula. I really do."

"You are. It feels so amazing to hold you again. It's not just about the sex but that was pretty incredible last night. Wasn't it?"

Steph gazed into the wild blue eyes and she was certain she saw Paula's soul. She nestled her cheek against Paula's shoulder and they started to dance with the music, turning a slow box step in the messy office. When the song ended, Paula kissed her hungrily and Steph felt her chest pounding. It was as if last night never ended. There was no awkward morning after or regret, only passion.

"Are the others coming over today?" Steph asked between kisses.

"No, they all had to go back this morning. We're all alone."

"You're sure Shelby's not coming back?"

"Positive."

"Did you save any of the mattresses or are they burned to a crisp?"

She answered by pulling her into her old bedroom. Although the Tinkerbell comforter had been sacrificed, the plain fitted sheet still hugged the old mattress. They slid on top, their hands greedily searching each other's flesh, not satisfied until their clothes formed a heap at the foot of the four-poster bed.

"You're absolutely beautiful. I love looking at you. And I must admit, that there's a definite advantage to bedding a woman of substance."

Steph laughed. "What the hell does that mean?"

Paula kissed her shoulder lightly. "It means that I'm so grateful for all of the fine oils, lotions and body wraps that you must treat yourself to. Your skin is absolutely delicious."

Steph thought she remembered Paula's touch but nothing she'd imagined compared to the soft fingertips that traced the curve of her neck. She suddenly felt terribly deprived, having spent years pressed against a rough beard and enduring smelly armpits.

Paula drew her body over Steph's until their hips rocked together in unison.

"I've never made love in the daytime," Steph said unsteadily. "Hell, I've never made love twice in twenty-four hours."

"That's just shameful," Paula concluded as she fondled Steph's breasts. "This body shouldn't be ignored."

"I'm probably a little self-conscious. I know this might sound ridiculous but Lawrence believed in a schedule and he had certain rules about sex, at least when it came to me."

She traced a circle around her areola. "Ah, well this will be a new experience for you. I love sex in the daytime. Remember that day in my bedroom?"

Steph rolled her eyes. "Of course. I was terrified."

"Are you terrified now?" she asked, the heat between them increasing.

Steph wasn't sure how much longer she could converse. She imagined that soon her body would do all of the talking. "No, I'm not afraid but I don't know you anymore. It's been so long."

"What do you want to know?"

"Everything. Uh, who's your favorite rock group?"

"U2. What about you?"

She chuckled. "It's still Rush."

"I remember that. What's your favorite food?"

"Anything French. I love French food. Where's your favorite vacation spot?"

Paula smiled sadly. "I don't have one, really. I'm always working. How do you feel right now?" she asked. Her fingertips roamed across Steph's belly, flipping switches of passion that she had thought were off for good.

"Fabulous."

"Does it bother you that we're totally naked on a rickety old bed in the light of day? We're not even hidden under a sheet. All of our wrinkles and crow's feet are entirely exposed," she added dramatically.

She gazed up at Paula whose face beamed in the sunlight. She grinned and flipped her on her back, settling their hips together like two puzzle pieces.

"What are you doing?" Paula asked innocently.

"Well, after my abrupt departure from this room seventeen years ago, I owe you. And you're gonna love the way I pay you back."

CHAPTER THIRTEEN

Paula pulled into the small parking lot behind the lawyer's office, a converted house that served three different tenants. She admired the beautiful old columns and sturdy bricks, grateful that Eugene was smart enough to change the zoning laws when the center of town shifted. All of the businesses that lined the one-way streets were residential homes in a past era, but instead of destroying them in the name of progress and erecting tacky strip malls, the city planners opted to preserve the history. It was one of the things she loved about Eugene.

"Hey, thanks for coming with me," she told Steph. "I'm not sure what Ted's going to tell me. It could be really bad news. Maybe Mom owes a ton in back taxes."

Steph laughed. "I seriously doubt that, given how frugal and careful she was, and if she does owe anything, I think you'll be able to cover it with all the quarters, dimes and nickels sitting in the hallway."

"You're probably right. I'm just glad you're here. I know I keep saying that but I am."

"I need to thank you for the best morning of my life. I've never felt so…refreshed."

Paula stroked her cheek. "That's what morning sex can do for you. It's totally invigorating." She quickly added, "I mean I hope you thought it was great. I shouldn't be so presumptuous."

Steph answered with a sizzling kiss before she hopped out of the Malibu. Paula blinked, steadying herself before she tried to exit. Steph completely unraveled her every time they touched. She was lost in a black hole, caught between the love she felt for Steph—and it was love—and the common sense that ruled her personal life and told her that *straight women always go back to their husbands.* But was she really straight? What about those afternoons behind the rock?

She closed the black hole and joined Steph on the sidewalk. When they entered the Law Offices of Ted Ruth, Esquire, no one was there to greet them in the waiting area but a man's laugh resonated from the interior office. He was obviously on the phone and speaking to a client. Paula felt slightly uncomfortable listening to someone else's confidential business and she hesitated to sit in one of the overstuffed chairs.

"Do you think we should wait outside?" Steph asked. Her conscience was clearly facing the same dilemma.

Paula shrugged. "I don't know. You'd think he'd close the door if it was important."

Steph nodded and they sat. Paula couldn't help herself. She leaned over and kissed Steph, savoring her lips.

A deep cough caught her attention and she realized that Mr. Ruth had a clear view of their display of affection. His eyes met hers but his expression showed no sign of disapproval, merely curiosity. He was obviously a multitasker, able to listen to his conversation and absorb information visually.

She'd always remembered him as a smart man and he'd spent a lot of time at their house, especially after her father's death. He and Francine had been incredibly close and he'd enjoyed plenty of her mother's cooking, usually arriving thirty minutes before dinner with papers in his hand. He'd always worn a three-piece suit, as he did now, but in the casualness of their home, he'd taken off his jacket and rolled up his sleeves, offering to help her mother prepare a salad or a side dish.

"I always wondered if there wasn't something between Mr. Ruth and my mom," she whispered to Steph.

"What?" she asked, looking up from the old magazine she'd grabbed from the coffee table.

She threw a glance toward Ted. "I mean he was always around looking dapper and well…very traditional."

Steph nodded. "That doesn't surprise me. I remember one time my mother tried to get him to write a nasty letter against one of our neighbors who'd called the police about her singing on the porch. The guy said she was a public nuisance." Paula laughed, remembering Debbie's endless serenades. "She must've thought that a letter from an attorney would get him to back off but Ted wouldn't do it."

"He wouldn't?"

"Nope. He quizzed her about how loud she was, and she said she was as loud as the song demanded, and he asked her when she sang, and she said whenever she felt like it. And he asked if that included early in the morning or late at night and her response—"

"Was that it depended on the song?" Paula guessed.

Steph pointed at her. "Exactly. Ted wouldn't help her because she was violating the law. She was hopping mad at him but she also respected his scruples. Told him he was a stand-up guy and if she ever really needed an attorney, she was calling him. He was the most honest man she'd ever met."

Paula nodded, thinking about why they were there. "Good to know."

They heard him finish the phone call and he appeared at the

door. He'd buttoned his jacket to greet them and Paula thought he looked dapper.

"I'm so sorry to keep you waiting. Please come in. Can I offer you something to drink?"

They both shook their heads and took a seat. Ted returned to his chair and quickly scanned a yellow notepad full of notes before folding his hands on his desk.

"I'll be blunt, Paula. Your mother's will is shocking."

"Really? Why?" She shifted in her seat and didn't even realize she was bobbing her leg until Steph placed her hand on her knee.

"Your mother's generation, *my* generation, is very private about personal matters. If you knew the particulars of today's discussion, you probably would've contacted me sooner. And when we're done, I hope you won't hate me. Remember that I'm just the messenger."

"I understand that, Ted. Please just tell me what's in there. I'm beginning to think my mother was an ax murderer." She tried to be funny but her voice cracked.

He picked up the Last Will and Testament and held it out to her. The first few pages were introductory, line after line containing confusing legal jargon. She hoped Ted didn't expect her to read or understand all of it. She got to the fourth page which listed the assets. There were several numbers and addresses, much more than she thought.

"I guess I don't really understand what I'm reading, Ted. What are these three other addresses underneath Mom's house?"

"Those are your mother's holdings."

"Her what?"

"She owned other pieces of property, Paula, not just the house."

She looked at him incredulously. Had he mixed up this will with someone else's?

"What are you talking about? My mother wouldn't spend money on real estate."

"Oh, she did," he said, opening his own copy of the will.

112

"After your father died I advised your mother that she needed to diversify her portfolio. Your grandparents left Francine a sizeable inheritance and when Paul was killed at the prime of his life, your mother received a substantial settlement. She couldn't leave all that money sitting in a savings account, which was what she was inclined to do."

Paula instantly thought of the coin jars and cash hidden throughout the house.

"I convinced her that real estate was the best investment and she listened. And I was right," he added, with a note of pride. "Eugene has grown significantly and her investments proved quite profitable."

She couldn't believe it. Her mother had never said a word about investments and she'd always lived like a pauper. "So, you're saying my mother had some money," she summarized.

"Paula, your mother had a *lot* of money. These three other addresses are a commercial property, a rental house near the university and a lighthouse."

"My mother owns a lighthouse?"

He nodded.

She fumbled with her collar and craved a cigarette. "I just don't understand. How can this be? She was a tightwad who never spent a dime unless it was entirely necessary."

"I know," he said softly. "She could be quite stubborn." His professional tone vanished.

She knew he'd been close to Francine and quite upset at the funeral, arriving late and leaving early. "What do you mean?"

He cleared his throat. "You'll have to pardon me. I knew your mother for a long time and I'm sorry she's gone." He set three large file folders in front of her. "Each of these contains the pertinent information about the other properties I've mentioned. I assume you've located all of the paperwork on her house."

Paula nodded. "Yes, it was in her desk." *Along with eight hundred dollars in cash.*

"Then you should have all of the necessary documents. There will need to be transfers of title, new deeds, et cetera, and I'll be happy to help you with that or you could hire your own attorney. It's up to you."

The idea of wading through voluminous documents and paperwork made her ill. "I'm fine with hiring you, Ted. You've navigated my mother through these investments so you'll have the most familiarity. She also spoke very highly of you so I trust you."

"Thank you," he replied, unsteadily.

She saw tears in his eyes. "Is everything all right? You seem distraught."

He shook his head. "I'm fine. I suggest that you review these files so you can see exactly what you're going to own and we can discuss options."

"What if I just wanted to sell everything?" she asked.

Ted shrugged. "I suppose we could do that but I'd advise against it, considering these are tangible assets making money. And it wouldn't be easy to unload a lighthouse in this economy."

Paula sifted through the folders until she found the one labeled *Tillamook*. Her eyes widened as she read the first page.

"My mother owns the Tillamook lighthouse?"

"That surprises you?" Ted asked. "You knew she loved lighthouses, correct?"

"Well, yes, and I love shoe shopping but that doesn't mean I've gone out and bought a boutique."

"You could now," he replied. "Apparently the lighthouse is where your mother would like her ashes to go. A few years back she and some other investors made Tillamook a final resting place for people who loved lighthouses or the sea. It's proven quite profitable."

"Fine. I'll take her out there myself." She glanced at Steph who nodded in support.

Ted leaned forward on the desk. "Now there is one more thing."

His voice sounded ominous, whereas a minute before he'd been welcoming and friendly.

"Just say it."

114

"I said your mother's will was shocking. I've shared with you the holdings that you are to receive but there is a condition. And please remember that I'm only the messenger." He took a deep breath before he said, "About three years ago your mother came to me and added a codicil to her will after she learned you were a lesbian."

The room seemed to get a little smaller and warmer and Steph pressed her hand against Paula's knee. This time Paula took her hand and held it. Ted dropped his gaze to their laced fingers.

He opened another folder and handed Paula a paper. It was a short paragraph of only a few sentences. She scanned it, unsure if she understood the legal jargon sprinkled among the words she knew—lesbian, relationship, forfeit and charity.

"Why don't you just say it plainly," she said.

"Essentially your mother has decided that if you pursue a long-term lesbian relationship, the bulk of the estate, except for the house you grew up in, will transfer to several charities that she's designated."

"I see."

Her mind was reeling and she thought she might be sick. She yanked her hand away from Steph's, as if her mother were watching her. When she looked up at Steph, she expected to see a look of reproof but all she found were her kind eyes. She repressed the urge to run out of the room.

"You might as well start contacting those charities, Ted. I don't think I can stop being a lesbian."

"I understand but I would be remiss if I didn't urge you to think about this carefully. You're a very wealthy woman and you could be set for life. I suggest you take some time to learn about what you've inherited before you make any rash decisions. And I'm happy to help you, once you've had a chance to process all of this. I know this is a shock to you."

She watched his eyes, full of sadness. His hands busied themselves by rearranging the other papers on his desk, as if he were preparing for his next client meeting and her exit.

"Ted, can I ask you a personal question and you can tell me to mind my own business if you want."

"Of course," he said, unwilling to meet her gaze.

"How close were you to my mother?"

"Very close."

"More than just attorney and client?"

"Yes. I considered your mother a friend, a dear friend."

"Were you lovers?"

"Paula," Steph said sharply.

While Steph had been offended, Ted showed no emotion. He fingered his gold pen, not answering. He still had not looked up.

"It's just that I remember when I was growing up that you were around a lot, especially when my dad died. But even after his death you spent time with my mom."

"I always wanted to support your mother," he said softly. "She was a wonderful woman, except for this decision. Please know how hard I tried to get her to reconsider. I find her decision absolutely reprehensible," he added, his voice filled with anger. He wiped a hand across his face to steady his emotions. "Why would you think we were involved, Paula?" He finally looked up and she smiled slightly. His face fell. "How did you know?"

"Mostly it was little things. You showed up to deliver papers right when we were sitting down to dinner and then you'd stay after I went to bed. Once I saw you holding her hand when she was crying. And that wasn't anything significant in itself but I remember that you didn't let go for a long time."

"Just so you know, your mother and I didn't get involved until after your father's death. I wanted to marry her but she wouldn't."

She should have guessed the truth but she'd never wanted to know. She couldn't imagine Francine giving up her freedom, her weekends when she went off to lighthouses alone. "I like my independence," she'd once told Paula.

"I wasn't good enough for her," he concluded.

She shook her head. "I don't think that was it." She didn't

want to know any more. She had her own grief and he had his. She held up the folders. "So, bottom line. How much will the charities get?"

Ted tilted his head. "Um, well, I'd guess about one and a half."

"One and a half what?"

"One and a half million dollars, Paula. Your mother was a millionaire."

She nearly fell backward. Then she looked at Steph, who was shaking her head.

"You've got to be kidding? My mother? The woman who never bought a single item that wasn't on sale or clearance? Was this lighthouse a Blue Light Special because that's the only way my mother the cheapskate ever would've paid for it!"

She laughed heartily while Steph and Ted remained stoic. But there was nothing amusing about any of this, and she abruptly stood up, taking Steph's hand in her own.

"Ted, I appreciate your help. I'll call you after I read through all of this. I doubt I'll change my mind, though."

Ted's gaze again fell on their intertwined hands. "Just think about it, Paula. It's a lot of money. Um, are you two involved?"

Steph immediately dropped her hand and shook her head. "No, we're just friends."

Paula frowned but refused to respond. She looked back at Ted. "One more thing. Do you have the combination to her safe?"

He looked quizzical. "I didn't even know she had one."

Paula started to go but turned around in the doorway. "And for the record I think you were plenty good enough for her."

CHAPTER FOURTEEN

They pulled back into Francine's driveway but Paula remained still, holding the manila folders on her lap, staring out the windshield. She'd asked Steph to drive and then said nothing else. Steph couldn't imagine what she was thinking. While her life was a mess and she'd hated it for a long time, she'd only had one curve ball thrown at her—Eric. The rest she'd signed up for. Paula had been blindsided.

Paula made a guttural sound, jerked open the car door and threw up. She raced into the house, discarding her fortune on the front seat. After Steph hosed off the driveway and collected the folders, she went inside. Paula wasn't in the bathroom but Steph noticed the mouthwash had been left on the sink.

"Paula?" she called.

Paula screamed and there was a tinny thud. Steph jumped and knocked the mouthwash bottle onto the floor. She ran through the house and found her in the office behind the desk, wielding a sledgehammer. She brought it down against the safe barely making a dent in the top. Bleary-eyed, she bashed the metal repeatedly with little effect. Her screams evaporated as she concentrated on her swing. When she could no longer lift the hammer over her head, she dropped it and rested against the desk. She'd managed to break off the dial and crack the door but she couldn't open it—even with a crowbar.

"You fucking bitch!" she yelled. She kicked the safe several times until she grabbed her foot in pain, falling onto the carpet.

"Shit, Paula."

Steph took off Paula's shoe and checked her foot, which was already turning black and blue but didn't seem to be broken. She tossed the crowbar and sledgehammer out of reach and pulled her into her arms.

She sobbed. "I suppose you think I'm insane."

"No, I'm stunned by what your mother did with her fortune and the will. I don't even know what to say."

"Well, I do. She was a horrible, prejudiced, awful woman who obviously never loved me." She wiped her eyes on her shirt and stared up at her. "I don't care about the money, Steph. I really don't. In fact I don't want anything from her—not one cent."

Steph said slowly, "I can't even imagine how hurt you are but I think you need to think this through clearly."

"I am," she said confidently. She stood up. "Let me show you something."

They wandered into the guest bedroom and she picked up a picture from the dresser. It was a black-and-white photo of her and Steph on the day Paula won the regional spelling bee. They stood arm in arm, staring into the camera.

"Tell me what you see," she said.

Steph chose her words carefully, fearful that any response could cause Paula to hurl the photo into the dresser mirror. "It's us on the day you won the regional bee." She squeezed her arm.

"I was so proud of you."

"Do you remember the dress you're wearing?"

She looked closely at the gingham dress. "Oh, yeah. When my mom found out I could go with you to the County Courthouse, she insisted I have something worthy of such an important occasion. She was so worried I'd embarrass you or Francine."

Paula laughed maniacally. "I was the embarrassment. Your mother took you out to buy a new dress. Do you know what *my* mother did? Nothing. She said my pink skirt and white blouse were fancy enough. It wasn't like I was meeting the governor."

Steph looked closely at the picture, noticing the difference between their expressions. Paula's smile was tight, almost painful, while she was joyful over Paula's good fortune.

She stepped behind her and wrapped her in a hug. "Hey, it doesn't matter. You won, regardless of what you wore."

She shook her head and stepped out of the embrace. "I won but I was totally humiliated. When I went to take my place on the stage before it started, the woman who was running the bee gave me this disapproving look and pulled me into the bathroom. She grabbed some paper towels and soap, trying to shine my scuffed shoes and rub out a paint stain on the sleeve of my shirt. She told me that she thought it was great that a poor girl like me could be so smart. Maybe I could get a scholarship to college." She picked up the picture and Steph thought she might smash it against the dresser, but instead she tossed it into a nearby box. "Apparently my mother had enough money to buy properties and lighthouses but she didn't care enough about her own daughter's pride." She stared at Steph, her eyes on fire. "You weren't even in the fucking bee and Debbie made sure you looked nice."

She went back to the office to work on the safe but the door wouldn't budge. "I don't know what the hell is in here but I don't need any more surprises. She probably hired a PI to take pictures of me kissing my girlfriends."

For the next hour they tried to pry the door with any tool they could find. Admitting defeat, Steph went to the kitchen and retrieved the bottle of scotch Paula had found. It reminded Steph

120

of her father, who preferred scotch to any other drink.

"I can't understand what the hell your mother sees in that terrible JD crap," he'd often said.

She took the bottle and some highball glasses with ice to the office. Paula was on the floor, propped up against the wall, looking dejected. She handed her a drink and sat down next to her.

"You must think I'm an ungrateful bitch," she said, gulping the scotch.

"No, I think I get it. You had this whole understanding of your life and it's not true."

Paula reached for the bottle and poured another glass. "It's more than that. That codicil was the most hurtful and terrible thing she ever could've done. She's slapping me from the grave." She turned and faced her. "I won't lie. I'd like that inheritance. It's security for the future. But I won't pay the price. By adding that condition she proved that it was more important to control me than make a better life for me once she was gone."

"You're right," Steph agreed. She sat quietly next to her. There was absolutely nothing she could say to help and she was just as mortified by Francine's homophobia.

Paula swirled the scotch, watching the brown liquid melt the ice. "Right now your mother is looking like a fucking saint."

She had a point. After Steph moved to Scottsdale and had Eric, Debbie was a decent grandparent, always sending gifts and calling. Even when she came and visited she never embarrassed Eric or Lawrence.

"I'm not sure I'd use the word saint but you're right. Debbie wouldn't do anything like this. She's not mean, she's just…"

"Debbie."

They finished their drinks, staring at the safe. She wondered if Paula was right and it contained the proof of her lesbianism.

"How do you think your mother found out about you? Was it just a hunch?"

Paula shook her head. "I know exactly how she figured it out." She laughed. "Well, she didn't *figure out* anything. I'm positive my ex told her."

"Shelby?"

"No, Nia. She was the only other woman I've ever loved, other than you."

She was stabbed with jealousy. "Why would she do that?"

"Hell hath no fury…"

"Did you break up with her? Was she pissed?"

She set down her glass and crossed her legs. "The simple version of the story is that I wouldn't tell my mother about us. We were deeply in love and looking to spend our lives together. Nia even wanted to have a child. I'd almost convinced myself to call my mom and tell her the truth but every time I picked up the phone, I couldn't punch in the numbers. My hand froze. Nia got angrier and angrier. Our worst fight happened when she threatened to call Francine herself. I was enraged and threw things. I scared her and she backed off for a while but soon we were fighting again. Eventually she walked out and I couldn't blame her."

"But why do you think she told Francine?"

She sighed. "She told me she had. A week after we broke up she called me from a bar. She was wasted. She said she'd done me a huge favor and told Francine the truth. I hung up and immediately called Mom but she seemed entirely normal on the phone. I assumed Nia was bluffing and didn't think about it again. I wouldn't believe that someone I'd loved so much could ever do something so cruel. Apparently she did."

"So she thought you chose preserving your mom's delicate nature over a life with her."

She offered a guilty smile. "Didn't I?" Steph opened her mouth but she waved her off. "I did what I had to do. Nia didn't know Francine and she'd never seen all of this." She gestured toward the antique desk and the old-fashioned chairs that sat in front of it. Steph's favorite accessory was the nineteen-sixties era stapler that was heavy enough to be a weapon.

Paula took a breath and looked at her. "Do you think I did the right thing?"

She kissed the side of her head. "I can't answer that, sweetie."

She thought of Eric and her decision to keep him—and the role Francine had played in that decision. "We all do the best we can," she said.

"That's true," she agreed.

Steph sighed. "Look, I don't think anyone is all good or bad. Francine had a tough road, dealing with your dad's death and raising you alone…" She let the sentence fade away. She wouldn't deny what she knew was the truth. She'd told Paula a hundred times during their youth that she envied her relationship with her mother. Francine was *normal*.

"She certainly had her faults," Paula said flatly.

She wanted to move Paula away from the suffocating darkness she faced. "Yes, but did *your* mother ever spike the punch at a high school dance when she was the chaperone?"

Paula couldn't stifle the laugh brought on by the effects of the scotch. They were both feeling no pain. "God, that was so funny. And do you remember how Principal Drury drank the most? He thought it was the *greatest* punch he'd ever tasted."

They snuggled together and eventually Paula fell asleep, her chest rising and falling. Steph closed her eyes and thought of the hundreds of times she'd joyfully trudged up the hill, relieved that she'd escaped Debbie's chaos. So often Paula had anticipated her arrival and was sitting on the window seat against the huge bay window near the front door, usually reading a book. Steph would stand on the sidewalk, watching her beautiful face through the glass until she looked up and laughed. It was a little game that they played for years.

She thought that bay window was her looking glass inside the Kemper house. She thought she understood Francine and the kind of person she was. She'd believed that as Paula saw her family raw and exposed, she'd seen hers. She never fathomed that Francine's kindness and decorum were intertwined with a moral superiority that she wielded like a knife, excising pieces of Paula's self-esteem and pride.

As the day paled into twilight, splashing light and dark across the office, she gently pulled away from Paula and went to the living room. She gazed out the window at the well-manicured yards surrounding the Kemper house. It was a lovely picture and perhaps that was why Paula was always smiling when she saw her on the sidewalk. It was her chance to look out and forget what existed over her shoulder.

CHAPTER FIFTEEN

Several hours later Steph loaded Paula into her car and drove her back to Heceta Head. They trudged up to Victoria's Room, Paula's arms wrapped around her shoulders. Steph was reminded of her childhood and carrying Debbie up the stairs after her nightly binges. She tucked Paula in and debated whether to crawl underneath the cozy comforter with her but decided against it. She didn't want to complicate her living situation with Caroline and Rick.

Steph fell into her own bed certain that she would face another sleepless night. She hadn't put three thoughts together when her eyes closed and she was on the light rail in Phoenix going through a tunnel. Francine was next to her, holding her hand as she did the day she went to her for advice. The train's lights flicked off and she was lying next to Eric in the racecar bed he owned when he was eight. He wore a look of terror from a bad dream. She kissed his head and stroked his hair until he fell back to sleep. She turned over and Lawrence was next to her, kissing her and pulling at her panties. He mounted her and pushed her deeper into the darkness until she fell through a hole and landed on the path to Heceta.

Fog enveloped her and she could only see the outlines of trees and plants. The beacon flashed and she moved toward it, unsure of every step. If she veered too far to the left, she could tumble down the steep ravine that bordered the trail. The mist thickened and she could barely breathe. It was as if a length of crepe cocooned her, a veil over her eyes. The sensation disoriented her and she was dizzy.

Then she heard a woman's laugh and a figure brushed past her, directing the fog toward Heceta Head. Wild hair fluttered in the mist, surrounding a faceless visage. The beacon grew closer, its light brilliant and comforting. She stepped forward, freed from the mist—and found herself at the cliff's edge. She lurched backward, a scream bursting from her lips, and fell onto the soft grass. When she gazed up at the lighthouse, two figures stood against the glass next to the giant lens—her mother and Paula.

She sat up in bed covered in sweat, the sheet wrapped around her body like a swaddling blanket. She untangled herself and padded to the kitchen for a drink of water.

Standing at the window she gazed at Heceta, a stalwart sentinel in the distance. A chill passed through her and a low giggle nibbled her ear. The glass slipped through her fingers and shattered on the tile floor.

"What happened to you?" Caroline asked as she hobbled into the kitchen the next morning.

She leaned against the counter, favoring her left foot. "I had a little accident with a glass last night and I cut myself but I'm pretty sure I got it all picked up. You don't need to worry."

She'd been barefoot trying to maneuver around the broken

glass in the dark kitchen and she'd stepped on a large shard when she went for the dustpan. It took nearly an hour to clean everything up since her hands shook so violently. She was certain she'd heard a giggle and it kept repeating in her brain as she attempted to make sense of it.

"Rue didn't startle you, did she?" Caroline asked.

She whipped her head to the side and saw Caroline's smirk. "Of course not. I'm just a klutz."

Caroline grabbed a melon to slice, the smirk sliding into a grin. "It wouldn't be the first time she's made somebody jump. I thought Rick cut his finger off one night when she giggled in his ear."

Steph gripped the counter and said nothing. Feet on the staircase made them both look over at Paula, who hugged the handrail. "I could really use some aspirin," she mumbled.

"First shelf of the cabinet over the toaster," Caroline said.

Paula shuffled past Steph, planting a kiss on her lips. "Morning."

"Good morning," she said, eyeing Caroline, who wore an amused expression.

She said nothing and Steph assumed her morning baking duties, albeit slowly.

"What's wrong with your foot?" Paula asked.

"Rue scared her," Caroline said before she could respond.

"She did not. There's no such thing as ghosts."

"I disagree," Paula said, downing four aspirins. "I'm a big a believer in the spirit world. And I'd think you'd be happy to finally have an exchange with Rue, seeing as you're the only one who hasn't seen her."

"I didn't see her this time, either. I only *heard* her," she conceded.

Caroline laughed. "I knew it. That means she likes you."

Steph thought about the odd dream and the wild-haired woman leading her down the path to Heceta. *Was that Rue?*

"What are your plans for today, Paula?" Caroline asked. "Don't you leave in a few days?"

"On Friday."

Steph looked down, hoping Paula couldn't see her sad face. Despite the madness that surrounded her mother's death and her own divorce, being with Paula was heavenly. And the idea of her friendship—and her lips—drifting two hundred miles away instantly depressed Steph.

"I still need to make more progress on the house but I'm curious about the other properties my mother owned."

"What other properties?" Caroline asked, and Paula updated her on the will, carefully avoiding the codicil. Caroline nodded and said, "I think I heard your mother bought Tillamook. I'd just forgotten."

Paula wrapped her arms around Steph. "Will you go with me and look at these places?" She kissed her cheek and Steph laughed. "Please?"

"Sure, but I promised Caroline and Rick I'd help them with some gardening first."

"A lot of help you'll be now that you're injured," Caroline said.

"I'll pick up Steph's slack," Paula offered. "I'm really tired of packing boxes." She nuzzled her neck.

Caroline shook her head. "God, it's like when the two of you were teenagers."

"Really?" Steph asked. "Were we that obvious?"

She snorted and picked up the beverage tray. "You were inseparable. It was the late eighties so I don't think people immediately thought you were gay but you fawned all over each other *all the time*. And I'm not counting on either of you being much help outside," she added as she left for the dining room.

Once they were alone, Paula's mouth found Steph's. Her kiss turned Steph to mush. She groped her breast and pressed against her.

"Why didn't you stay with me last night?"

"You were too drunk to do anything and I didn't want Caroline and Rick to know."

"Oops. Sorry." She stepped back and leaned against the opposite counter.

"I think it's a little late." Steph thought of the minutes ticking away until she flew back to Seattle. She didn't want to waste any time so she floated back into her arms. "What if you don't finish by Friday?"

"Then I'll have to come back." A smile broke through Steph's depression and Paula caressed her cheek. "Would that be okay with you, if I spent a little more time in Eugene?"

She kissed her again, Paula's hands stroking her shoulders, her arms. Steph heard a car door slam and ignored it. If Rick was back from the gym, he'd just have to enjoy the show. She intended to kiss Paula much more—and frequently. She buried her tongue deep in her mouth until she moaned.

A pounding on the window made them both jump. "What the hell!" a voice boomed.

It took Steph a few seconds to recognize the people on the other side of the glass. She fell away from Paula's embrace and stared at Lawrence's face, red and irate—and the slack-jawed expression of her son.

She rushed through the house, stopping them at the front door before they could disturb the guests, who would be coming down for breakfast. Lawrence seemed twice his size, his rage and surprise inflating him like an inner tube. Eric was just the opposite. He hunched over and his gaze remained glued to the ground, his hands in his pockets. Steph couldn't imagine how embarrassed and betrayed he must feel.

"You're not even going to let us inside?" Lawrence bellowed.

She led them around to the side yard, cradling her body, feeling suddenly chilled. She looked at Eric, who followed slowly, dragging his feet through the grass.

"I'm so sorry, son. I know you must be shocked."

"Mom..." His voice broke apart. He obviously couldn't put words together to explain what he saw. She reached for him and he stepped away. She thought she might collapse at his abandonment.

Lawrence paced back and forth, making a tread through

the grass. He stared at the ground, his arms crossed. It was his customary response to an uncomfortable situation. Steph was used to it but the hospital executives had to constantly remind him about appropriate bedside manner since his patients didn't appreciate his cold and often tactless summation of complications that occasionally arose after a gastric bypass or face-lift.

She took a breath. "Putting aside the little show you saw in the window—"

"What the hell is going on with you?" Lawrence bellowed. "Since when do you kiss women?"

Steph noticed Eric was standing off to the side, holding the fence. At the sight of her only child helpless and hurt, she started to shake and sob. She could care less about Lawrence but Eric's pain was unbearable.

Lawrence clearly saw her tears as weakness. He grabbed her wrists and pulled her close. "I came to take you back, to plead for your forgiveness and this is what I find?"

She looked at Eric. "I'm sorry. I didn't mean to hurt you," she said between sobs.

Eric shuffled back to the rented Hummer and climbed inside. Steph moved to follow him but Lawrence tightened his grip on her wrists.

"You leave him alone. What are you now, a lesbo?" He spewed the question through clenched teeth and she barely understood him.

She glanced at the Hummer's windshield but she couldn't see Eric. Anger flared in her belly and she leaned closer to him. "You get your hands off me or I'll knee you in the balls."

A sick smile crawled on his face. "Is that what you learned with your dyke friend? How to play rough? I like rough," he said, shoving her away so hard that she almost fell to the ground.

"Why are you here?" she asked slowly, trying to control the tremor in her voice.

"Like I said, we came to get you back. Eric wants his mommy," Lawrence said, frowning like a child.

She shook her head. "That's bullshit. Eric's accepted our

130

divorce. He hates your guts. He's the one who encouraged me to leave you. How did you get him here?"

Lawrence grinned wickedly. "I told him that I was so distraught that I might do something to myself or get so drunk on the plane that I'd be arrested. He felt sorry for me." Lawrence stuck out his lower lip.

"You are horrible. You deceived your own son. You lied to him to get him to leave school and come here."

He snorted. "I'm thinking now he'll forgive me. I may have been his least favorite parent five minutes ago but I think you're at the top of the list now."

She wanted to smack the smug expression off his face but a seed of vulnerability lodged itself in her heart. She'd rarely talked to Eric about gays but she knew he was rather open-minded and mature. *But he's also seventeen.* It had to be shocking to see his mother making out with another woman.

"Why are you really here?"

"I'm telling the truth. I want you back. I kicked that slut out of the house so we can get on with our lives."

"Really."

"Really," Lawrence said. He moved toward her and rubbed her shoulders. "C'mon, baby, you know you want me back. Don't you miss me?" He pulled her against him and she could feel his erection. "And for the record," he added, "you can bring any woman you want into our bed. I'm all for threesomes. Just the thought of it makes me hard."

She jerked away, disgusted. *Think, Steph. Why is he here?* Then it hit her.

"What did your divorce attorney say? He agreed with mine, didn't he? Arizona is a community property state and I'll get half the practice. As much as you want to kick me to the curb, you can't. I get half and I *deserve it*, Lawrence. A judge would see that."

His smug expression vanished and he pushed his glasses further up on his face. He chewed on his cheek and pursed his lips. She'd figured out his motive and now he was thinking, analyzing, doing what he did best. Lawrence was an asshole, a cheater and a terrible father but he was brilliant. He had the best mind of anyone she knew and his business acumen had transformed his father's simple surgical practice into a multimillion dollar corporation. And he didn't believe she deserved a penny.

He turned to the Hummer and stared at it for a long time before he faced her again. When he did, his expression had softened, devoid of emotion.

"Okay, cards on the table. Yes, I came here to get you back because it's cheaper for me. And I still think we should get back together, Steph. We're a good team, even I'll acknowledge that. You look good on my arm when I have to go to all those stuffy charity dinners and medical conferences. I wish you'd get your boobs done again," he added, "but they're still pretty perky for a woman who's had a child."

"Thanks."

He lifted his hands in surrender. "Sorry, I know that didn't come out right. Look, if you keep on with this divorce, it'll hurt, and until I peeked through that window I couldn't think of what you'd gain from divorcing me." He pointed at the house. "Is she the reason we're over? Did you leave me for her?"

"No, Paula is an old friend. We've gotten close. I didn't intend for it to happen but it did. I left you because I don't love you and you don't love me."

Recognition crossed his face. "That's Paula? Francine's daughter? How interesting." He clasped his hands behind his back and attempted humility. "Well, you'll do whatever you want but this new lifestyle certainly doesn't help your position—not with the courts or your son."

Her mouth went dry as his master plan became clear. That kiss in the kitchen could be quite costly.

"Arizona courts don't look too kindly on lesbian romances, particularly if it's the cause of the problem." He spoke like an attorney making a case before the judge.

"But that's not true. My divorce doesn't have anything to do with Paula and there aren't any other *romances* as you put it."

He shrugged. "You say that but I don't know if you're telling the truth," he said, an innocent look on his face. "You say that but Paula was your *best* friend during your youth. Perhaps the two of you experimented a little, huh? And I seem to remember a certain tennis pro who became your best buddy. What was her name? I wonder how hard it would be to find her and make her testify in open court." His eyes turned to ice. "Don't mess with me, Steph. You'll lose. Come home. Do it for Eric. It'll be the only way he'll forgive you. Call me when you've changed your mind."

He walked back to the Hummer and drove away.

When he was out of sight, she collapsed to the ground. As a child she'd sometimes run behind the granite rock at night and gaze up at the sky. She'd imagine how many other people were craning their necks in awe of the bright stars or full moon at that exact same moment. She pictured people in San Diego lying on the beach or a family at a campsite in Colorado sitting by the fire while the father or mother pointed out the Little Dipper or the W of Cassiopeia. Whenever she needed to feel connected to the universe or she wanted to stave off the terrible loneliness that came from being an only child, she gazed at the heavens above.

The grass swished and crunched as someone approached.

"He didn't stab you in the back with a knife, did he?" Paula asked sarcastically. When she added a nervous chuckle, Steph knew she was genuinely concerned.

She pulled her up and they headed back to the house. "No, he's already done that," she said, answering her question. "He came to make threats and try to rattle me."

"Did he succeed?"

She nodded slightly. Her heart was pounding and she couldn't stop shaking. She put her hands in her pockets so Paula couldn't touch her and feel her vulnerability. *What if he's not kidding? What if he can find the tennis pro?*

"I'm definitely concerned that he saw us kissing," she said, carefully choosing her words. "That could hurt my standing with the court."

Paula scowled. "Why would the courts care?"

133

She took a breath, trying to be patient. "Paula, you've lived your entire life in the Pacific Northwest, a place that openly accepts gay people. I live in *Arizona*. It's a little different there." She'd raised her voice unintentionally and taken a sharp tone. "I'm sorry," she added, climbing up the porch steps. "I just need some time to think."

"Do you still want to take a drive with me today?" Paula asked before she could slip inside. "I thought we could go up to Tillamook with the ashes and maybe spend the night. It'd be nice to get out of here."

Her heart was splitting in half. She wanted to spend every minute with Paula but she pictured them pulling up to a diner for lunch just as Lawrence and Eric came out.

"I don't think so. Not today. I know I promised I'd go with you but I'm not feeling well."

Paula looked away, saying nothing. Steph knew that she wasn't a good liar and Paula wanted to call her on it like when they were kids. But Paula always swallowed her tales since they usually involved an embarrassing moment with Debbie. She recognized that sometimes Steph just needed to save face.

She hesitated at the door, drawn to Paula's beauty and the desire to please her—to be pleased *by* her, but her mind reverted to the last image she had—the two of them cuddling in the kitchen, their lips igniting their passion and the look on Eric's face when she realized he was watching. She quickly went inside, unable to look at Paula again.

CHAPTER SIXTEEN

The sound of the screen door smacking shut between them reverberated in Paula's ears as she drove out of Eugene. Steph had promised to help her with Francine's ashes, but at the sight of her husband, she'd abandoned her. At least that was how it felt.

Steph's choice probably was an indicator of what she'd do about her life—return to Arizona with Lawrence and Eric. The strong Steph that scurried up the cheerleading pyramid and thrust out her pom-poms twenty feet in the air was gone, replaced by a woman whose entire adult life revolved around serving two males. Paula felt terrible that she'd missed out on Steph's life for so long. They'd supported each other in childhood and her heart hurt imagining Steph's confidence whittled away year after year, stuck in that upper-crust Scottsdale life.

"And you're such a great catch," she muttered, thinking about her own unemployment and potential disinheritance.

How could she ever compete with a rich plastic surgeon? She turned the Malibu down Spruce Street toward the university. She was suddenly grateful that she hadn't yet mentioned to Steph that she'd been fired. Based on the events of the last few hours, she decided to visit her mother's other holdings before going up to Tillamook. If a life with Steph was impossible, would endless one-night stands be so bad? At least she'd have sex and money.

The rental property Francine owned was a three-bedroom bungalow south of the U of O. She pulled up on the other side of the street and was surprised by the curbside appeal. Most of the houses near the university were often in disrepair since the tenants were usually students who didn't make time for upkeep. This one seemed to be the exception. The lawn was mowed, the hedge trimmed and bright flowers lined the front porch in colorful pots. The tenants were definitely neat freaks and she could picture her mother personally reviewing the applications and choosing whom to interview to ensure only quality people inhabited her property.

The house was quaint and sat on a small lot, necessitating that it be built up and not out. She imagined the rooms were tiny but served their purpose to students. She remembered how little time she spent in her dorm room and later her college apartment. There was always a study group meeting or a party happening. She'd loved college. *And you certainly enjoyed your share of women, too.* She blushed even though she was alone. Her roommates referred to her as Casanova's sister because she'd bedded so many co-eds.

Steph had missed almost the entire collegiate experience. She pictured her sleepless nights after Eric was born. Instead of dancing until two in the morning, she would've been nursing her newborn son or tending to his colic. While Paula pulled all-nighters studying for finals, she would have been planning Junior League events and acting as the perfect wife for Lawrence. Her life revolved around other people and she'd never had any time for herself as an adult. She imagined the thought of being alone scared Steph immensely.

She stared at the house and wondered how long her mother had owned it. She picked up Ted's file and thumbed through the property details. It had been built in 1946 and Francine bought it in 1990, after Paula was done with school. It pleased her to know that her mother hadn't owned it when Paula was still in Eugene. Somehow it made her deception bearable.

She headed downtown toward the heart of old Eugene and the commercial building that was her mother's next investment. It sat on a corner at a prime location. The other three corners had already received major face-lifts, the buildings newly painted and parking lots repaved. There were no chain stores and the area seemed dedicated to the local businesspeople making a play for loyal customers or clients who might actually walk or ride a bike.

She immediately liked the sturdy old red brick building and large windows that faced the street. Three brown doors indicated a place for three tenants. Paula noticed the largest space was unoccupied. She peered through the window at what was once some sort of eating establishment. She could see a kitchen area and service counter and a few discarded pieces of furniture sat in the corner. She guessed her mother had been without a tenant for a while.

Maude's Closet, a vintage collectible and antique store, occupied the middle space. A bell tinkled when she pushed open the door and she automatically smiled at the old hobby horse that greeted her. She'd had one when she was very young, a gift from her father. Somewhere in the old family photo album was a picture of her riding the horse—Bart. Every inch of floor space was packed with memorabilia and display cases. She could imagine her mother sifting through the treasures for hours.

An elderly lady emerged from one of the aisles carrying an antique vase. "May I help you?"

She wore a lavender pantsuit and Paula thought of a nearly identical outfit that she'd tossed into the bonfire. Perhaps this lady and Francine shopped together.

"Um, well, I'm Paula, Francine Kemper's daughter?"

She stuck her hand out and the lady met it hesitantly. "It's nice to meet you. I'm Geraldine Appleton, the owner of Maude's Closet. I'm sorry for your loss. It's always difficult to lose a parent, regardless of what kind of person he or she was."

Paula blinked, taken aback by her forwardness. "I guess you didn't get along with my mother?"

"Nope," she said on her way to the register. "Francine wasn't what I would call an excellent landlord."

"What do you mean?"

She smiled sympathetically. "Sweetie, I don't want to be telling stories on the dead. It's not right."

Paula picked up a spinning top that could've belonged to her great-grandfather. "No, I'd really like to know. This building may be part of my inheritance so if you didn't view my mother as a good landlord, I'd like to know why. It could help me."

Geraldine seemed to weigh her request against her understanding of good manners. "Well, considering you may become the boss and you *are* her daughter, if you want to know I'll tell you."

Paula nodded. "I want to know."

She stared at her icily. "Your mother was a cheapskate. She did as little as possible to keep this building operational. Last summer we went almost a week without air conditioning. Drea, that's the owner next door, had to threaten Francine's attorney with another attorney."

Paula was shocked. "Really? People thought my mother was the epitome of kindness and I can't imagine she'd let you suffer in the heat and humidity."

"Oh, she made a point of telling us that we'd brought it on ourselves."

"How?"

"One day she came by and saw that I'd set the thermostat a little lower than she liked and she gave me this lecture about conserving energy and watching costs. So when the compressor blew the next week, she blamed us for overworking the unit. Can you believe it?"

She rubbed her eyes. She could believe it. She was reminded of the many days during her teen years when her mother wouldn't turn on the A/C. "We live in Oregon," Francine argued. "We don't need air conditioning." And sometimes that was true, but at the peak of summer it was helpful.

"I'm sorry that it hasn't been easy for you. I'm not sure if I'll inherit the store but if I do I'll try to always be considerate."

Geraldine smiled at her sincerity. "So why wouldn't you inherit? Is there some sort of long-lost relative who's trying to take it from you? I thought Francine only had one child."

"Yeah, I'm it." She toyed with a cute figurine on the counter and avoided her gaze. "There are some provisions in the will and I'm not sure I want to follow them."

Geraldine narrowed her eyes and gave a slight nod. "I hear you. I imagine my life with Francine was only a slice of the pie that you had to eat."

Paula said nothing but headed toward the door. "Oh, who was Maude?"

She grinned. "Maude was my old dog, bless her soul. She used to sleep in the closet. I saw her there one day and I thought it would be a good name for the store. I'd picked my brain for months and then I saw her and I liked it. That's Maude right there," she said, pointing behind Paula.

When she turned, she nearly jumped out of her sneakers at the sight of the stuffed Greyhound standing at attention. "Oh, what a beautiful dog. Well, I should be going. I'll let you know what happens." She offered a slight wave and headed out, trying not to giggle.

A neon fluorescent sign hung over the door at the last storefront. She assumed it was a hair salon since the name was Cut Upz. Sitar music greeted her and the smell of incense was heavy. The shop was small with only three cutting stations. A punker sat in the waiting area reading a guitar magazine, his head bopping to the music of his iPod while he quietly sang along.

The furniture was eclectic. A row of movie theatre seats faced two chairs that had obviously been part of an airplane at one point. She chuckled when she saw the oxygen masks dangling from the ceiling above them. Across the room a woman in a tiny miniskirt that barely covered her bottom hunched over a large man at a sink. The tattoos on her arms wiggled as she scrubbed his hair.

"Be with you in a minute," she said flatly without looking up.

Paula sat down across from the iPod guy in another empty barber chair and noticed the wall behind him, which contained rows of shelves displaying vintage lunchboxes. There was Snoopy on a lunchbox shaped like his doghouse but most were the traditional rectangles with the plastic handles. Scooby Doo, Six Million Dollar Man, E.T.—even soccer great Pele had been memorialized in tin. Most were used and very old.

"Did you have one as a kid?" the woman asked as she approached.

Paula pointed. "Third one from the top. Donny and Marie."

"Poor you," she said dramatically. "Somebody *gave* me that box. I never actually had to carry it."

Paula chuckled. "My mother was into wholesomeness." She held out her hand. "I'm Paula and my mother was Francine Kemper."

"Drea."

Her perfect lips formed a slight smile and Paula could tell she rebelled against traditional good looks. Purple streaks raced through her white-blond hair and thick black eyeliner hid the rich gold of her irises. It was more important to be punk than pretty but her physical beauty was evident despite her attempt to hide it behind excessive makeup.

"I heard about your mother. That sucks."

"Thanks. So what did you think of my mom?" she asked, prepared for a tongue-thrashing.

Drea laughed. "Well, if you've already been over to Geraldine's shop then you know your mother wasn't easy to get along with. I had all sorts of ideas for this place, how to really liven up the atmosphere, but if it involved painting the walls, adding lights or anything permanent, Francine said no. I had to beg for the lunchbox collection." Her eyes twinkled. "Now that I've met you, I wonder if she agreed just to preserve Donny and Marie's memory."

Paula grimaced. "It wouldn't surprise me."

She gazed at the many plants scattered throughout and the various simple touches. The unblemished white walls detracted from the look Drea wanted to achieve and no amount of flora or cute displays could erase the hospital-like environment. She smirked at her mother's stubbornness. Why would she object to a little action? She immediately rolled her eyes. *C'mon, Paula, this is your mother.*

"I think this is an awesome place," Paula said and Drea beamed at the compliment.

"Too bad you're not the landlord, or are you my landlord now?" she asked as an afterthought. "I suppose somebody's got to inherit. Please tell me it's you!"

She instantly liked the idea of being Drea's landlord—and knowing Drea. And if it weren't for Steph, she'd definitely make a pass at the lunchbox lady who she was rather certain swung both ways.

Paula took a deep breath. It was too difficult to explain and it would cast Francine in an awful light.

"Maybe," she said. "There's still some stuff to work out."

Drea stepped closer and Paula noticed her tiny nose stud. "Well, I really hope it works out."

She smiled seductively and Paula stared at her black lined lips. She knew women who paid thousands for collagen injections to achieve the sculpted little pout that naturally formed on her face. Suddenly feeling as though she were sucking the air out of the room, Paula nodded and quickly left.

She stood on the sidewalk and breathed deeply. An image of Steph wiped Drea away and she smiled.

She returned to her car and started up I-5 toward Tillamook. The weather was fabulous and she longed for her convertible Mercedes, the open road and the wind blowing through her hair. The cramped quarters of the enclosed Malibu did little for her growing restlessness. She'd had a day to comprehend the implications of the codicil and she now appreciated Ted's advice. She was glad she didn't immediately sign a document to give away her inheritance, particularly after the little drama with Lawrence and Eric. She knew Steph hated Lawrence but she'd do anything for Eric. She'd lived her life for her son and if he couldn't handle his mother being with a woman, Paula grudgingly acknowledged that Steph would again give up any chance of happiness to secure his love.

She popped a CD mix into the slot and smooth jazz calmed her nerves. She was assuming the worst. She'd shared some amazing moments with Steph this week so maybe she needed to give their past a little credit. But when she thought of the intervening seventeen years and how *long* they'd been apart, she held little hope she'd win in the competition for her love.

And if Steph went back to Arizona would Paula ever want anyone else? She frowned at the truth. Other than Steph and Nia, Paula had never been with any woman for longer than six months and usually her mini-relationships were littered with one-night stands or quickie affairs designed to doom any long-term liaisons. At least that's what her shrink said.

So if Steph went back to Lawrence there really wasn't anything keeping her from accepting the inheritance, other than her principles, which desperately wanted to tell Ted Ruth where her mother could shove it. But her principles didn't have to buy groceries or find a job in a tight market. How hard would it be to sign some sort of legal paper promising never to fall in love?

But what if Steph changed her mind?

That wouldn't happen.

If Steph returned to Lawrence it would be like stepping into a time capsule and sealing the door shut. There would be no turning back and she doubted Steph would even want to remain friends. It would be as if the last few days had never occurred.

She needed some type of assurance immediately. She flipped open her phone and called Steph. When her cell went to voice mail, she called the B and B and got Caroline.

"She's not here, Paula. She went out."

Paula heard the hesitation in her voice. She was hiding something. "Oh, she told me to call her this afternoon. She was going to take the safe in and we wanted to do it before five."

"I see." Caroline's guard came down and she sighed. "Well, she should be back from Ted's office in just a little while."

She was seeing Ted Ruth, probably asking about her court case, wondering if her new affection for girls was going to ruin her divorce settlement.

"Okay, well, I'll catch her on her cell," she said casually, hoping her voice wasn't cracking. "Um, has Lawrence called? I've been really worried all day. He and Steph had a big argument this morning."

She made it sound like she was privy to the entire discussion and Caroline sighed in frustration. "He's called at least five times. I finally gave the phone to Rick who had a few choice words for him. What happened?"

"Just divorce details. I'll call her cell," she said and quickly hung up.

She glanced down at the speedometer and realized she was cruising at ninety miles an hour, passing every car in her path. Oregonians were some of the most law-abiding, patient people who never hurried to get anywhere. She let up on the pedal and watched the road before her. An idea gnawed at her brain and she focused on the blacktop in front of her.

Like a word jumble, her epiphanies often needed reordering. She waited patiently until the idea came into a logical formation. She should take the inheritance. Doing so would keep the status quo of her life. She'd forsaken Steph, refused to fight for Nia and extinguished any possibility of other relationships because it would've meant standing up to Francine. She wouldn't stand up to her in life so why would she bother now? She glanced at the tin box sitting on the seat, containing Francine's ashes. Her mother had controlled her personal life for the last twenty-five years and it looked as though it would continue if Paula wanted

143

any semblance of a rich life.

She laughed out loud. "You win, Mom! I get it now!"

With a new sense of freedom she turned onto the 101 and drove the last stretch of highway to Tillamook. It was already three o'clock so she doubted she'd be able to see the lighthouse today. She needed to check into a motel and take a shower.

She'd be thanking Ted Ruth for his sage advice. She'd already thought about ways to help Geraldine and especially Drea, who'd be thrilled to know she could paint the walls any damn color she wanted, and she couldn't wait to see the lighthouse. A small pebble of regret lodged in her heart that she couldn't shake. To forsake true love in writing was difficult to absorb. She thought of Mr. Darcy and Elizabeth—and Steph.

She pulled out a map she'd found in her mother's desk and began to search for the Terrible Tilly Motel. Her mother had made pencil notes in the margins and Paula remembered she'd mentioned it once to Debbie. She turned onto Main Street and found the simple motel, a Sixties-style two-story where all the doors faced the pool. The office was attached to a house but when she went inside it was vacant. A curtained doorway behind the desk suggested a connecting point between the house and the office and she was rather certain she heard the theme song to the *Andy Griffith Show*. She politely dinged the bell but no one appeared. She waited for the final bars of Andy's whistling and dinged again.

"Just a moment," a woman's voice called.

The canned laughter disappeared and a petite, ancient woman emerged from between the curtains. She smiled brightly and in an incredibly articulate voice said, "Hello. Welcome to the Terrible Tilly Motel. My name is Estelle and I'm one of the proprietors. Will you be staying with us this evening?"

Paula was reminded of her mother and a level of courtesy and politeness only found in older generations. She swallowed hard and returned the woman's pleasant smile. "Yes, I'd like a room, please, and directions to the Tillamook lighthouse."

The woman held up a finger and reached for an old-fashioned guest book. "First things first. Let's get you registered. Will you please sign?"

Paula signed her name on a thin line at the bottom of a page. "It looks as though you have a lot of people staying here right now."

"We do. In Tillamook it's all about the cheese." She said this in a whisper, as if it were a well-kept secret. Paula doubted that anyone who visited a grocery store didn't know about Tillamook cheese.

Estelle gave her a key on a homemade wooden key fob. The number four was burned into the side and Paula guessed she'd just been handed somebody's seventh grade shop project.

"Room four is our last vacancy tonight. Just out the door and to the left."

Paula looked at her quizzically. "Don't you need to take my credit card information or write down my license plate number?"

Estelle scoffed. "Oh, sweetie, you look trustworthy. Besides I don't understand all of the new fangled machines like computers and faxes. I've never sent an e-mail in my life and I'm proud of it."

"You're not missing much."

"I didn't think so. I do enjoy those funny dog and cat pictures that my niece gets on her e-mail. You know, the ones that show a bird pecking at a dog's head or some such nonsense. And there's always a humorous caption? Have you seen those?"

"Oh, yes. Many times."

She laughed heartily. "They're a hoot." She caught her breath and added, "My niece is the one who understands how to run the computer." Estelle flipped her thumb toward the small desk and Paula noticed a very old machine. "When you check out in the morning, she'll take care of you." She put on her reading glasses and looked at the entry in the guest book. "Ms. Paula Kemper." She looked up, curiously. "Now why does that name sound so familiar?"

"My mother was Francine Kemper. I think she probably stayed here before. She owns the Tillamook lighthouse."

Recognition flooded Estelle's face. "Of course! You're the spitting image of her. How is your mother?"

Paula had prepared herself for that question. "Unfortunately, she passed away recently."

Estelle's face dropped. "I'm so sorry, dear. She was a wonderful woman and an excellent guest. We had some lovely conversations about Tillamook and lighthouses…" Her voice faded away as her memories filled her mind. She took a deep breath and gazed at Paula again. "You'll have to excuse me, sweetie. When you're older, it's difficult to hear of death. It's like someone sending you a reminder notice, you know?"

"I understand. You said you spoke to my mother about Tillamook?"

Estelle seemed relieved to change subjects. "Oh, yes. I remember when your mother was considering the purchase. They'd come up here several times and couldn't decide whether to do it. It was risky, you know?"

Paula narrowed her eyes. "Why?"

Estelle gestured to an array of pictures on the wall behind Paula. "She isn't called Terrible Tilly for nothing. She's a tough nut."

Paula realized that the Tillamook Rock Lighthouse sat on a treacherous rock away from the shore. Several of the pictures depicted the waves battering the rock and the lighthouse. The dangerous rock stair-stepped two hundred feet to a plateau where Tilly sat. Paula imagined it had been extraordinarily difficult to build.

"So my mother obviously decided to purchase it. What's the story behind it?"

Estelle stepped to the end photo of the rock without the lighthouse and gestured as if she were a tour guide. "Some say Tilly is shaped like a sea monster. It's the place where sailors go to die. In the late eighteen hundreds, surveyors decided the rock would be a good place for a lighthouse. The locals disagreed

146

and threatened to sabotage the project. They refused to help and workers who were unfamiliar with the area were acquired."

Paula could tell from the dramatic quality of Estelle's voice that she'd given this tour before. She stepped to the next picture, one of Tillamook under construction. "It took two hundred and twenty-four days to level the rock for the lighthouse to be built. The only transportation was by boat and at one point a nor'easter hit and nearly killed them all. They were found clinging to the rocks by a ship that was nearby. But Tilly wasn't done. She would claim what was hers."

The next photo depicted the finished Tilly in all her glory. "Five hundred and twenty days later Tillamook Rock was completed but it came with a price—the death of the foreman. The lamp was lit and over the years she earned the name Terrible Tilly. Storms got so bad that rocks would break off and pelt the lamp room, shattering the glass. Sometimes the whole place would flood, filling with seaweed and debris. Repairs became a way of life. Keepers wouldn't stay. No one with any mental instability lasted long, and there's one story that said a keeper went after one of his helpers during a severe bout of anxiety."

Estelle stepped toward a framed newspaper article from the thirties. "Then in nineteen thirty-four, the greatest nor'easter imaginable came to Tillamook. The four keepers, for one would never have been enough, couldn't control the damage. The place was flooded and the Fresnel lens was destroyed by flying debris. Bolts that anchored the lighthouse were ripped from the rock. When the storm subsided, it was decided that Tilly's lens wouldn't be replaced."

Estelle bowed her head and her voice was reverent. She moved to the last photo, a modern-day color picture of Tillamook. She sighed before she began what Paula suspected was the last chapter. "Tilly's ownership changed hands several times, like an unwanted pit bull. Rich folk would invest without ever seeing her, in love with the romantic notion of a lighthouse. Then when they visited they were sorely disappointed. A company bought Tilly and turned her into a columbarium—"

"A what?"

"A place to house urns. They thought it would be a wonderful final resting place for those who loved lighthouses, like your mother. Unfortunately they lost their license and Tilly became the victim of vandals and thieves." Estelle looked up with a smile. "Then Francine came along and gave Tilly a new chance. She purchased Tilly and I believe her intent was to make the columbarium proper and regain the license. That's what they always talked about."

Paula held up a hand. "Estelle, you've said *they* a few times. Don't you mean *she?*"

Estelle shook her head. "Of course, sweetheart. I know he died and it was your mother's money."

"What? Who died?"

Estelle looked confused. "Well, John, darling. Your mother's beau."

Paula froze. She only knew one John. "John who?" she asked quietly.

Estelle looked at her as if she should already know the answer. "John South, of course. He came up here with your mother all the time."

There wasn't anything to support Paula and she thought she might faint. She held tightly onto her purse and breathed deeply. It helped when Estelle took her arm and steadied her.

"Sweetheart, are you all right? You look pale."

She closed her eyes as she realized the truth, the puzzle pieces coming together. It all made sense.

Please, God. There can't be any more secrets or surprises. I may be under fifty but I'll die of a heart attack.

John South, Steph's father, was her mother's lover.

CHAPTER SEVENTEEN

"I very much appreciate you seeing me on such short notice, Mr. Ruth."

"That's not a problem, Mrs. Rollins. Eugene isn't like big cities. We move at a slower pace and have more time on our hands."

She smiled pleasantly at the truth. Eugene was about enjoying life, not just living it. "Please call me Stephanie. I'm in the process of getting a divorce and I won't be Mrs. Rollins for much longer." Even as she said the words she realized they may not be true.

He raised an eyebrow. "Oh? I didn't realize you were separated. I'm sorry. You have an attorney in Arizona, don't you?"

"Yes, but I'm hoping you can answer some simple questions since he's at a conference this week and I've had an emergency arise."

"Of course. Just give me a second," he added, his eyes scanning the paperwork.

She nodded and stared out the window. Ted had a great view from the third floor. The sun clambered over the tree line and light streamed into the room. There was no need for lamps as nature provided enough for him to read the fine print of her divorce petition. It had all seemed easy to her. She hadn't felt so good about a decision since Berkeley—and then Lawrence had showed up.

He flipped back to the first page. "It seems very standard and reasonable. I know Arizona divorce can be a little thornier because of various influences, but as a community property state you have a right to fifty percent of everything you've acquired during the marriage. So what is it that you're worried about?"

She wet her lips, unsure of how to phrase the question. "I'm wondering if there are circumstances that could jeopardize that decision."

His eyes narrowed as he pondered the question. "I'm not sure I understand. To what kind of circumstances might you be referring?"

He poised his Mont Blanc fountain pen over the legal pad, ready to take copious notes. She noticed he sat in "perfect penmanship position," as Ms. Riley, her third-grade teacher used to say. Clearly Ted Ruth was a straight arrow who always colored inside the lines.

"What about infidelity?"

He exhaled. "Did you cheat on your husband?"

"No, he cheated on me."

"Legally, that's good for you. It casts you in a favorable light. You were a hardworking mother trying to make a good home for your family while your husband advanced his career..." He waved his hand, expecting she could finish the thought.

"Would his adultery be enough to counterbalance something I did?"

"Meaning?"

There was no easy way to explain and she knew he'd seen

Paula take her hand when they'd visited him the other day—right before he told her she'd lose everything for being in a long-term lesbian relationship.

"Can I ask you something, just between us?"

He set his pen down. "Of course."

"Why did you agree to that awful codicil in Francine's will?"

He looked stunned. "But I didn't. I tried several times to get her to change her mind but she was so hurt. She felt so betrayed after years of Paula's lies. I tried to get her to see past her anger but she said she couldn't."

Steph threw up her hands. "If you thought her position was so reprehensible, why did you agree to do it?"

He looked away and she could see that she'd asked a question he'd pondered many times. Silence filled the room and she waited patiently. After a deep sigh he said, "There were probably many reasons but I knew that if I didn't help her, she'd go to someone else. She was so blinded by her anger then that she would have gone down the street to the first lawyer she found and aired her dirty laundry. And then there would've been gossip, and lots of it. Eugene's a small town and both of their names would have turned to mud. I couldn't let that happen."

His loyalty to Francine was clearly unwavering and she nodded her understanding.

He folded his hands in front of him and looked at his notes. "Now, tell me about this issue or obstacle that you fear will affect your divorce settlement."

Steph took a deep breath, hoping she could remember her rehearsed speech. "Mr. Ruth, since I've returned to Eugene, Paula Kemper, who was my dearest childhood friend, has become my lover." She watched his reaction, which remained unchanged. "I want to stress that absolutely nothing occurred prior to filing my divorce papers. Filing for divorce stemmed from my husband's infidelity and dissatisfaction with my marriage. However, this morning my husband and son arrived at an incredibly inopportune moment and observed us kissing. He's threatening to hold this over my head during the divorce proceeding. And my son, who used to be my ally, won't speak to me."

Her voice cracked and she lowered her head, thinking about the ten messages she'd left on Eric's cell phone.

Ted stroked his face thoughtfully. "I'm sorry for your predicament, Stephanie. I think the world of Paula and I'm sure you're both hurting immensely." He gazed at her with a serious expression. "Homosexual conduct remains one of the greatest wild cards in the judicial system. It's incredibly problematic because it's not acknowledged as a protected class by the federal government and most state governments. As you can imagine, Arizona supports few rights for gays. Thus, legal decisions often boil down to the effectiveness of attorney argument and judicial prejudice." He held up a hand and added, "I'm not implying judges ignore laws but when there aren't very many on the books they are left with their own interpretations."

"So this could affect the outcome of the divorce."

He pinched the bridge of his nose. "It's hard to say. If your husband chooses to make this an issue for discussion you might be in financial trouble. Your son won't be a legal issue because he's nearly an adult. If he were a minor you would probably lose custody. That's the sad truth. Your result will be affected by the factors I mentioned and only your Arizona attorney will be able to help you analyze the judicial culture you'll face. I'm sorry I can't help you more."

She hung her head. "No, you've confirmed what I suspected."

"May I ask you a personal question?"

She nodded and looked up into his kind eyes. "Do you love Paula?"

She smiled slightly, hearing another person say the words out loud. "I'm not sure. We were so very close when we were young. It's hard to know whether our feelings now are just residual or something special." She stood to go. "Thank you for taking the time to see me."

He shook her hand and then escorted her out to the BMW. "Do me one favor, will you?" he asked, opening her door like a true gentleman.

"Of course."

"When you have an answer to my question, the one about Paula, will you please let me know?"

She was somewhat taken aback by the request. He wanted an update on her personal life and she couldn't imagine why. He didn't seem like a gossipmonger who sought titillating details but perhaps she'd given him more credit than he deserved.

"I'm not sure why that's any of your business." Her tone was more puzzled than hostile.

He held up a cordial hand. "Of course. I'm sorry for being so forward. I just worry about Paula."

She drove on autopilot back to Heceta Head, numb to her circumstances. Years of living in Eugene must have ensured she wouldn't be killed on the road, because when she pulled up behind the B and B, she had no recollection of the drive at all.

She couldn't get out of the car. She felt incredibly vulnerable and exposed. She couldn't win regardless of the path she chose. It was like the road that stretched past the B and B. Travelers could trudge up to Heceta Head or down to the shore. Both views were pleasant but entirely different and choosing one usually meant forsaking the other. People wanted the seashore or they wanted the view of the cliffs. She always chose the view beyond the horizon at the cliffs.

The wind kicked up and she heard the scream of the weather vane as it reacted. Rick had promised to fix it but he hadn't yet managed to climb on the roof. The sound drove her onto the trail toward the turning beacon. What did she want? What did she need?

But her needs had always seemed so insignificant. She wasn't trained in anything particular. The fact that she'd spent her life helping a doctor establish his practice and raising a son gave her great pleasure. It was important and meaningful. She rationalized that some people lived their lives as the supports for others. Not everyone could be the world-famous doctor. Someone had to be the triage nurse or the orderly. While many aspired to be wealthy actors, most were personal assistants or behind-the-scenes types.

It was late in the afternoon and only a handful of tourists marveled at Heceta's view, the tours for the day completed. She waited until the last visitor had started back down the path before she unlocked the door to the tower and climbed the steps alone. It was the greatest advantage to living there—constant access to the light without a chaperone. Some days she would bring a chair and sit next to the Fresnel lamp, as if she were the keeper and someone important to the continuance of the mighty beacon. She faced the ocean and stared at the waves, kneading her index finger. According to Lawrence she had the onset of arthritis and periodically a few of her finger joints would start to ache. It made baking difficult and she could only imagine what it would be like in twenty years.

Where will you be in twenty years? That was a difficult question that she couldn't answer. She envied those who had long-term goals. Perhaps it became easier to create new ones, like a frog jumping from one rock to another. She'd lived vicariously through Lawrence and what he'd wanted—to build his father's practice, to become Chief of Surgery at the hospital and to sit on several prestigious boards and foundations. And at his kindest moments he'd acknowledged she was a significant reason for his success, a fact her attorney had hammered on in the divorce petition.

She propped herself against one of the windowsills, pressed her forehead against the cold glass and was instantly chilled. She became one with the blue water in the distance, her senses comforted by the hypnotic, repetitive sound of the waves merging with the shore.

This was why she loved the ocean. It was dependable and constant just like Heceta. The tides came in and out and could be forecasted months ahead. It was stable. When Rick and Caroline looked at Heceta, they saw the romantic symbolism, but Caroline had said it best. "You see what you need to see in Heceta."

She needed a home and she wouldn't ask Paula to forego her inheritance. She was too old to change her life alone. While she loved Caroline and Rick, they were not the center of her life. Eric and Lawrence filled her existence, and while she loved the

154

dream of Paula, she needed to go home. If she chose to fight she would be alone, as alone and solitary as a lighthouse.

But you're not alone, dear, and neither is Heceta. She has me.

Icy breath floated across her face. She glanced to her right—into a blank face with blazing green eyes.

She jumped and fell to the floor. She quickly sat up unable to get her bearings. She was still in the lighthouse and at some point she'd fallen asleep—she thought. *Are you sure?* She wiped her sleeve across her face but she couldn't rid herself of the cold breath and the glowing green eyes.

CHAPTER EIGHTEEN

Paula drummed her fingers on the steering wheel and crept along with the bumper-to-bumper traffic that crawled south on I-5. She hadn't noticed the roadwork earlier in the day on her way to Tillamook, too focused on her problems with Steph.

"C'mon," she growled. "How much longer can this take?"

They'd been reduced to a single lane for the last two miles as a road crew made improvements to the highway—at least that's what a large orange sign proclaimed at the beginning of the construction zone. She didn't see the necessity and was losing valuable time. She checked her watch again. Five o'clock. The handyman who agreed to pry open the safe said he'd hang around his shop until six to give her the contents. Otherwise, she'd have to wait until tomorrow—and she didn't think she could.

After Estelle had revealed Francine's affair with John South, Paula lost all interest in seeing the Tillamook lighthouse, particularly since Estelle told her that no one could visit the lighthouse except by helicopter.

"It's really quite sad for Tilly," Estelle said forlornly. "She's a majestic lighthouse but she's so isolated up on that rock, which is practically uninhabitable and dangerous. Everyone who's ever lived there just wanted to leave. I can't imagine what it would be like to be that alone."

She spoke as if Tillamook were a person and Paula realized that some people did in fact have that life. She'd be one of them if she took the money.

Paula grilled Estelle with a few more questions and asked to see her old guest books. She scanned several pages covering the months she knew Francine preferred to travel and found at least two entries where Francine and another person had checked into the motel. Her mother had always said she traveled alone, which was obviously a lie, and Estelle had described John South perfectly.

As the Malibu crept down the highway, pieces of the puzzle fell into place. Steph's father was frequently out of town. How hard would it have been to take a few extra trips? She thought of the many barbeques she and Francine had attended at the South's when she was younger. Before her father died, he was always flying somewhere, leaving his family alone, but the Souths always invited them over on the weekend.

She remembered how handsome John was and a memory of Francine sitting in a chair next to him while he stood at the grill made her mouth go dry. They were both laughing heartily and he leaned over and kissed her forehead.

Paula had thought nothing of it. It was one of those gestures where context was critical and an outside observer could easily miss the meaning—just as everyone had failed to see the meaning of her affection for Steph.

And the bottle of scotch. Both of them had found it terribly odd that Francine kept scotch in her cupboard. Only John drank scotch. The fact that it was an unopened bottle suggested an abrupt ending to the relationship. Had he ended the affair? Did Debbie find out? Had it ended when he died?

The traffic came to a complete halt as a large dump truck backed up across the road. She could hear the annoying beep-beep from her position fifty yards away. She checked her watch again, watching the second hand speed past the twelve. Another minute was gone.

Her cell phone rang. *Christian.* She'd answered so many calls and texts from him during the last few days, all of which began with, "I hate to bother you..." And then he did exactly that.

"Hello, Christian," she said.

"Paulie, I hate to bother you..."

His sentence died and she rolled her eyes. She didn't say anything but she could tell he was on speakerphone. That was unusual.

"Paulie, I'm sitting here with Lenny. Surprising, huh?" Surprising wasn't the word she'd pick. "Are you there, Paula?"

"Yes. Hello, Lenore," she said coolly to her former client.

"Hey, Paula. I'm sorry to hear about your mother."

"Thank you. Is there something I can do for the two of you?" she asked, moving straight to business.

He cleared his throat. "Paulie, we're calling because Lenny and I have had a real heart-to-heart for the last few hours. I'm talkin' some real 'Kumbaya' moments. Anyway, she's convinced that you're the heart and soul of the team and she wants you back."

The phone fell from her hand into her lap. She made no effort to pick it up. She closed her eyes, unable to believe that she was being un-fired.

"Paulie, are you there?"

She took a drink from her bottle of water and did some quick mathematical calculations. This was going to cost him—big time.

She grabbed the phone. "Yes, I'm listening. You don't want to fire me."

"Aw, Paulie, don't say that word. Firing is so harsh, so tsunami-like. You were never really *fired*."

"I wasn't?" she asked, wide-eyed. "When you tell an employee that someone else will take over her office in two weeks, I'm pretty sure that's a firing."

"Paula," Lenny interjected, "I don't know what Christian said to you, but this is my fault. I gave him some really mixed messages. If anyone's to blame, it's me."

She shook her head. There wasn't any point in arguing. The back story, the second story, the real story—it was all relative in PR. The truth only existed in the moment. She knew that.

"I appreciate you calling and I'll think about it."

"What's there to think about?" he argued. "C'mon, Paulie, this is home. You know I need you."

"Well, a lot's happened in the last few days and I need some time to think."

"Are you talking about Shelby?" Lenny asked.

She sat up at the mention of her ex. "What are you talking about?"

"Well, I heard through the grapevine that you two broke up. You know how people talk."

Her tone was so light, as light as cotton candy. As smart as he was, she doubted that Christian had picked up on the double-meaning of Lenny's question but Paula had. There was an entire unwritten contract in her return. If she wanted her job back she'd sleep with Lenore Kerry and Lenny was letting her know that up front.

"I'll get back to you," she said, hanging up.

She cranked the stereo up and U2 wailed throughout the car. She checked her watch. She had less than half an hour to get to the locksmith and she was stuck behind a Subaru, the Oregon choice of automobile. Yes, she was stuck. Nothing in her life was moving, at least not in the direction she wanted. She gripped the steering wheel tightly, feeling terribly claustrophobic in the confined Malibu. She closed her eyes and screamed.

159

It had taken five minutes of pleading and an extra hundred bucks, but she'd convinced the locksmith to wait for her at his shop until seven. He'd opened the safe and she quickly dumped everything into a plastic grocery bag and headed for the house. It took all of her restraint not to pull onto the side of the road and rifle through her mother's secret life.

She raced into the kitchen, flipped on the light and let the contents spill onto the table. A quick inventory revealed a bundle of letters, three manila envelopes, four jewelry boxes and some loose photographs. A five-by-seven black and white photo caught her eye—of her and her father. She was a baby and he was holding her in his arms, wearing his pilot's uniform. She saw the pride in his eyes and how much she looked like him. Francine had always called him handsome and claimed she fell in love when she saw him walk into a little bar outside of San Diego, where he'd initially been stationed during his Navy days. On the back of the photo was a date—July, 1975. Paula had been a year old.

The other loose pictures were of various family members, some she recognized and some she did not. Fortunately Francine had written captions and dates on the back. An old color photo caught her eye—she and Steph in each other's arms at high school graduation. They both looked so happy and young. It warmed her heart to think that her mother thought so much of Steph that she kept the picture in the safe.

She picked up the bundled letters and postcards, recognizing the overseas postage stamps. These were from her father who'd spent most of his time flying internationally. She hesitated, unsure if she should read the private thoughts of a husband to a wife, particularly her parents.

She set the piles of pictures and letters out of the way and reached for the velvet boxes. She took a deep breath. Her heart was racing. She could feel it pounding in her chest.

The largest jewelry box contained a gold necklace with a single ruby stone, one she'd remembered her mother wearing during her childhood. She was certain her father had given it to her mother. She found her mother's wedding ring and what she thought was her grandmother's wedding ring in the smaller boxes. When Paula was a child Francine had constantly made reference to her inheriting the rings one day and having to choose which one she'd want for her own engagement. She realized the jokes and comments had stopped around the time her lover Nia had disappeared from her life.

She opened the last box and discovered an emerald and diamond bracelet, one she'd never seen. The box was from a jewelry store in Portland. The bracelet was gorgeous and expensive. Her heart sank as she thought of the implications. A remnant of a conversation at Steph's house reminded her of emeralds, but she couldn't place the memory... something about loving emeralds. Was that Debbie or her mother?

She turned her attention to the three brown envelopes. If there were any other secrets, she imagined they resided in there. The first one contained all of the important papers she expected Francine to have kept inside the safe—birth certificates, her father's death certificate, passports and the deed to the house.

The second one contained brochures, pamphlets and photos of lighthouses. Most were from Oregon but several were from California and Washington. On the back of each photo Francine had carefully written the name of the lighthouse and the date. Each photo showed a tiny Francine standing next to a different lighthouse. Her mother was barely recognizable as the photographer had to stand far away to include the entire lighthouse.

So who took this picture?

It occurred to her that her mother's initial story was plausible and these pictures were taken by strangers that she'd stopped randomly as many tourists did.

She held up the third envelope, which was much newer than the others. She took a deep breath and ripped it open. A stack of letters and photos toppled onto the table, secured by a beautiful satin bow. She pulled it free and the truth stared up at her. Her gaze fell to a close-up shot of an embracing John and Francine, their heads cocked together on the deck of a ship. Paula could see the railing and the sea behind them. She turned it over and read the caption in her mother's meticulous handwriting. *Alaskan cruise, 1982.*

She picked up the next picture, one of John standing behind Francine, his arms resting on her shoulders. It looked like they were in front of a log cabin. The caption read, *Lake Tahoe, 1995.* She no longer cared about the pictures, only the dates. She turned over all seventeen photos and put them in chronological order. She had one photo for each year from 1980 to '97. She knew John had contracted prostate cancer and been dead by '99.

Francine had been ill and unable to come to his funeral, at least that's what she'd said. It occurred to Paula that she was probably sick with grief and guilt. She couldn't imagine her mother ever facing Steph and Debbie. She turned over all of the photos, putting aside the notion of her mother having a seventeen-year affair with her best friend's father, and stared at the pictures. Many were taken at lighthouses but some, such as the Alaskan cruise photo, suggested more exotic vacations to the Bahamas, the Grand Canyon and Las Vegas.

She searched her memory for hints that her mother had traveled to these places, a souvenir or a haphazard comment—but nothing came to mind. There had been times when she'd spent an entire week at Steph's while Francine claimed to visit a relative in another city. Perhaps those were the times they'd vacationed.

They'd clearly been discreet, another quality of their generation. Affairs were not flaunted and the feelings of the spouses were protected. She was almost certain her father had never suspected and poor Debbie was so caught up in her own world of booze she never would have known. *Or would she?*

She closed her eyes and shook her head. When she opened the package of letters, her fingers were greeted by luxurious stationary from several different hotels in cities all over the United States. She scanned one letter from 1981, written in a sharp, angular script. John. The words were sweet, rehashing one of their trips to a lighthouse—Heceta Head. She dropped the note and checked all the pictures carefully until she found one of them standing in front of the B and B. *Steph would die if she knew this.*

She returned to reading the note which included perfunctory mentions of work and family. She smiled after a lengthy paragraph in which John detailed a mishap that occurred at school between Steph and a bully. Paula remembered it well. Someone was picking on a younger student and Steph came to his defense. The bully turned on her and Steph popped him in the mouth. She smiled. Steph was always a firecracker.

John clearly saw the same spark in his daughter for he praised her for challenging the bully and having the courage to stand by her convictions. In the last paragraph he told Francine how much he missed her and hoped that she and Paula were well. It was signed, *All my love.*

Paula set the letter down and went for the remaining scotch. She wanted to hate John. He'd cheated on Debbie and betrayed her father, a dedicated pilot trying to provide for his family. Yet John's love for Francine and Steph was genuine.

She spent the next two hours reading the letters and sipping scotch until her vision blurred. All of the letters said basically the same thing and she recognized that John composed them when he was legitimately out of town, away from his family and Francine. That was why the stationery was repetitive. He stayed in the same places when he traveled for his company. He certainly wasn't a great writer but she doubted her mother cared. She suddenly realized how little her father had written to his wife. She compared the two piles and Paul's was significantly shorter. Of course he spent a lot of time in the air, but he certainly could've composed more correspondence than he did.

She stretched out in the chair. "What did you do, Mom? You think *I'm* fucked up?"

She imagined her mother caught in John's charms, for he was a fine gentleman and she was horribly lonely. How many nights had she heard her mother quietly weeping in bed? No doubt she regretted marrying someone who was always out of town but divorce was taboo. And then Paul died and John was right there.

She was drunk and in no condition to drive back to Heceta Head. Steph expected her to be at Tillamook anyway, and if she showed up at Heceta, she'd be questioned by Steph, who would definitely know something was wrong.

She was certain Steph knew nothing of her father's indiscretion. She could tell from the way Steph compared Debbie and John. She clearly believed John had been the superior parent.

She grabbed the photo from high school graduation, hauled herself into her old bedroom and dropped onto the old mattress, smiling when she remembered her morning delight with Steph. She stared at the picture, focusing on Steph's confident expression and blazing eyes. Maybe that person was still there, just buried beneath Junior League fundraisers, PTA meetings and charity auctions. How could she find out and did she really want to know? Could she stand to have Steph break her heart again?

She closed her eyes and hoped she'd have a dream that would tell her what to do.

CHAPTER NINETEEN

Steph couldn't imagine what would compel her to visit her mother more than once in a week. She'd never given helpful advice. Steph had once asked her if she should tell a friend that her boyfriend was cheating on her and Debbie's response was, "Ignorance is bliss, kiddo. It's not always good to know everything. Who wants to?"

Paula had scowled when she relayed Debbie's response, and consequently Steph had ignored her mother's advice and told the friend, who'd subsequently dumped *her*—not the boyfriend—as payback. Apparently Debbie understood teenagers better than Steph did.

She knew Debbie thought highly of Lawrence. Once she'd gotten past the fact that he'd knocked her up, she focused on her daughter's marriage to a doctor and that pleased her immensely. Debbie especially enjoyed the ritzy dinner parties Steph threw when she visited Scottsdale, usually alone without her father. For some reason she seemed to drink less when John wasn't around.

Steph found her in her room doing a crossword. She was surprised to see her engaged in such a simple, benign activity.

Debbie peered over her glasses. "What are you doing here? It's not Monday." She looked around with dramatic anxiety. "Am I dead?"

Steph chuckled. "No, Mom. You're not dead and it's not Monday. I came by to ask your advice."

Her mother took off her glasses and stared at her. "Are you *sure* I'm not dead? The last time you asked me for advice I told you it was okay to go to a dance braless. You didn't speak to me for a week." Steph nodded. "Now, about twenty boys called you for a month after that," she said. "I never even got a thank you."

"I wasn't interested in those boys."

Her mother stared at her and smacked her puzzle book on the table. "You weren't interested in *any* boys. All you wanted was to spend time with Paula." She let her observation hang in the air. "The two of you were inseparable. Always at Francine's or hiding behind your rock. You and your rock," she said almost wistfully.

Steph looked at her, astounded. "You knew we were out there hiding from you?"

"Of course I knew. I was only a *little* drunk. I'm a *lot* self-absorbed. I just wanted yours and Daddy's attention and it seemed the only way to get it, especially from your father."

"How can you say that? Daddy was the one who constantly cared for you. Do you know how many times we carried you up to bed? Can you guess how many times we changed our plans because you were in no condition to go somewhere? Mom, you were always the center of attention."

"And you resented it."

"Of course. Your drinking controlled our lives."

"Did it? Are you sure?" She raised her eyebrows and Steph

knew she'd hit a nerve. "Which came first, your father's constant *business* trips or my happy hours?"

She'd always assumed her father had taken the out-of-town sales accounts *because* of Debbie's binges.

"Did he start sleeping with another woman before I fell in love with Jack Daniels or after?"

Her jaw dropped. She'd never known her father was unfaithful.

Her mother eyed her shrewdly. "What's the matter, missy? Cat got your tongue?"

"I'm surprised. I just never knew…" Her voice faded off into memories of her father. "Who was she?"

Debbie looked away. "That's not important. It's all in the past."

"So you know who this person was? Did you ever confront her?"

She bit her lip. "No. It was complicated." She walked to the window and stared out. "I'm sorry I opened my big mouth. You didn't need to hear this. They gave me a new medication for my arthritis and now I'm crabby. I've got the shits like nobody's business." She made a fist and gently pounded the wall. "Sometimes I just got so jealous of your feelings for him. I guess I still do. He wasn't the saint you thought he was, Steph, but it doesn't matter. Don't worry about it. He's gone and I forgave him. There's no sense living in the past. It's over." She pointed a steady finger at her. "You'd be wise to remember that. Your life with the doctor-asshole is over. Look to the future and focus on my grandson."

Steph stared into her eyes. They were clear and focused. "What's wrong?" she asked suspiciously.

"It's just that I haven't seen you so sharp and…thoughtful."

Her mother returned to the chair and motioned for Steph to lean closer. "Can you keep a secret?"

"Uh-huh."

"No, I mean a *real* secret."

Her patience was waning. "What's up, Mom?"

167

She sighed. "I just know your sense of righteousness and morality sit on a higher plane than mine does."

"That's not hard, Mom."

She scowled. "Do you promise?" she asked again, her expression almost child-like.

"Okay, I promise."

"I'm not really nuts. It's an act," she whispered.

She couldn't hide her shock. "What?"

"There's nothing wrong with my mind, Stephanie. My thoughts are crystal clear. I just *pretend* to be soft."

She was stunned. "Why would you ever pretend to be mentally unfit?"

"Are you kidding? Do you know how much I get away with around here? If I jump up in the middle of bingo and start singing, they just ask me to sit down. I don't get in any trouble. If I *accidentally* wander into Mr. Krumholz's room while he's having his sponge bath, they just escort me out with a smile. And let me tell you," she added, "Mr. K still has a decent body and quite an attractive package."

Steph shook her head. "This is unbelievable. You've been faking dementia."

"Partial dementia," she corrected. "I go in and out of it. That way nobody's surprised if I have a coherent moment and I shuffle over to the TV and change the channel or if I eat Lois Pfeffer's chocolate pudding."

"You're stealing food from other patients?"

"It's not stealing. Lois never eats it. She likes vanilla. But if I were *normal*, I'd get in trouble for taking seconds. Heck, if I wasn't putting on this act, you'd be getting phone calls all the time."

"So you're really doing me a favor."

"Absolutely."

Steph sighed, telling herself she shouldn't be surprised by anything. This was Debbie the actress.

"Now, don't forget. You promised you wouldn't tell. I like it here, Steph. I don't want to move into a different wing. These people need me. I'm their entertainment."

That she could believe. "Does anyone else know?"

"Only my boyfriend, Steve, the orderly you met."

"He really is your boyfriend?"

She smiled wickedly. "Oh, yeah. He's packed better than Mr. K."

"Oh, God. I think I'm going to be sick. I can't believe you."

Her mother's playful smile vanished. "What can't you believe, Stephanie? That I'd do whatever the hell I please? Why not? What do I gain from depriving myself? I'm not cheating anyone. I pay a lot of money every month to stay here and I'll remind you that I'm sober."

That was her trump card. Moving to Waverly Place had indeed dried her out.

"Is that why you came here?"

The question seemed to hurt her and she recoiled. "Partially. I didn't know what else to do. I needed help and there was no one. I was alone and I've never liked being alone." She grinned. "Just know I'm spending your inheritance. I figured that married or divorced you wouldn't need it since you're attached to a rich doctor."

Steph rubbed her temples. "So what about all those times when you tell stories and you get it wrong, like the jellyfish story you told Paula?"

She leaned closer. "Threw you off, didn't it?"

"Oh, God."

There was a knock at the door and a timid but handsome young man approached, carrying a copy of *The Sun Also Rises*. His volunteer badge identified him as Sean.

"Hello, Mrs. South," he said in an elementary school voice. "Who's visiting you today?"

In a millisecond her mother's expression went blank and her eyes glazed over. She pointed toward her with a quaking finger.

"My daughter."

The fresh-faced teenager flashed a perfect smile and extended his strong hand to Steph. "I'm Sean. I'm a senior at Eugene High

169

doing some community service. Your mom is one of my favorites. She loves to have me read to her."

"I'll bet she does."

She grinned at Debbie, who turned away from Sean and stuck out her tongue.

"Your mom convinced the manager to let my swim team practice here on Saturday mornings. She's the best."

"How nice," Steph said, her voice dripping with goodwill. She pictured her mother sitting out by the pool, sipping her coffee and eyeballing the hot, tanned bodies wearing only their tiny Speedos.

"Sean, could you come back in an hour? My mom's having a really lucid moment right now and I don't want to miss it. She's been remembering all the wonderful times we baked brownies and strung popcorn on the Christmas tree. It's been so touching."

She thought Sean might cry as he nodded and headed out, shutting the door behind him.

She glared at her mother. "You're a horse's ass."

"You're probably right, Steph." She patted her hand. "Honey, I know you're surprised but the truth is that all of those ridiculous clichés are right. You only get one ride and you need to make the most of it. Don't wait until you're sixty-eight to figure it out. Now, what's going on with you and Paula? Is she still in Eugene?"

Steph sat up straight, realizing that she hadn't gotten away with anything—not since Debbie had arrived at Waverly Place, not in her entire life. Behind cloaks of inebriation and fake dementia, she'd watched her every move.

"Paula and I aren't speaking right now."

Her mother clucked her tongue in disapproval. "Again? Oh, for Christ's sake, Stephanie, get it right this time. The woman's loved you her entire life. You screwed it up before. Don't do it again."

She struggled for a response. "Maybe if I'd had a little better role modeling about relationships—"

"That's it," her mother said harshly, in a searing voice Steph had only heard a few times in her life. "I've waited long enough for you to appreciate me. It's obviously not happened so I'm speeding the process along. I demand that you understand me!"

Steph held up her hands and shrugged. "What do you want from me, Mom? What don't I understand?"

"That your life isn't my fault. I'll admit I was a lousy mother, probably unfit at times. But at some point it's not about me anymore. I've barely seen you for the last seventeen years. If your life is a mess, it's yours, baby. Whatever skills or equipment you didn't bring to the party were my fault but you have to adapt to your surroundings. You have to adjust to your own life, and if you waste whatever time is left, you'll regret it. So put on your big girl panties and fix it!"

She started to cough and reached for a glass of water. Once she could speak again, she smiled and said, "So how was my tough love speech?"

Steph smiled wryly. "Probably about twenty years too late."

Her mother shook her head. "You'd never have heard me. That's the great thing about growing older. We really do get smarter, whether we like it or not." She stopped and looked up. "And why is that? It finally all makes sense when you're too old to really use it. What a crock."

"You never settled for what you had, did you?" Steph asked.

She rolled her eyes. "Settled? Are you kidding? Settling is giving up. It's for cowards. Don't believe all that crap on TV and particularly those TV psychologists. They act like they're trying to help you but all they're really doing is making you feel like shit. It's like getting bit in the ass by a dog. And you turn around and go, *Shit!*" She stopped and glanced at her. "So what did you want to ask me? What sage advice can I give you?"

Steph squeezed her hand. "You already gave it to me. Thanks."

"Good." She pushed herself out of the chair and headed for the door. "Now, let's get out of here. I know where the keys to the golf cart are."

When Steph returned to Heceta, Paula still wasn't back from

Tillamook. Caroline and Rick were out at the lighthouse and the B and B was vacant. She thought of Rue and her appearance in her life. She stood in the middle of the living room, waiting for her to tell her something else but she was either ignoring her or busy thinking up new ways to taunt the guests.

Steph decided to do what she always did when her troubles weighed her down—bake. She went to work in the kitchen making another loaf of banana bread for the Steiners, unwilling to mail them one that had possibly visited the spirit world. She was immersed in flour and sugar when her cell phone rang. She answered it automatically, hoping it was Paula and disappointed to hear Lawrence's voice.

"Stephanie? Have you had a chance to think about our situation?" No cordial greeting, just the question. It was all about the bottom line for him.

She prepared the mixer and added the flour. "I've thought about it but I haven't come to any definite conclusions."

He sighed. "I see. Well, I did have a chance to speak with my attorney yesterday afternoon and he assured me that your little peccadillo could be very costly for you, both in terms of your reputation and your financial settlement."

"My little peccadillo? Is that what you're calling it?"

"No, that's what he called it, actually. And it seems that's what Judge Witherspoon called it during one of his rulings last year. You remember Judge Witherspoon, don't you? He's *our* judge? The one granting your divorce petition and deciding on the financial award?"

She wanted to scream at his smug superiority but she said nothing and turned on the mixer. Perhaps it would shorten the conversation.

"Ah, you're baking. How nice. I know what that means."

Damn. She kept forgetting that he knew all of her idiosyncrasies, worries and habits. She was nervous and he would capitalize on it.

"You need to give me a final answer, Steph. Eric needs to get back to school and he wants you to come back with us."

She set the mixer down, her hands shaking. She took a deep breath and said, "May I speak with him, please?"

"He's not here right now. He went for a run. He said he needed to clear his head. This has been terribly confusing for him."

She groaned. "You make it sound like he's ten. Why in the hell did you bring him up here? He needs to finish his studies and get his diploma. He needs to be in school."

Lawrence snorted. "Oh, he got quite the education yesterday morning."

She gritted her teeth, wishing she could reach through the phone and strangle him.

"Steph, you need to wave the white flag and come home. I didn't want to tell you this but Eric's talking about not finishing. He's really upset. He thinks you've lied to him—about everything. I don't know what he'll do next."

Like return to drugs. She forced herself to breathe, thinking this was probably a manipulation technique. Eric knew lots of gay people. *But you're his mother.*

"I need to talk to him," she said, hearing the quake in her voice.

She heard a voice in the background and Lawrence said confidently, "He just got back. I'll put him on."

They exchanged the phone and she could tell Lawrence had placed his hand over the mouthpiece while he coached Eric. She scowled, knowing this wouldn't be a fair fight.

"Mom?" His voice was subdued, questioning.

"Hi, son. Hey, we need to talk." She hoped she sounded open and honest, which is what they'd always been with each other.

"Well, I'm not sure I'm ready for that. I don't know what to think right now. You really shocked me."

"I know, baby. It's been really surprising for me, too. I need to see you."

"How long have you been gay? Dad said something about the tennis pro. Did you have an affair with her?"

She seethed silently, her hatred for Lawrence growing by the

173

second. "I won't lie to you, Eric. Yes, I had an affair, a single affair. What's happened between Paula and me was a surprise I wasn't expecting." She stopped and caught her breath. This wasn't how she wanted to explain this to him. She needed to regain control of the situation. "Please meet with me. Talk to me."

"You should've told me," he whispered. "I thought we were friends, too, not just mother and son."

Tears streamed down her face. During his months of therapy they'd worked intensely on trust issues. It was vital to his sobriety. "We are, baby. Look, can we meet and talk without your dad?"

"I'll think about it," he said in a voice that sounded as though he'd already made up his mind.

"Well, I was hoping we could do it soon since you need to get back."

He acknowledged her with a small grunt and she knew there had to be some truth to Lawrence's statement that Eric had grown ambivalent about school. "Please, son," she pleaded.

There was silence and then muffled voices again. He'd handed the phone back to Lawrence.

"He needs more time. You'll just have to be patient. The best thing you could do is come back with us, Steph. You're much more likely to make headway at home and I imagine that he'll be willing to return to school if he knows you're nearby."

She was sick to her stomach. She pushed away the mixing bowl and leaned over the counter, her legs buckling underneath her. The phone fell onto the counter and she heard Lawrence calling her name.

She thought of her mother's words, ones that were easy for her to say—ones she hadn't followed. What Steph had learned from Debbie today, what was left unsaid, was a simple fact: her mother had remained in a loveless marriage for her. John had been with someone else but she didn't divorce him. How could she expect Steph to turn her back on Eric?

CHAPTER TWENTY

It was still impossible to believe that John South had had a seventeen-year affair with her mother. Paula paced back and forth across the old shag carpet. She hadn't slept at all, the bed too uncomfortable. She couldn't understand how she'd ever stood the lumpy old mattress whose age preceded her birth. She longed for her pillowtop queen bed in Seattle. She imagined Steph laying next to her, naked, the twelve hundred thread count sheets kissing their bodies. She nearly tripped over the ottoman lost in her thoughts. She righted herself and closed her eyes for a second, willing the vision to go away.

Steph hadn't called and Paula hadn't found the courage to call her. Time seemed to freeze in a moment that was nearly two decades old. How many days had she stood in her grandpa's kitchen that summer after high school, holding the receiver, her fingers ready to punch in Steph's number—only to slowly place it back on the hook? She'd been a coward then and she was a coward now.

She continued to pace. She was a hostage in the house until Goodwill arrived to take the furniture that was left. She'd finished most of the packing after she decided that sleep was futile. It was amazing what a burst of energy and solitude could do for productivity. She'd packed almost sixty boxes and decided to abandon the rest for now. She looked around and chuckled. She wouldn't win any awards for neatness, having randomly tossed things into boxes, leaving half a shelf or an entire corner untouched.

There were several items that sent her mind into a quandary. She'd pick something up, like the porcelain elephant her father won at the fair for her, stare at it, set it back down and then pick it up again. She decided that if an item didn't automatically go into the box without a second thought, it needed extra consideration and she was too fatigued to decide right now. She'd need to come back to Eugene and finish the task before the house was put up for sale.

In the hour it took the Goodwill truck to arrive, she planned her departure from Eugene. She'd already scheduled another appointment with Ted but she needed to go back to the motel and settle the bill and return to Heceta once more to claim her things. She realized she'd probably run into Steph, but the idea of slipping in and out during the dead of night seemed extremely childish.

Once the cheerful and grateful Goodwill people had emptied the house of the boxes and furniture, Paula walked aimlessly from room to room, feeling as though her childhood had driven away as well with the Goodwill truck. She leaned against a doorway and cried again.

When Paula pulled up to the B and B, Caroline was finishing her gardening.

Caroline wiped her hand across her brow and left a dirt smudge. "It's unusually warm for this time of year," she commented. "How was Tillamook?"

"Enlightening." Paula stuffed her hands in her pockets and her gaze landed on Steph's BMW.

"She's up in the lighthouse," Caroline said, reading her thoughts. She leaned against the Malibu and folded her arms. "What's going on between the two of you? Steph's hardly said two words since you left yesterday and she's spent most of her time out on the cliff. Did you have a fight?"

She shook her head. "No, we didn't fight. She had a fight with Lawrence. He wants her back and I think she'll go."

Caroline looked surprised. "Really? Why?"

"Because he usually gets his way and she's afraid of what's between us. But mainly I think she's worried about her son. He saw us kissing."

"Oh. She didn't mention that."

Paula wasn't surprised. She imagined that when Steph held up her lesbianism like a newspaper for Eric to read, he screamed and ran away from the headline. "I don't think she's strong enough," she said.

Caroline studied her for a moment and turned to Heceta. They saw Steph inside the tower. It was clear she loved the place and felt a kinship to lighthouses—just like Francine.

Paula glanced at Caroline. "Did you know my mother stayed here?"

After a long pause Caroline replied, "I did."

"Did you know she was with a man who wasn't my father?"

Caroline didn't look at her. "Yes, I've seen the past guest books."

Paula knew she didn't need to ask any other questions. She figured that Caroline and Rick had learned the value of confidentiality.

"There's no reason to tell her," Caroline said slowly.

"I know."

Caroline started toward the back door but stopped and

turned to face her. "Are you staying?"

She didn't answer right away. Her gaze drifted to the tower. Steph looked like a princess who needed to be rescued. Her feet automatically shuffled to the lighthouse. She made her way up the tiny ladder and stuck her head through the hole in the lantern room's floor. Steph sat in a folding chair next to the glass, gazing at the ocean.

"Do you want some company?"

Steph offered a slight smile. "Sure."

She climbed up carefully, making certain her feet found purchase on the floor. She hesitated, unsure if she should go to her or keep a practical distance. When Steph rose and hugged herself just as she had done so many times when they'd sit on Paula's patio, Paula stepped behind her and massaged her shoulders.

Steph exhaled and a sigh escaped her lips. "He wants me back, not because he loves me but because divorce will be far too expensive for him."

"Wow, what a romantic guy. I can see why you stayed with him for so long."

"It wasn't about him," she said quietly.

"I know. I shouldn't make jokes. I can tell that everything you've done has been for Eric. He's all that matters to you."

"That's right. He's all I have."

Her shoulders heaved and Paula knew she was crying. She bent down beside her and stroked her hair. "I don't even have him anymore," she said between sobs. "The one person I loved walked away from me."

"It's going to be okay, Steph."

"You can't say that. Eric was horrified by what he saw, not that he hates gay people. That's not it."

"No, he just never counted his mother as one of them."

"I'm not."

She laughed. "C'mon, Steph. Be honest with yourself. It's like Caroline said. We've been all over each other since we were kids."

She looked away. "That was just curiosity."

"And what was it the other day? Was that just curiosity?"

"That was answering a question, one that was asked a long time ago."

They gazed at each other until Paula kissed her softly. "I always felt like we ran away from something. Actually you ran away and I chose not to run after you. As stubborn as I am, I ran in the opposite direction." She paused before she added in a sad whisper, "I've always regretted that."

Steph shrugged. "You should've let go. I did. We were just kids who couldn't explain our feelings—"

"No, I knew exactly how I felt about you. It was everything else I was unsure about—where to go to college, if I really wanted to go into public relations..."

Steph went to the window as if she weren't really listening.

Paula shook her head and kicked at the floor. "You are one of the most brilliant women I've ever met. You could've done anything, including medicine. I understand your choice to keep your baby but that didn't need to be the end of your dreams."

Steph offered a condescending smile. "You know nothing about my life, remember that."

"And whose fault is that?"

She burst out laughing. "Oh, please, Paula. We just fell out of touch. It happens."

Paula's face reddened at her simplistic explanation. It suddenly mattered that the record be set straight. It was important to her that they admit their true feelings, even if Steph exploded and it ruined their newly formed bond.

"I won't let you rewrite our history," she said fiercely. "We didn't fall out of touch. You couldn't deal with your feelings for me. After that last afternoon in my room, everything changed. I felt it happen. And then it all fell apart."

She'd picked up a mirror and held it in front of Steph's face, forcing her to see the truth she'd avoided for most of her life.

"I'm sorry," Steph said. "I was very confused and I didn't know what to do. I know you suffered and I'm sorry. I hope you'll accept my apology."

Paula shook her head. "No, I don't. This isn't some petty issue between you and your Junior League buddies that you can smooth over with a few words. This is me, the woman who was a finger's length from becoming your first lover." She grabbed Steph's wrists and pulled her against her. "What the hell happened to you? Where's the go-getter I knew in high school?"

She exhaled. "She got up and went."

Her anger evaporated and she released her. "How? You were the most driven and focused person I knew. How does that change?"

She shrugged. "Slowly. I didn't realize it was happening. After Eric was born I thought I'd get back on track in just a few years, once he was in school. Then Lawrence became the chief of surgery and there was a new house and parties to plan and expectations as the chief's wife. A few years became a few more and I still thought there was time. When I looked in the mirror I still saw me. I saw that girl who was on fire. I knew she was there.

"Then Eric got older and there were soccer games and PTA presidencies and volunteer work with the Junior League. I was a socialite and much was expected. Five years later when Eric was about fourteen, I looked in the mirror and I realized the girl was gone."

She stared at Paula. "I know you don't understand. You've known what you wanted your whole life and you never let anyone or anything interfere. I wish I had your vision."

"No you don't," she said quietly. "Nobody gets everything she wants. I sacrificed a lot for my career and a lot of good it did me," she added.

"What do you mean?"

She shook her head. "I've never had a serious relationship because I wouldn't give up the work—and I wouldn't come out to my mother. I feel as alone as you, Steph. So you see we're really very similar. We've both spent our lives unsatisfied, not getting what we want."

"What is it you want, Paula?"

She offered a sad smile. "I'm not even sure anymore." Acting on impulse, she stepped across the lantern room and gazed toward the B and B. She turned to Steph, a wicked smile on her face. "Come here."

She placed her hand on the back of Steph's neck and pulled her closer. Steph froze just as their lips were about to touch.

"No, Paula. I'm so sorry."

Steph leaned against one of the enormous windows and stared at the ground. Paula knew she'd lost and her worst suspicions were confirmed.

"What are you going to do?" she asked.

"Go back, I guess."

"Can I ask you a question and can you promise you won't get angry?" Steph nodded and met her gaze. "You'd already left Lawrence and moved to Heceta before I got here. Were you always planning on going back? Was this just some kind of ploy to make him treat you better?"

"No, I never could have predicted...*this.*"

They stood in silence, contemplating the meaning of her words. The waves hurled themselves against the shore and Paula imagined her battered heart withstanding much the same.

"Look," Steph said brightly, "If I go back everyone wins. My problems with Eric evaporate and you can claim the inheritance and Lawrence will be eternally grateful to me. Knowing him, I'll get some great jewelry and probably a fabulous vacation somewhere exotic, maybe Bermuda."

She tried to sound hopeful and wildly excited and Paula knew it was her attempt at optimism but the words hurt and her eyes glistened with tears that blinded her.

"Everyone wins but you," Paula said.

CHAPTER TWENTY-ONE

Paula clambered down the ladder and Steph made no effort to stop her, even when she craned her neck and gazed at the top of the tower. Steph imagined she was the reason people like Francine loved lighthouses were because they were unique and symbolic of hope and courage. They were fearless.

She headed back toward the B and B feeling miniscule and defeated. Fear had ruled her life. Paula was right. She could've had Eric without Lawrence but she'd been afraid. It would've been crazy trying to juggle the demands of college while raising a small child but instead of meeting the challenge, she avoided it. At the time she'd rationalized that it couldn't be done because she didn't have the support system. Her mother couldn't help because she was a drunk and her father was too busy helping her mother.

But that wasn't the truth. She could've continued her pursuit of a medical degree but she was afraid. And she was afraid now. She knew that but she didn't know what to do. Seventeen years had passed and she still didn't know how to run her own life on her own terms.

"You're pathetic," she murmured as she picked up the pace.

As if he could hear her thoughts, Lawrence's rented Hummer pulled up beside the Malibu and he hopped out, dressed casually in jeans and a button-down shirt and jacket. Seeing her on the path, he stood at the top and crossed his arms. As she drew closer, she could see the corners of his mouth turn up slightly. He knew he'd won. They'd lived together for nearly twenty years and he knew her body language and expressions.

"Why are you here and where's Eric?" she spat.

"It's nice to see you, too, Stephanie. To answer your first question, I'm here to take you home. I want you to come with me right now to the hotel. We've got plane reservations for the morning. As for Eric, he's packing. He's already missed three days of summer school because of this nonsense. If nothing else, I know you don't want his studies to suffer because of your theatrics."

She wrapped her arms around herself and gripped her body, resisting the urge to charge into him. "I never understood why he came in the first place."

"Honestly? Because I asked him to. I knew you'd never agree to come back with me if it was just me asking. I'm sure he'd like to stay on my good side since I'll be paying for college."

She shook her head, still unable to believe the depth of Lawrence's manipulative nature.

He looked around. "Where's your little girl toy? Is she coming back to Arizona with us? She's quite a looker."

His hard expression dissolved into a fluid mess and his features shifted. He always looked that way whenever he eyed a beautiful woman and Paula was certainly beautiful. She slapped his face and he stepped back.

"You are absolutely disgusting!"

She turned around and went back toward the cliff, unwilling to enter the B and B with him in tow. As she approached Heceta, she couldn't decide if she was moving toward or away from something. The wind was picking up, making each step a challenge. It was all happening too fast. Five days ago she'd been content with helping Caroline, sleeping in her little room and torturing herself once a week with a Debbie visit. Since Francine's death her copacetic life had exploded. She'd slept with Paula and Lawrence had reappeared.

He caught up to her in less than a minute, the hike to Heceta far easier than his daily five-mile run through Phoenix. He grabbed her arm and turned her around. "Be reasonable. How will you live knowing Eric hates you? Has he called you? Will he speak to you?"

"No," she admitted, and the tears began. "But he didn't say he hated me," she added between sobs.

He held her tightly and she cried. "You need to come home. You need to forgive me. I'm a terrible husband, I know, but I want it to work for us. I'm willing to go to therapy," he said loudly, fighting to be heard over the raging wind.

She stared into his face, probing his honesty. Ten years before, when she'd suspected he was already cheating, she'd asked him to go to a counselor but he'd blasted psychology and said it was ridiculous. If he was truly willing to work on their marriage, it was a huge leap. He could see her lip trembling, a symbol of her shaky resolve, and as he had done so many times during their marriage when she was upset—usually with him—he took his finger and with the gentle touch of a surgeon, traced her lips slowly.

"You're so beautiful," he whispered against her ear.

He leaned toward her, waiting for permission. She raised her eyes and the decision was made. Their lips met and in a matter of seconds his tender kiss turned fierce and he consumed her. Her eyes closed, Heceta's bright beacon imprinted on her mind. Lawrence's tongue pushed into her mouth, demanding that she acquiesce to him forever. The beacon turned its three-hundred-sixty-degrees—around and around—while his hands brushed against her breasts and lingered on her hips. The light dimmed. Lawrence pressed against her and in the moment she thought to pull away and remind him that they were in a public place, the beacon extinguished and darkness surrounded her. Astonished, she broke free. He was laughing, obviously pleased with himself.

"Well, I'd say we still have some chemistry." He looked like a little boy, his head drooping with a silly grin on his face. He put his hands in his pockets. "Please, Steph? Can we try? If it doesn't work, I promise I won't stand in your way. I'll even help you pack and I'll sign whatever divorce papers you shove under my nose." She said nothing. She only stared into his amazing green eyes, glowing in the late day's sun.

She'd brought very little so it took only a few minutes to repack her things. Lawrence handed her clothes from the bureau, determined to expedite the process.

"Is this yours?" he asked, holding up a gold jewelry box.

She nodded, hiding her disappointment that he didn't recognize her mother's special trinket box that had sat on her dresser throughout their marriage.

She froze when someone knocked on the door. Lawrence opened it and a smug smile covered his face as he motioned for Paula to come inside. He'd won and was gloating.

When their eyes met, Steph realized Paula had been crying and she wondered how much of the little show Paula had seen on the lighthouse trail. Had she seen him groping her? Kissing her? She was certain he'd think it was nothing more than payback for the other morning. If he was subjected to watching then she should be too.

"Will you give us a moment, please, Lawrence?"

"Of course. I'll take these out to the car."

He picked up her packed suitcases and faced her, standing between her and Paula. When he leaned forward she almost backed away, but she held her ground. She'd made her choice. His kiss lingered on her lips far too long. When he stepped away she was intensely aware of Paula's stare and the tears in her eyes. Steph stood perfectly still until he left the room, more ashamed and sad than she'd ever been in her life.

Paula's gaze flitted around the room and she tugged nervously at her shirt collar, clearly embarrassed. Eventually she looked at her and offered a little smile.

"I guess this is goodbye again," Paula said.

Steph almost fell to the floor. She put her hand on the dresser and took a deep breath.

"Are you all right?" Paula asked, coming to her, resting her hand on her shoulder.

"I'm fine."

They stood there, suspended in the moment, listening to the roaring wind outside. The creak of the weather vane provided an awkward soprano line to the melody rushing between the tree limbs.

"He said he'd go into counseling," she offered. "He wants to make it right."

Paula stared at her blankly, showing no emotion, her lips a straight, unreadable line. Steph was becoming more uncomfortable by the minute, half of her fearing that she was making the wrong decision and the other half terrified of facing the dark future, the one where Heceta's beacon had extinguished.

Steph removed Paula's arm from her shoulder and a surge of emotion poured out of her when Paula stared at her, turned and headed for the door. If it was at all possible, Steph was certain Paula had kidnapped her passion, lust and desire.

Paula's beautiful chestnut hair disappeared around the corner and Steph dropped to the bed. The wind pitched to a new octave, higher and more forceful. An odd sound overhead, like wood ripping, jolted her eyes to the ceiling, and in the time it took to gaze upward, she pictured the roof flying off the B and B. But nothing was different.

A second later an enormous crash made her jump. She ran out the back door and nearly ran into Caroline who was standing on the small porch staring at the cause—the old weather vane protruded from the Hummer's windshield. Half of it was buried deep inside the front seat but the north and west spokes waved at them from the hood of the car.

"Too bad it didn't just hit the top," Caroline said acidly. "It would've bounced off."

Steph knew how she felt about gas guzzlers and vanity vehicles. Her attitude was shared by most Oregonians who pioneered the green movement. Lawrence, though, was from Arizona, the state with more golf courses than recycling bins.

Where was he? She raced down the steps as he and Rick crossed in front of the car, examining the damage. Neither of them seemed overwrought by the entire incident, only amused.

He looked at her and gestured to the destroyed Hummer. "I guess the great green god is trying to tell me something," he said. "We'll need to take your car."

He and Rick resumed their small talk while he transferred her suitcases from the Hummer to her BMW.

Caroline turned toward her, her face full of concern. "You're sure about this?"

"Not at all." She embraced her. "Thank you so much. Your friendship is priceless and I promise to keep in touch."

"You'd better." She glanced toward the window of her little room. "I think I'll leave that place alone for a while. Just in case." Steph nodded, grateful. "Are you going to see Debbie before you leave?"

She snorted and shook her head. "Are you kidding? I'll just call her when I get home. It's easier to deal with her scenes from a few thousand miles away."

Lawrence was already in the car, the engine running. He couldn't wait to get her away from Oregon and Paula.

She offered a slight wave to Caroline and Rick as they backed out and started down the drive. In the side mirror she glanced at Heceta, receding in the distance, and she felt her heart sink. As Lawrence made another turn, Heceta disappeared out of view and was replaced by the picturesque front of the B and B. Movement caught her eye. The upstairs drapes parted, revealing a figure in a white dress. She whirled around to stare through the back window, but as quickly as it had appeared, it was gone.

Lawrence touched her shoulder. "You okay, honey?"

She closed her eyes momentarily, wondering if the last vision she'd had of the Heceta Head Lighthouse was that of a ghost.

CHAPTER TWENTY-TWO

From the windows of Victoria's Room, Paula had watched the entire encounter between Lawrence and Steph on the trail. As someone who was a smooth talker, she recognized the quality in others and judging from the exchange between the couple, she knew Lawrence's persuasive tactics were exceptional, and from her vantage point his behavior was entirely transparent. His gestures and body language fluctuated from wounded puppy to macho caveman. She imagined that the topic of conversation was Eric, the greatest weapon in his arsenal. She knew Eric would be her undoing. She couldn't compete with him. Steph wouldn't be happy anywhere if she believed her son hated her.

Paula's stomach knotted when Lawrence kissed her, grabbed her—and won. She turned away from the window and fell onto the bed. It was over and she would leave. A part of her was furious with Steph for not asserting herself but in another second she thought of Eric. Yes, he was nearly an adult, but she remembered how *young* seventeen really was.

The scene in Steph's room had been half-hearted. She knew she'd lost and so did Lawrence. The only one who didn't seem to recognize there'd been a contest was the prize herself. She willingly let her husband kiss her in front of her lover and she made no apologies, no declarations of love. She had done nothing to ease Paula's pain.

The weather vane falling into the Hummer had been fabulous comic relief and she laughed out loud. She wondered for a split second if Lawrence was inside. She'd actually frowned when she realized he was still alive and then shook her head in shame. She stood by the side window and watched the car pull away.

A noise from above caught her attention. Someone was in the attic but she couldn't imagine who. Caroline and Rick were outside with Lawrence and Steph. Who would be in the attic without them? The guests were off sightseeing, strolling on the beach or gazing at Heceta.

She glanced up as the floor above her creaked. *Rue.* She didn't want to think about it and she didn't care. *If I'm lucky she'll grab something really heavy and send it through the ceiling. It can kill me quick. Let the charities get all of my mother's money.* She flopped down on the bed and closed her eyes, falling into a deep sleep.

"Paula?" a voice asked, accompanied by a knock.

She sat up. It was nighttime and the windows were dark. "How long have I been out?"

Caroline smiled sympathetically. "It's about eight."

About six hours. "Crap." She wiped her eyes and stretched her arms. She'd slept in an uncomfortable position and her body wasn't thrilled about it.

"I thought it would be best to let you rest. You seemed so tired and I know you've had a hell of a week."

Paula glanced at her, her meaning clear. "Thanks."

"Uh, well, two things. First, if you want something to eat, I left some pot roast for you in the fridge and Ted Ruth is downstairs. He'd like to talk to you if you're available. He says you missed an appointment with him this afternoon."

She nodded. The scene with Steph had consumed her.

"Do you want me to tell him you'll call him tomorrow?"

"I'm leaving tomorrow," she murmured. "I need to get back."

"Of course," Caroline said softly. "Why don't I just tell him you'll call?"

She waved a hand in the negative. She wanted to leave Eugene without any loose ends.

She went downstairs and found him gazing at Heceta through the window. "Hello, Ted."

He turned and nodded. "Hello, Paula. Have you made a decision?"

Somehow it seemed harder to say the words out loud. There was such finality in her decision and she could see her mother nodding from heaven—victorious. She'd managed to stave off her daughter's sick lesbian tendencies. *Not really. I can have as many one-night stands and meaningless affairs as I want. That'll be more fun. Mom's ashes can spin in her little urn while she watches.*

"I'll take the inheritance," she said swiftly. "What do I need to sign?"

He blinked, clearly stunned. "I'll admit I'm surprised. You seemed so sure of your decision the other day when you were in my office with Stephanie."

She remained expressionless, unwilling to discuss the details. She wanted to sign, ask him to leave and head home in the morning—back to her great job, a new salary and endless opportunities with fabulous women like Drea. He motioned to the dining room table and they settled into the antique chairs. He removed the codicil from his briefcase and presented it to her. She reread the short paragraph that stated she agreed to refrain from long-term relationships as determined by Mr. Theodore Ruth, Esquire or she'd forfeit everything. Her eyes drifted to his kind face.

191

"Before I sign I'd like to know what you really think of this. You've said that you tried to dissuade my mother from writing it but you're determined to enforce it. How can that be?"

Ted cleared his throat and stared at the paper. "There are unpleasant tasks in every profession. This was one of them. And honestly, I'm not sure if I agreed because of my professionalism or my need to please your mother."

When he looked up, his eyes were full of pain.

Paula smiled wryly to break the tension. "So, what if I meet Miss Right? Any chance you'll look the other way?"

Ted's tight smile conveyed discomfort. "I couldn't do that, Paula. I'd be ignoring the wishes of my client, regardless of what I think of her choices," he said softly.

She took the pen he offered and quickly signed the document. "I'll be leaving for Seattle tomorrow. So you'll need to fax me any other papers I need to sign."

"I thought you weren't leaving until Friday."

Paula shook her head. "Everything's packed. I need to get back." She leaned back in the chair. "I do have a question for you, if you don't mind."

"Of course."

"Did you know about my mother and John South?"

He seemed to shrink in his chair, hanging his head. She'd definitely caught him off-guard. He wiped his hand across his face and looked away. "How did you find out?"

"She kept everything in a safe. I had it opened."

He shook his head and exhaled. "Why am I not surprised? She couldn't let it go, not even when she should have."

"Why do you say that?"

He looked at her thoughtfully. "I don't know how much I should tell you."

She snorted. "You can tell me everything, Ted. There's nothing you could say at this point that would surprise me. Was my mother a streetwalker? Did she pole dance on Saturday nights?" He didn't laugh at her jokes and she looked down guiltily. "I'm sorry. I know you cared about her."

"Can we take a walk?"

She followed him outside. The beacon showered the trail with just enough light to illuminate the path but Paula was grateful that the severity of her expression and the depth of her pain remained hidden in the overwhelming darkness. The wind had died and she thought rain might soon follow.

"Your mother and I began our affair after your father's death but by then her heart belonged to John. She'd been having an affair with him for several years but neither of them had any intention of leaving their respective spouses. I think that was largely because of you and Stephanie."

"I don't understand. Why did that matter?"

"The two of you were best friends. Your parents worried that it would destroy your friendship and they couldn't stomach that. You were children, innocent victims to their passions. It wasn't right to involve you."

"I suppose." She knew he was right. It would've devastated them and fingers of blame would've pointed in all directions.

"So they continued on with their little charade. Your father was absent so much that he never suspected anything when he was home."

A thought occurred to her. "Do you think Mom was grateful he died?"

"Absolutely not," he insisted. "Your father's death devastated Francine. She loved him and if he'd been around more often I don't think she ever would've given John a second look. Your father was a handsome, dashing man but absence didn't make the heart grow fonder."

"Did Debbie know?"

He frowned. "Debbie was a victim. She knew if she demanded a divorce it would crush Stephanie. It was easier to drink so she did."

Paula shook her head. "How do you figure into this triangle?"

He chuckled. "There wasn't a triangle. There was only John and Francine. I was no part of it. Debbie wasn't either, really.

John and Francine were a true love story and the rest of us were bystanders. I was naïve enough to think that your mother might choose me over him since I was actually single and she was a widower. I was a respectable attorney and in love with her."

Paula stared at him. In the light of the beacon his goodness surrounded him. His mild nature, pleasant face and shrewd intellect made her question her mother's sanity. "She should've picked you. You're a catch."

The compliment drew his sad face into a smile. "Thanks." They reached the lighthouse and settled onto a bench underneath the beacon. "If it were only that simple," he continued. "Your mother only had eyes for John. For a while she dated both of us but eventually she told me to step back."

"Weren't you angry? Did you think about going to Debbie?"

He held out his hands. "And say what? She already knew. There was nothing I could do except bow out. Making a scene would've only hurt you and Stephanie. Your mother belonged with John. I really believe that now. Their love was timeless."

She rolled her eyes. "Please."

"I'm serious. Once I got past the hurt and pain of losing her I saw the truth. Do you know that she visited his grave every day after his death? She brought him flowers once a week and would sit in front of his tombstone, telling him about everything that was happening in her life. It was the kind of romance that movies are made about."

"And Stephanie never suspected."

He looked up, panicked. "Are you going to tell her?"

She shook her head. "I don't think any good could come from it. Besides I'm leaving tomorrow. I can't see devastating her and then walking away." She hung her head and added, "I've already done that to her once."

He glanced at her. "So I guess things with Stephanie didn't work out?"

"No. She's gone back to her husband." She swallowed hard and changed her tone. "I'll probably come back in a month to clean out the rest of the house. I'll need you to recommend a good real estate agent."

It surprised her how quickly she shifted to business and how easy it seemed to talk about. She stood to go, assuming their business was concluded, but he remained on the bench.

"Is there anything else, Ted?"

"Has Stephanie left Eugene?"

She took a deep breath. "Tomorrow, I imagine."

"Do you think there's any hope for the two of you?"

Paula chuckled. "Doubtful."

"Doubtful doesn't mean hopeless," he said. "Sit, please." She joined him again, realizing that the glorious beacon was like a spotlight and Ted could plainly see her anguish.

"Paula, your mother knew she was dying."

"What do you mean? I thought she had an unexpected heart attack."

Ted nodded. "It was unexpected in terms of the exact time, but your mother had seen a cardiologist a few months before. She had severe issues with artery clotting and they told her she only had a little while left. She took comfort in the fact that she would go quickly. She came to see me and told me that she'd made a few more decisions."

Paula sighed. "Fabulous. Another codicil?"

"Not really a codicil, but it was a letter clarifying her wishes." He pulled an envelope from his jacket pocket which she took but didn't open. "She also said that she wasn't going to tell you. She'd made arrangements with Mrs. Gunn next door and it would be Mrs. Gunn who would contact you."

Tears pooled in her eyes. "Why would she do that? Why wouldn't she tell me?"

"She believed you would insist on coming home for the duration to care for her, to be present when it happened and to do everything in your power to delay it from coming."

Paula nodded fiercely. "Damn right. That's exactly what I would've done."

"And she didn't want that." He offered a gentle smile. "She was ready, Paula. She'd made her peace. She didn't want to disrupt your life for something you couldn't control or change. She knew that despite the differences the two of you had, you were an amazingly loyal person who loved her. She felt that in her heart."

Tears streamed down her face and she took some deep breaths. "Yes," she said finally.

He handed her his handkerchief and patted her knee. "Knowing was enough for her. It completed her, if you will. She didn't need you to prove your love by leaving your job and moving back. Your mother, for all of her faults, loved you until the very end and she believed you were a person capable of great love." He pointed at the envelope. "You need to open that."

She fumbled with the seal and removed a single sheet of her mother's stationery. She almost cried again when she saw her mother's elegant old-school handwriting. With the glow of Heceta behind her, it was easy to read in the darkness.

Dear Paula,

I imagine you cannot fully describe your feelings for me at this moment—but I can. Betrayal, anger, sadness, bewilderment and shock are just a few of the emotions I know you've experienced since my death. You see, I've had much more time to imagine my passing and its effect on you. It's one of the unavoidable activities that engage the mind of the elderly each and every day. Now that my life is ending there is much time for reflection since all I'm doing now is waiting for the moment when I see your father and John again.

You'll be surprised to know that I'm not evaluating my life or judging my choices. What would be the point? Everything is in the past and I cannot change it. All I can think about is how your life will be affected and the pain or joy my existence will bring to you.

I will admit that I do not understand your love of other women. I did not raise you this way. I cannot help but think that somehow I caused this. After I learned of your lifestyle, I spent so many mornings staring out the kitchen window while I drank my coffee, thinking about what I could have done to make you normal. I do regret that I was unable and unwilling to discuss this with you but I could not. Perhaps it was too embarrassing and potentially painful.

I am certain that you do not approve of many of my choices as well, including the codicil in my will. I imagine it hurts you to be judged so harshly by me, and since I have learned of my imminent death, I have questioned my decision and found a sense of peace in the middle ground.

Amid all of those mornings at the kitchen table I thought as much of Stephanie as I did of you and I started to wonder why. After much thought it occurred to me that you loved her, and when I replayed all the important moments of your youth, Stephanie was always there. She loved you too, even if she didn't know it.

She may have told you that she initially came to me when she got pregnant and I urged her to keep the baby. At the time I didn't know what she meant to you or you to her, but the child was all that mattered. I still believe that. However, she promised me that one day she would return as your friend. The fact that you are reading this letter means that this has happened. Stephanie has returned to your life.

While I do not condone your lifestyle, I love Stephanie almost as much as you do. She brings out the very best in you, darling. She is a beacon of light for you, and if I had been paying attention, I would not have needed an angry phone call from your insane ex-girlfriend to convince me. (What could you have ever seen in her? She didn't seem to be anything like Stephanie.)

I'm rambling now. I have reread what I have written and I have yet to state the point. Such is the price for growing old. Here is my final decision: if you choose to spend your life with Stephanie, you may have the entire inheritance—every penny. She belongs with you. If you find someone else, the codicil stands.

I understand how hypocritical I sound and I don't care. I don't expect you to understand how I could love two different men just as I don't understand your lifestyle. I'm old, outdated and dying. I can decide whatever I wish. I don't know anyone else you may choose to love but I know Stephanie. While I don't approve of your lesbianism, I do approve of Stephanie. She is to you what John was to me. Be with her, honey. Love her as she loves you.

All my love,
Mom

After reading the letter twice, she looked up at Ted, mouth agape. "She's nuts."

"She's certainly complicated."

She looked down at the pages again. *She belongs with you.* "Why did you show me this? Steph's going back to her husband."

A smile crossed his lips. "Incentive."

CHAPTER TWENTY-THREE

Steph's fingers trailed over the luxurious soft cotton terry cloth robe that covered her flesh. She wandered out to the balcony of the Eugene Hilton and stared westward toward Heceta. Only a trace of the afternoon's severe wind remained and it cooled her skin and wet hair. She sipped the scotch and thoughts of her father surfaced.

He'd cheated on Debbie and she'd known but she'd stayed with him anyway. She knew who the woman was and she still stayed. An idea desperately tried to ignite, like two pieces of flint that just wouldn't catch. Steph knew she was missing an important detail but she couldn't see it.

She leaned over the balcony and stared into west Eugene. Only Lawrence could secure a suite at one of the nicest hotels on a big football weekend, but he almost always got his way.

"He certainly does," she muttered into the highball glass.

He'd talked nonstop from Heceta to the hotel, catching her up on all of the hospital gossip and planning a trip to Belize—not Bermuda. He made a quick stop at a drive-through liquor store, complaining that the second-rate hotels in Eugene didn't have a decent minibar. When he requested a bottle of Glenlivet for her, the rest of the evening became clear. She knew his expectations and after everything that had happened he knew what she'd need to get through it.

She drained the glass and stumbled back inside to search for the bottle and change the radio to an upbeat station. Once she'd poured her fifth drink of the evening, she returned to the balcony with the bottle and propped her legs up on the table. The robe slid open and she was grateful Eric was out with Lawrence, enjoying a steak somewhere.

When they'd arrived back at the hotel, Eric was holed up in his room, the door locked and music blaring. Steph imagined Lawrence had given him specific instructions to stay away. Lawrence poured her a double, which she downed quickly while he prepared the bed. She guzzled another one and was quite tipsy when he finally came for her. Her mind went elsewhere, to the beacon at Heceta, but when she tried to imagine the huge lens washing across the land and sea, all she could see was the light dimming and flickering until it finally went out.

"I'm sure you'll enjoy it more when we get back to our regular life," he said when it was over, kissing her on the cheek before he disappeared into the bathroom. She lay in the bed, listening to the mood music he'd selected, a classical guitar.

When he reappeared, she quickly took his place and locked the bathroom door. She used only the hot water, scorching her body, ridding herself of him. When she finally stepped out, angry red blotches covered her back and torso from the powerful spray of the showerhead. She opened the bathroom door slightly but Lawrence had left, probably with Eric. A rushed note confirmed that they'd gone out for a "boy's night dinner" and would be back in a few hours.

She leaned back in the balcony chair, allowing the robe to slide open indecently, the cool breeze a welcome kiss to her overheated skin. She tried to look ahead to what awaited her back in Phoenix.

After a three-month absence, she had undoubtedly been replaced by others for her committee chairmanships. Her exceptional doubles ranking at the tennis club was gone and she was certain that there would be a lengthy period of awkwardness between her and the other members of their social circle, as they continued to whisper about what a horrible wife she'd been to Lawrence and how ungrateful she was, despite her marvelous life and beautiful home. It would be annoying for a long time but then all would be forgotten, probably by the time the Christmas parties began. Then they would all impress themselves with their ability to forgive her and welcome her back into the group. Leslie, her doubles partner and true friend, would keep her sane. She knew Lawrence and hated him.

She finished her drink and poured another. She lost track of time and didn't care. What else could she do? The answer was simple—nothing. Pink's "So What?" blasted from the speakers and she sang along as she trashed her ex-husband. Anyone coming out on a neighboring balcony was in for quite a show—a drunken woman flashing everyone with her open robe and belting out a song.

She was so into the performance that she didn't notice Lawrence step onto the patio until the song ended and he applauded wildly. Eric leaned against the wall, frowning. She quickly set the glass down and covered up, wondering how much of her body she'd exposed to her son.

Lawrence's face held that same sexual expectation that he'd worn earlier when they'd arrived from Heceta. His hands caressed the back of her neck and he kissed the top of her head.

"You're very talented," he said. "Just like your mother."

She shot him a look. "What?"

He noticed the change in her voice. "I'm just saying that you look like Debbie, singing and drinking."

201

The comparison nearly debilitated her. It was true. How many times had she seen her mother, highball glass in hand, serenading people with Debbie's Dinner Theater?

He kissed her cheek and headed inside. "I'm going to go for a run since it's so nice. Why don't the two of you enjoy some time together?"

She looked over at Eric, leaning against the doorway, a hesitant smile on his face. She really didn't want to have a conversation with him while she was drunk and practically naked. He was long past the age when she could disguise her foibles. He was an adult now—a sharp one—and she wasn't at the top of her game for their first discussion since he'd seen her kiss a woman. Yet she doubted she'd get another opportunity to speak with him alone.

"Do you want to talk?" she asked, pointing to a chair.

He shrugged. "Sure."

He sat down, his hands clasped in his lap. It was his nervous body language. She remembered that the last time she'd seen him this way was the night she and Lawrence had confronted him about his cocaine usage. That image was enough to propel her forward and accept her decision.

"Eric, I'm very sorry that I didn't tell you about Paula, that's my friend's name. I can't really explain to you what happened. She's gay and she was very upset. She'd just lost her mother. I guess I just went a little out of my head for a while but I never meant to hurt you or deceive you. You're the most important person in the world to me."

She put her hand on his knee and stared into his deep green eyes. Genetically he'd inherited them from Lawrence but she'd always seen a kindness that was unique to him. He smiled slightly and covered her hand with his own. He stared at her with a look of innocence tainted by wisdom. She could tell he wanted to believe her simplistic story but he knew she wasn't telling him the whole truth.

"Is everything okay, Mom?"

She flashed a weary smile. "I'm tired," she said, reverting to the timeless mom response that instantly explained everything. "I'm ready to go home," she added, hoping he would be convinced.

She knew he wanted to say more and she'd learned that with enough time he'd give voice to his feelings. He took a breath and said, "Mom, about that morning—"

"There's no reason to talk about it. Just forget it, okay?"

"I don't want to forget it. I mean, I was really shocked, that's for sure. But if I step away from my feelings and just look at it objectively, you were really into her. Dad says she was an old friend. Is that true?"

She nodded, somewhat uncomfortable by how much he'd really noticed. "Paula and I have known each other since we were little. We grew up together." She finished her drink and turned to him. "We don't need to say any more, son. I'm just so sorry you saw that."

"Are you sorry you kissed her?"

It was a loaded question, and if he was still eight-years-old she could avoid it by changing the subject or jumping out of her chair and claiming a large bug had just scampered across the patio. Both tactics had worked before when she wanted to avoid a subject with him. By the time they'd addressed the distraction the original topic was forgotten. That wouldn't work now.

She summoned the voice she used to comfort him when he fell off his bike, the serious expression that reassured him that he really would get into college and the persuasive tone which convinced him that he could beat his drug addiction.

"It was a terrible mistake. Now, we're going to go home and get you back in school. Okay? That's all that matters."

She squeezed his hand and went directly to the bathroom. She sobbed silently for several minutes and decided to take another shower to mask her tears. When she emerged again, he was back in his room, talking on his cell phone. She sighed deeply and felt hunger pangs. She found the room service menu and ordered a sandwich. Realizing she had no money for a tip, she burrowed through Lawrence's pockets, looking for his wallet. She pulled a five out and a book of matches fell onto the coffee table.

They'd come from the Camelback Inn, a luxury hotel and

spa in Phoenix. It was one of his favorites and he'd taken her there to celebrate their fifteenth wedding anniversary. On the inside cover of the matchbook he'd written a room number. It was relatively new and probably acquired during one of his trysts with a prostitute while she was away. He couldn't be deprived of sex—ever. A niggle of suspicion tickled her mind and she reached for his cell phone, which he never bothered to take with him on his runs despite her protests.

She found the main number in his contact list and the operator connected her with the room. She recognized the voice immediately. Marta's eastern European accent was quite distinct.

"Is someone there?" she asked irritably.

"Hello, Marta."

She could hear her gasp two thousand miles away. "Shit!" And she hung up.

Three seconds later Lawrence's cell phone rang and Steph grinned. She picked it up and laughed. The picture that popped up on the Caller ID showed Marta naked from the waist up. She sported a cute, blond haircut, but what instantly caught Steph's attention was her recent augmentation. While Marta had never been flat-chested, her breasts weren't her best feature—until now. She'd added at least two cup sizes, probably to a double-C.

"Marta?" she answered gleefully.

Marta stammered until she asked, "Where's Lawrence?"

"He's out running right now. He left his cell phone and I've been admiring the lovely picture of you that he's included on his display. Are those double-C's?"

"D's," she said dumbly.

Steph poured another drink. "Ah, of course, that's the size Lawrence likes the most." She paused and when Marta didn't comment, she continued to stick the knife deeper. "I know you're a little shocked right now so I'm just going to tell you a story and you let me know which parts are wrong. Okay?"

Marta grunted and she took a huge slug of Glenlivet. "So after I left, you and Lawrence played house and he performed some work on you, but when he found out from his attorney I'd get half of his wealth, he told you I had to come back or your ride on the gravy train would come to a crashing halt. He set you up at the hotel and came to get me but he assured you that it wouldn't take long before he could convince me to let you back in the house and everything would be back the way it was. He could fuck you every Wednesday afternoon while I played tennis and got my massage. Did I get it right?"

There was a pause and Marta said softly, "Except that I get an all-day visit to the spa every week."

Steph smiled. "Of course. I'm hanging up now."

When she dropped Lawrence's cell phone onto the table she noticed her hands were shaking. She sat down and closed her eyes. Nothing had changed and she wasn't surprised.

"Mom?"

She whipped her head to the side. Eric stood in the doorway to his room, his hands in his pockets. She had no idea how long he'd been standing there or how much he'd heard. She was drunk and she knew that like her mother, she got much noisier when her sobriety was compromised.

She looked down and said, "I ordered a sandwich. Did you want anything?"

He came and sat next to her. "I haven't been a very good son."

Her eyes widened. "What are you talking about? You're the most amazing person. I couldn't ask for a better son."

He shook his head. "I really don't know where to start." He took a breath and organized his thoughts. "I always knew Dad was a bastard and that he cheated. But when he came to me a few days ago and said he wanted to make it right, I believed him. He'd been pleading with me for weeks to forgive him, and when he asked me to go with him to get you, I said no at first. Then he said he might do something foolish and I got a little scared."

She smoothed his hair and touched his cheek. "Of course you did, sweetie. He's your father and you'd never want anything bad to happen to him. You wanted to believe him."

"That shouldn't matter. I'm a recovering addict and one of the cardinal rules is that everybody lies. Anyway, I only came because I was worried he'd hurt himself. I meant it when I told you to leave. He's not good for you. But then I saw you and your *friend*..."

His voice trailed off and she said, "We don't have to talk about this, son—"

"Of course we do! Mom, you're a lesbian and you're in love with a woman. And you're about to go back to Scottsdale and live with someone you hate."

She couldn't speak. He'd called her a lesbian, a word she couldn't even call herself. She took another drink and poured him half a shot. He nodded his thanks and downed the liquor.

"I was just talking to Jameson about this."

"Oh, why?" Jameson was Eric's best friend and the person who convinced him to get help for his addiction.

He looked at her like she was dumb. "He's gay, Mom."

"He is?"

Eric chuckled. "Mom, sometimes you're a little dense. You'll have to work on your gaydar if you're going to be a lesbian."

"My what?"

He shook his head, the chuckle turning into a real laugh. It felt so good to see him laugh. "Mom, Jameson helped me realize that I needed to let you live your own life and be *happy* for you. I need to support *you*."

She shook her head. "That's not your job. You're my son. I support you."

"Mom, that was great when I was nine but I'm a grownup. We have to be here for each other, starting right now."

He took her drink from her hand and put it on the table and held her hand. "Do you love your friend...sorry, what was her name again?"

She was overcome by so much that tears dripped from her cheeks. She was so proud of him.

"Paula," she whispered.

He kissed her on the cheek. "Just by the way you say her

name I know how you feel. Can I meet her sometime?"

She nodded. "Of course."

He looked around and checked his watch. "Well, I think we'd better get you out of here. You don't need another scene with Dad."

She agreed. She quickly repacked while he called the front desk and secured another room several floors below. He promised that he would deal with Lawrence and she made a point of leaving the matchbook and his wallet visible. He'd get the message.

They met at the door with her things and she threw her arms around him. "I love you. It doesn't say enough but it's all I have."

"I know, Mom. I love you, too."

She picked up her suitcases and set them down again. She gazed at Eric who eyed her quizzically. "Son, sometimes adults don't always behave well. There's a part in each of us that doesn't mature past the age of twelve. Inside we're still kids who sometimes choose to do the wrong thing."

He grinned. "I know. You don't have to explain Dad's behavior, Mom. I get it."

"That's not what I'm talking about, sweetheart."

She disappeared into the bedroom and returned with Lawrence's garment bag. He always traveled with an expensive suit regardless of where he went, including their vacations. As Steph became a savvy participant in their marriage, she surmised that he brought his dress clothes to pick up women, and she couldn't imagine how many nights she'd lain in a lonely bed while he rode a stranger somewhere else in the hotel.

She took the bag out to the balcony and pulled the zipper down, exposing the tailored Armani suit. It was gorgeous. She hefted the bag over the balcony and with all her strength, threw it out into the night sky. Eric quickly joined her at the railing and they watched it plummet ten stories—and land in the gurgling hot tub.

She looked at him with a pout. "Do you forgive your mother?"

He laughed so hard he cried.

CHAPTER TWENTY-FOUR

Paula exited the FedEx office, the five boxes of family memorabilia on their way to Seattle. Her flight wasn't for another seven hours and she debated how to spend the rest of her time. It would only take three hours to drive back to Portland, return the rental car and check her bags. She'd already said goodbye to Caroline and Rick, promising to keep in touch. She'd hired Rick to finish the packing, ensuring that she wouldn't need to return to Eugene herself.

She turned toward the Cascades, a scenic backdrop to the city, and decided to take a short hike on one of the trails near the highway. She and Steph had spent a lot of time in the mountains, enjoying the pine-scented air and great views when they were in high school.

She swallowed hard, wondering how long it would take to erase the last few days from her mind. All she could think about was Stephanie, who filled her entire heart with pain and longing. She'd thought of nothing else except her mother's letter since her talk with Ted. She knew she'd lost Steph but the anger she'd felt toward Francine was gone. Knowing that her mother approved of her love for Steph balanced her homophobia. It was enough.

She'd just passed Springfield when her cell phone chimed. She didn't recognize the number but the call was local. "Hello?"

"Paula! It's Debbie. Are you still in Eugene?"

She stumbled in surprise. "Uh, hi, Deb. Yeah, I'm still here for another hour or so. Then I'm off to Portland to catch my flight."

"Terrific! Look, I know it's a huge inconvenience but is there any way you could drop by my place before you go?"

She grimaced, grateful Debbie couldn't see her. She didn't want her last memory of Eugene to be a senior center but Debbie was like family. Without another thought she said, "Yeah, I can stop by, but only for a few minutes, okay?"

"Fabulous! I'll see you in a short shake."

She disconnected before Paula could say goodbye.

She took the next exit and turned around, heading back up the interstate toward Waverly Place. She wondered if the subject of John and her mother would come up and she didn't know how she would handle it. Would Debbie be mad at her because her mother was a home wrecker?

She realized her thoughts were ridiculous as she turned into the parking lot. Most likely Debbie just wanted to say goodbye and Paula realized it would probably be the last time she saw her. It was apparent her memory was failing and she wondered how long it would take before her physical health followed. Then Steph would experience the loss of her mother too. It was different for a woman to lose her mother. Both of their fathers were dead, and while that was painful, particularly since it had happened at such a young age for Paula, it had been much worse to lose her mother. She imagined it would be the same for Steph since both of them were only children.

"I'm here to see Debbie South," she said to the receptionist who gave her a suspicious look.

"You're not one of those séance people, are you?"

"Uh, no," Paula said, surprised by the question. "Debbie had a séance?"

The woman snorted. "There isn't much Deb hasn't done since she's been here. Last week Madame Somebody-or-other arrived complete with her crystal ball and tarot cards. She set up shop in the ballroom and totally freaked out the residents. Mrs. Higgs nearly swallowed her dentures when she thought she'd had a *vision* of her dead husband. One of the orderlies had to give her the Heimlich maneuver. The director put a stop to it and kicked the madame out when she saw her passing a hat and the residents emptying their wallets into it."

Paula snorted and pictured the havoc that Debbie had caused. She was certainly a force. "No, I'm not here to conduct a séance or anything else. Just a visit."

The woman sighed heavily. "Good. I can't take any more today. I've already got a splittin' headache from the singing, if you can call it that."

"Singing?" Paula asked.

"Debbie brought in a karaoke machine this morning filled with moldy oldies—and I mean really old stuff." Paula guessed the receptionist was under twenty-five and she'd consider songs by Madonna to be oldies. "They've been out on the patio all morning rippin' through these *classics* with everything they got."

Paula chuckled and headed for the patio. While she was sure that most eighty-year-olds weren't the greatest singers, she imagined that it was incredibly boring to live in a senior center. And the smell of sanitizer made her slightly dizzy. She realized that with her inheritance she could avoid this type of place.

Through the glass she could see the backsides of a large crowd gathered in a semi-circle. Some were standing while others were in wheelchairs and a few sat on the perimeter facing away from the circle mouthing the words to an off-key version of Sinatra's

210

"Fly Me to the Moon" that bellowed through the speakers at an annoyingly high volume.

She stepped on the electrified doormat and the doors whooshed open. A woman sitting nearby in an iron patio chair shot her a glance and her eyes bulged as if Paula were King Kong. Paula stopped suddenly and stared at the old woman, who grabbed a mallet and smacked it against a small gong that sat next to her. The sound made Paula jump and she reflexively took a step away from the woman, who continued to pound on the gong.

Debbie emerged from within the circle and took the mallet out of the woman's hand. She leaned over and yelled in her ear. "Thanks, Iris. You've been a great help." Iris nodded fiercely.

Debbie looked up at Paula and held her arms out. Paula reluctantly embraced her but Debbie's hug was strong. "Thanks for coming, sweetie. I don't think you'll regret it."

Paula stared at her, a cynical expression on her face. "Debbie, what are you up to? Why would I possibly regret visiting you?"

Keeping her arm wrapped around Paula's middle, she led her through the throng of geriatrics to a makeshift stage, where Steph stood, a microphone in her hand. Paula suddenly stopped and swallowed hard. She'd resigned herself to never seeing Steph again and how she'd live with the loss, but as she gazed upon her face, the entire plan burned away like the bonfire at her mother's house.

The haunting bass notes of the Police's "Every Breath You Take" filled the patio and when Steph crooned the title, Paula remembered her beautiful voice and the many times she'd belted out whatever was on the radio whenever they cruised Eugene. She'd sung in the concert choir throughout high school, inheriting her mother's marvelous pipes. Of course, she'd never shared Debbie's flair for showmanship and cringed when Paula had suggested that she audition for *South Pacific*, the junior-year musical. Paula's motives had been selfish. She just wanted to see Steph dancing across a stage for three nights in a bikini.

The slow ballad shifted into high gear and Paula remained

motionless, lost in her lovely voice and pained expression.

Steph stepped off the stage and faced Paula. She stumbled with the lyrics, unable to continue. Paula smiled and they floated together for a soft kiss.

"Holy hell!" one of the residents cried. "What's going on?"

Paula heard Debbie comforting the shocked gentleman, who continued to rant about the idea of two women kissing, but she wouldn't let go of Steph.

"I think it's nice," another female guest commented. "You should be able to love whoever you want."

"You're absolutely right, Eunice," another voice said. "My nephew is one of the homosexuals and he's the only one who bothers to come and visit me. Everybody else in the family would be happy if I rotted away."

The kiss ended but they remained inseparable, their foreheads touching. Steph's sweet breath lingered against her face.

"You oughta be careful," another voice cracked and Paula couldn't tell if it was male or female. "Those kind burn in hell."

"Then they'll be in very good company," Debbie said, wrapping her arms around both Steph and Paula. "Well, you two look very happy again. I guess my little plan worked."

Steph looked at her mother with a raised eyebrow. "Your plan? This was my idea, remember?"

"You? I'm shocked," Paula said, nuzzling Steph's cheek with her own. "You hate performing in front of people."

"But I love you," Steph whispered in her ear. "I'm not afraid of the future, of us."

"And this is a tough crowd," Debbie added. "Stevie just gave Old Man Sherman a swig from his flask to get him to shut up. I should probably skedaddle and go help him." She kissed each of them on the cheek and went to help a resident out of her chair.

"She's really unbelievable," Paula said. "You're lucky to have her for your mom."

Steph nodded. "I know."

"What about Lawrence and Eric?" Paula asked.

Pride filled Steph's face. "My son proved what he's made

of. He wants to meet you. As for Lawrence, I don't care." She laughed and looked away. "We can both be penniless."

Many of the residents tottered away or wheeled themselves back inside. They'd obviously decided the best part of the show was over and it was time to go in search of the next sliver of excitement that might charge their pulses or tickle their bored minds.

"Still planning on flying back today?"

Paula looked into her eyes and saw the worry. She touched her cheek and there wasn't any doubt. She wanted to make up for the years and decades of absence. She vowed that they'd live a life as full and rich as possible. *It's what Mom wanted*, she thought, remembering Francine's last words—*love her*.

"I think," Paula began, "that we should go celebrate with an extravagant picnic filled with expensive foods and a marvelous bottle of champagne. We'll take it up to Heceta and eat it inside the lighthouse."

Steph eyed her curiously. "Is spending a lot of money a good idea, considering your mother's codicil and the bloodbath my divorce is about to become?"

Paula smiled and took her arm. "Honey, we have a lot to talk about."

CHAPTER TWENTY-FIVE

Three Months Later

The breakfast rush was winding down and the line at the to-go counter was only three deep. Mrs. Gunn shuffled to the register to pay her bill and Steph smiled at her most regular customer. She'd frequented the Lighthouse Bakery since the day it opened and always ordered the same thing—an apple tart and black coffee.

"Everything okay today, Mrs. Gunn?" she asked, anticipating her reply.

"Better than okay, Steph," she said. Her dentures had slipped a little but Steph decided not to say anything. "The sun is finally shining again, I'm still breathing and I've started my morning with the best apple tart I've ever had."

This was her standard answer to Steph's predictable question.

Once when another customer had asked Mrs. Gunn what her doctor thought about her breakfast habits, she'd harrumphed and said the sunset of life was about indulgence and happiness. The questioner had gone mute.

Steph held out her change and Mrs. Gunn glanced about the small dining area. "Where's your mother? I've been meaning to ask her when she's coming over to play poker again."

Steph stifled a chuckle, remembering that their last evening had been a strip poker game. Just as she started to respond, Debbie's cute red Miata pulled up in front of the glass window. She pointed. "You can ask her yourself."

Mrs. Gunn patted her hand and went out to greet Debbie, who threw her arms around one of her new best friends.

When Steph had agreed to let her help at the bakery, it was with great skepticism and she imagined her little business morphing into a vaudeville cabaret. Then Debbie reminded her that before Grandma taught her to bake, she'd taught Debbie. Steph had rarely seen her mother's domestic side since she was usually too plastered to follow a recipe. Now that she was sober she claimed that baking was like riding a bike and her end results proved she was right. Her pie crusts were ten times better than Steph's.

KT Tunstall sang "Suddenly I See" through her cell phone, an appropriate anthem for the change in her life. She automatically smiled when she thought of Paula still curled up in bed, the sheet immodestly covering her body.

"Why are you calling me?" she tried to sound perturbed but she immediately laughed. "You're supposed to be sleeping in," she continued. "Remember? You've worked tirelessly for the last three months."

It was true. Paula had decided to open her own PR firm and the University of Oregon was one of her first clients. They wanted an outsider to assess their public relations efforts and Paula's report had greatly impressed the Board of Regents and the university president. Undoubtedly she would get more work from them in the future. Today was her reward—a day of relaxation at home.

"I'm still in bed," she reassured her. "In fact I'm holding the slinky red teddy you wore last night. You remember it, don't you? Remember how I slowly peeled it from your body and kissed every inch of exposed skin that my lips could find?"

She shook her head. "You know you're torturing me, right? I'm here at work, laboring as a small business owner. Remember the small business you insisted I start?"

Paula sighed dramatically on the other end of the phone. "I suppose. Maybe I'll come by later after I meet with Phil."

Phil was the contractor building their new home. Although they were fortunate to have Francine's house as a temporary residence, the memories were still too strong for Paula, who sometimes broke down and wept whenever she thought of her mother. They were eager to move but their design—an architectural beauty that would soon be featured in a local magazine—required a battalion of subcontractors all of whom had their own schedules and quirky work habits. They'd be lucky to hang their Christmas stockings on their new mantel.

Steph quickly said goodbye when she saw that Lily, the overqualified college kid she'd hired, needed her help with the temperamental cappuccino machine. She was the type of girl she'd want for a daughter, a wonderful mixture of brains, beauty and charisma. Apparently Eric thought she was special too because he'd mentioned that they visited via webcam quite frequently.

They fixed the machine again and Steph settled onto a bench with the paper and a cup of coffee, prepared to take a break. She'd been at work since four a.m., the early hours clearly the downside of owning a business that relied on morning customers. However, thanks to Debbie's innovations, their sandwiches and salads were becoming quite popular as well, and the lunch rush almost equaled the onslaught they endured when the doors opened at seven.

She'd been shocked by the success of the Lighthouse Bakery. It had been Paula's idea to turn the empty store next to Maude's

Closet and Cut Upz into her dream job. Paula had spent hours convincing Steph that her lifelong hobby could be a profitable endeavor. Paula's unwavering confidence in her pushed her forward and strengthened their growing love. It helped that the shop had been a restaurant in a previous life and only needed minimal remodeling.

They'd kept it simple and homey, choosing oak chairs and benches for the dining area and spending the big money on the display of the food, purchasing refrigerator cases for cakes and cream pies and large baker's racks for the breads and pastries they created each day.

In addition to Lily, Steph had hired Felipe, an assistant baker and counter help who made deliveries. She knew she was lucky to live in a college town with so many eager and energetic young people who wanted to work.

The front door opened and Debbie's hearty laugh filled the room. She held Ted Ruth's arm and the two of them joined her at the table. She'd moved out of Waverly Place and into a small condo once Steph had employed her at the bakery, and she'd dumped Stevie the Orderly after reestablishing her friendship with Ted. They'd known each other all through Steph's youth, but Ted had loved Francine and Debbie had loved Jack Daniels.

Steph was grateful Ted was in and Steve was out. It felt a little prudish but she was glad that Debbie was dating someone her own age. Steph had also noticed recently that Ted's usual three-piece suit had transformed to khakis and open-collared shirts, an entirely acceptable look in the low-key professional world of Eugene.

"Hi, Ted," she said cheerfully. "How's business?"

Ted didn't answer the question but looked at her mother instead. "Do you want to tell her or should I?"

She raised an eyebrow. "Mom, what's up?" She knew Debbie was plotting something and she pictured poor Ted skydiving or climbing the Himalayas.

Debbie smiled and then giggled uncontrollably. "Ted and I are going to live together."

"What?"

Ted coughed and said, "Um, I would marry your mother, Steph, it's just that at our age and with our assets it could be a legal nightmare—"

"You don't need to justify it to me, Ted. I'm already living in sin."

"But wouldn't you marry Paula if you could?" her mother asked.

She didn't know how to answer that. Her last marriage had left a dark imprint on her psyche, one that would take a while to get over.

"Let's not pressure Stephanie, honey," Ted said. "She's got a wonderful life now."

Steph smiled at him. He really was a terrific guy and Francine had truly missed an opportunity. "Thanks Ted. I'm fortunate to have so much. Now what do the two of you have planned today?"

"I thought I'd help you make tomorrow's pies," Debbie said.

Steph shook her head. "Felipe's on it, Mom. You taught him well. Why don't the two of you go and have some fun? Do some shopping."

Debbie's face brightened. "I nearly forgot! Before we move in together Ted and I are taking a trip to Paris. Isn't that great? I always wanted to go there."

"That's great," she said, knowing her mother had never traveled abroad.

She glanced at Ted who gazed lovingly at her mother. She'd never seen any man look at her the way he did. She realized she knew the secret ingredient that had been missing from her mother's life—mutual affection. Whoever it was that her father had found to fill his life may have been a positive for him but it had subtracted from Debbie proportionally.

"Yes," she continued, "we're leaving in two weeks and we'll be gone for three weeks after that. We're planning on taking the train all over Europe." She rubbed noses with Ted and planted a quick kiss on his lips. "It'll be fabulous."

"It certainly will," Steph agreed. "You'll get to see the Louvre, and the Eiffel Tower—"

"Maybe," Debbie said, "if we ever get out of the hotel room. Teddy here is quite the lover." She caressed his face in her hands and kissed him tenderly.

Steph closed her eyes. "Too much information, Mom."

"What?" she scowled. "You're a middle-aged adult, Stephanie. Surely you don't think your mother's sexual urges have all dried up."

She bit her lip. "Mom, I don't think about your sexual urges *period*. It's the ongoing fantasy that all children have about their parents. We *want* to believe we were delivered by storks and our parents are asexual beings. It helps us avoid therapy." She shuddered and stood up. "Go have a good time today. After the lunch rush I'm heading home to see *my* lover."

Steph waited for her reaction but Debbie stared at her blandly. "What, Steph? You think I'll be shocked that you and Paula eat each other's pussies?"

She stood there stunned. Her mother's ear-to-ear grin reminded her that she would never best her when it came to embarrassment. For as long as she lived Debbie would continue to rule a land of raunchy humor where Howard Stern could be king to her queen.

Steph walked to her office unable to describe her emotions, which sat at the brim of her mind waiting to spill over. Gone were the anger of her youth and the pity over Debbie's alcoholism. She no longer felt either. The corners of her mouth involuntarily turned up and her shoulders lifted slightly. She knew what was coming when a sound passed through her lips. Before she could stop herself, she was laughing hysterically.

The lunch rush came in a cyclonic wave as everyone wanted something to eat all at the same time, unlike breakfast, which seemed to be a meal that drifted throughout the morning. She was ready to go, leaving instructions with Lily and Felipe for closing at three. While the worst thing about serving breakfast and lunch was the early mornings, the best part was the early closing, ensuring that the evenings were still open for fun and relaxation.

"Where do you think you're going?"

Paula stood at the counter dressed all in black—jeans, T-shirt and boots. Her crooked smile suggested this wasn't an impromptu visit. Steph leaned over the counter and kissed her.

"Hey, babe. You look hot."

"Good enough to eat?" she teased.

Her teeth set on edge for a second, as she remembered Debbie's playful comment.

Paula noticed. "Did I say something wrong?"

"No, my mother was just..."

"Being Debbie?" Paula finished.

She nodded. "So how's the house?"

Paula smiled. "It's going great. They've got the front glass windows in place and the cantilevered ceiling looks amazing. It's going to be magnificent."

Steph smiled at the thought of owning a home she'd actually helped design. Although she and Lawrence had designed their Scottsdale monstrosity, she wasn't consulted about any of the furnishings and he trusted the decorator's opinion more than hers. Eric had recently told her he'd suspected his dad had had an affair with the decorator since he caught them sitting in her Lexus one afternoon—in the backseat. As a ten-year-old he thought nothing of it when his father told him they were looking for something she'd lost.

Paula clasped her hands and stroked her fingers. "I have a surprise for you."

"For me?"

"Well, actually it's for both of us."

She followed her outside to her hybrid Toyota Highlander and she pulled their duffle bags from the hatch and tossed them into the backseat of Steph's BMW convertible.

"Get in," she said slyly.

"Where are we going?" Steph asked, thrilled that Paula wanted to surprise her.

"You'll see."

Paula snapped her fingers as if she'd forgotten something and went back into the bakery. She returned with two takeout boxes and set them carefully on the floor of the backseat.

"What's inside?"

"That's for me and Felipe to know and you to find out," she said, lowering the Beemer's top.

She zoomed onto the highway and headed west. It didn't take long for Steph to guess their destination. Driving down the interstate it was clear that Mrs. Gunn was right. The spring sunshine had finally arrived and she relished the welcomed shift in Oregon weather. After spending years in the constant Arizona heat, she'd forgotten about the long months of rain in the Pacific Northwest. She tilted her chin upward and imagined Vitamin D spilling over her. Apparently, Paula was watching. "There is nothing hotter than a beautiful woman cruising in a convertible," she said.

Her free hand slowly pushed the hem of Steph's dress over her knee until the tips of her fingers stroked her inner thigh. Steph leaned against the headrest and breathed in the new car smell, enjoying Paula's caress.

The car was her gift to herself after her divorce was finalized. Lawrence's threat to expose her lesbianism had been quashed by Eric, who made it clear that he would back his mother in court if Lawrence said a word, and he insisted that his mother receive what she deserved.

Lawrence acquiesced and Steph received a handsome settlement, which although it wasn't truly fifty percent of his wealth, it was enough to make her happy. And what he didn't know was that Eric planned to move to Eugene next fall. His relationship with Lily was all hot sparks as Paula liked to say, and absence really was making their hearts grow fonder.

When Paula reached the 101 and turned the BMW north, Steph was certain their destination was Heceta. When the lighthouse cliff came into view, she clapped her hands together like a child seeing Disneyland in the distance. The sun eventually disappeared when the road wended between the trees that lined either side and met in the middle.

They hadn't even opened the Beemer's doors and Caroline was running down the porch steps to greet them, arms outstretched for a hug. It had been nearly two months since they'd visited, although she routinely went to Eugene for various reasons, including shopping at the Lighthouse Bakery.

"It's so wonderful that you're here for the weekend," she said in Steph's ear.

"We are?"

She looked at Paula who pulled their duffel bags from the back. "Yes, that's the surprise. This is our romantic weekend."

Steph frowned. "What about the shop? Who'll do the baking and open?"

Paula gripped her shoulders. "Steph, you have a capable staff. Your mother's going to direct Felipe and Lily. It'll be fine, I think," she quickly added.

Steph gave her a worried look and Paula kissed her forehead. "We have to be able to leave and vacation. This is a good test for your mother."

Steph turned to Caroline. "Please tell me you have a really potent bottle of wine that I can consume."

"I most certainly do." She patted her on the back and accepted the pastry boxes that Paula pulled from the back. "And thanks for bringing dessert."

"Not a problem," Steph said. "I didn't even know I was."

They got settled in Victoria's Room and Steph looked about for Rue, remembering the figure she'd seen in the window all those months ago when Lawrence had driven her away from Heceta. So much had happened since then.

After a wonderful dinner with Caroline and Rick, Paula led her down the trail toward the lighthouse. The beacon showered the night with its strength and Paula grinned.

"What are you thinking about?"

She pulled her closer and kissed her in response.

They went up into the tower and stared at the ocean through the enormous glass. Paula held her tightly in her arms, her lips nuzzling her ear. It was heaven. Steph was happy and she felt incredibly strong.

"Being up here reminds me of this great story my mother used to tell me," Paula said. "There were these two battleships out on maneuvers for several days in terrible weather. One night the captain was out on the bridge with the lookout. They saw a light and the captain ordered the lookout to signal the other ship, warning them that they were on a collision course. He ordered the other ship to change course by twenty degrees.

"The lookout sent the message and it came back saying that *they* should change course twenty degrees. Well, the captain was angry and he sent another message saying that he was a captain and the other ship needed to change course. The reply came, I am a second-class seaman and you *must* change course. By then the captain was furious, and he sent the message, I am a battleship! And the reply came, I am a *lighthouse*. Needless to say, the captain changed course."

Steph laughed heartily. "I can see why Francine liked that story."

"We're all alone in this incredibly romantic place." Paula buried her fingers in Steph's hair and brought her lips against Steph's ear. "You've changed in the past few months, haven't you?"

"I've certainly learned a lot about myself," Steph chuckled. "I'm very certain about what I want."

"Oh, what do you want?"

Steph found a blanket in the storage bin and spread it out on the tiny expanse of floor. Paula stood motionless as she slowly removed her clothes, the light of Heceta casting a heavenly glow about her. She sat up on her elbows hoping she looked as sexy as she felt.

"I want you—right now."

Paula fell beside her, landing in her arms, laughing. "Take me, I'm yours."

She cuddled against Steph and slowly stripped off her clothes. Steph's heart was pounding in a rhythm filled with expectation and anxiety.

"Is this okay?" she couldn't help asking, as her hands caressed her breasts.

Paula cradled her face in her hands. "Honey, it's more than okay. It's forever."

Paula's words fortified her. As Heceta turned in the night, the confident woman Steph thought she'd lost so long ago reemerged and Paula's cries of delight wrapped a shell of contentment around her heart. It indeed would be forever and always with her. Time had stood still, and like the beacon their love had never extinguished but continued to evolve—lighting their route back to each other. At least that's what Steph thought about afterward, lying in her arms, staring into the rafters and holding hands.

Two hours later they climbed down the tiny ladder and traipsed back up the trail to Victoria's Room. A light breeze flew past their faces and Paula's thick hair floated behind her, giving her the appearance of an angel. The hike took much longer than it should since she constantly stopped and pulled Steph against her for a long kiss.

"I think we're looking at another fifty years together," she said. "Do you think you can stand me that long?"

"That would be fabulous," Steph said, almost giddy.

"Really? That doesn't worry you?"

She stopped. "Does it worry you?"

Paula smiled. "No, I've seen my life with you and without you. There's no comparison." She touched her cheek and started to say something but suddenly changed her mind.

"What is it?"

Paula took her hand again and resumed the hike, silent until they arrived at Victoria's Room. As she prepared to open the door, her hand froze with the key in the lock. Again she looked at Steph with that same hesitancy.

"Paula, are you okay? Is something wrong?"

"It's nothing," she said quickly and pushed open the door.

Steph went straight to the dresser and removed her jewelry, longing for a shower, but when she turned around Paula was staring at something on the bed. Paula looked up at her, her mouth agape.

Steph followed her gaze—to a diamond ring that perched inside an open velvet box. It was the most exquisite ring she'd ever seen, delicate but bold.

"That's absolutely beautiful."

Paula took a deep breath. "I'm glad you like it. It was my grandmother's and I wanted to give it to you."

"What?"

"I brought you here to propose. I was going to do it at the lighthouse but I lost my nerve. I couldn't bear it if you said no, so I left the ring in the room—"

"But you didn't leave it on the bed like this."

Paula shook her head slowly, clearly shocked. Despite her belief in Rue, Steph knew from experience that it was disturbing to have an encounter. "How?" Paula finally said.

"No one knows how but she's definitely trying to tell you something." Steph embraced her and rested her chin on her shoulder. "And my answer is yes, if you're still asking."

The smile grew on Paula's face and it was contagious. They hugged each other tightly, laughing like they did when they were kids, unabashedly and freely. It had been their remedy against all the world's flaws—Debbie's embarrassments, Francine's old-fashioned ways, Paul's death and John's constant absence. Nothing was unbearable if they were united and nearly twenty years had done nothing to change their laughter's potency.

Steph slid the ring onto her finger and Paula drowned her resurging giggles with kisses. They fell onto the bed, the thrill of being newly engaged extinguishing their fatigue and reigniting their passion. The raging wind muffled their sounds of pleasure and they cried out in ecstasy without any worry of waking Caroline or Rick.

Their energy toppled quickly and Paula fell asleep in Steph's arms while she listened to the wind rustle the trees. She couldn't be certain but an incongruous melody seemed to float beside it, an odd harmony. She closed her eyes to block out all of her other senses, just to hear *it*. It had nearly floated away, probably all the way to Heceta before she understood what it was—wild laughter.

Publications from Bella Books, Inc.
Women. Books. Even better together
P.O. Box 10543 Tallahassee, FL 32302 Phone: 800-729-4992
www.bellabooks.com

TWO WEEKS IN AUGUST by Nat Burns. Her return to Chincoteague Island is a delight to Nina Christie until she gets her dose of Hazy Duncan's renown ill-humor. She's not going to let it bother her, though...
978-1-59493-173-4 $14.95

MILES TO GO by Amy Dawson Robertson. Rennie Vogel has finally earned a spot at CT3. All too soon she finds herself abandoned behind enemy lines, miles from safety and forced to do the one thing she never has before: trust another woman.
978-1-59493-174-1 $14.95

PHOTOGRAPHS OF CLAUDIA by KG MacGregor. To photographer Leo Wescott models are light and shadow realized on film. Until Claudia.
978-1-59493-168-0 $14.95

SONGS WITHOUT WORDS by Robbi McCoy. Harper Sheridan's runaway niece turns up in the one place least expected and Harper confronts the woman from the summer that has shaped her entire life since.
978-1-59493-166-6 $14.95

YOURS FOR THE ASKING by Kenna White. Lauren Roberts is tired of being the steady, reliable one. When Gaylin Hart blows into her life, she decides to act, only to find once again that her younger sister wants the same woman.
978-1-59493-163-5 $14.95

THE SCORPION by Gerri Hill. Cold cases are what make reporter Marty Edwards tick. When her latest proves to be far from cold, she still doesn't want Detective Kristen Bailey baby-sitting her, not even when she has to run for her life. 978-1-59493-162-8 $14.95

STEPPING STONE by Karin Kallmaker. Selena Ryan's heart was shredded by an actress, and she swears she will never, ever be involved with one again. 978-1-59493-160-4 $14.95

FAINT PRAISE by Ellen Hart. When a famous TV personality leaps to his death, Jane Lawless agrees to help a friend with inquiries, drawing the attention of a ruthless killer. #6 in this award-winning series. 978-1-59493-164-2 $14.95

A SMALL SACRIFICE by Ellen Hart. A harmless reunion of friends is anything but, and Cordelia Thorn calls friend Jane Lawless with a desperate plea for help. Lammy winner for Best Mystery. #5 in this award-winning series. 978-1-59493-165-9 $14.95

NO RULES OF ENGAGEMENT by Tracey Richardson. A war zone attraction is of no use to Major Logan Sharp. She can't wait for Jillian Knight to go back to the other side of the world. 978-1-59493-159-8 $14.95

TOASTED by Josie Gordon. Mayhem erupts when a culinary road show stops in tiny Middelburg, and for some reason everyone thinks Lonnie Squires ought to fix it. Follow-up to Lammy mystery winner Whacked. 978-1-59493-157-4 $14.95

SEA LEGS by KG MacGregor. Kelly is happy to help Natalie make Didi jealous, sure, it's all pretend. Maybe. Even the captain doesn't know where this comic cruse will end.
978-1-59493-158-1 $14.95

KEILE'S CHANCE by Dillon Watson. A routine day in the park turns into the chance of a lifetime, if Keile Griffen can find the courage to risk it all for a pair of big brown eyes.
978-1-59493-156-7 $14.95

ROOT OF PASSION by Ann Roberts. Grace Owens knows a fake when she sees it, and the potion her best friend promises will fix her love life is a fake. But what if she wishes it weren't?
978-1-59493-155-0 $14.95

COMFORTABLE DISTANCE by Kenna White. Summer on Puget Sound ought to be relaxing for Dana Robbins, but Dr. Jamie Hughes is far too close for comfort.
978-1-59493-152-9 $14.95

DELUSIONAL by Terri Breneman. In her search for a killer, Toni Barston discovers that sometimes everything is exactly the way it seems, and then it gets worse.
978-1-59493-151-2 $14.95

FAMILY AFFAIR by Saxon Bennett. An oops at the gynecologist has Chase Banter finally trying to grow up. She has nine whole months to pull it off.
978-1-59493-150-5 $14.95

SMALL PACKAGES by KG MacGregor. With Lily away from home, Anna Kaklis is alone with her worst nightmare: a toddler. Book Three of the Shaken Series.
978-1-59493-149-9 $14.95

WRONG TURNS by Jackie Calhoun. Callie Callahan's latest wrong turn turns out well. She meets Vicki Brownwell. Sparks would fly if only Meg Klein would leave them alone!
978-1-59493-148-2 $14.95

WARMING TREND by Karin Kallmaker. Everybody was convinced she had committed a shocking academic theft, so Anidyr Bycall ran a long, long way. Going back to her beloved Alaskan home, and the coldness in Eve Cambra's eyes isn't going to be easy.
978-1-59493-146-8 $14.95